A PALMFUL OF SKY

A
PALMFUL
OF SKY

HUMEIRA AJAZ

The Book Guild Ltd

First published in Great Britain in 2021 by
The Book Guild Ltd
9 Priory Business Park
Wistow Road, Kibworth
Leicestershire, LE8 0RX
Freephone: 0800 999 2982
www.bookguild.co.uk
Email: info@bookguild.co.uk
Twitter: @bookguild

Typeset in 11pt Minion Pro

Printed and bound in the UK by TJ Books LTD, Padstow, Cornwall

ISBN 978 1913913 168

British Library Cataloguing in Publication Data.
A catalogue record for this book is available from the British Library.

To Asif

1

THE EMAIL THREAD COMPLETELY documented what a pain this entire project was for the team. It had been pending for weeks for want of one last-minute change or another.

First, it was the font that bothered the client's agent. Then, the colour of the font. Then, a descriptive word he wasn't comfortable with. Then, he noticed the background was too dull. Then, not enough commas. Then, too many commas. And finally, he'd suddenly grown fond of a faulty tagline that he'd been okay with changing from day one.

I checked the CEO's social media profiles and realised he was obsessed with English grammar. Most of his posts were memes that were snooty to that effect.

So, he was sensitive to language…

I called his cellphone.

"Hello, Akbar Gill here," someone sounding perpetually cross with the universe answered the call.

"Akbar Sahib!" I trilled. His ad agency was one of many that outsourced creatives to firms like ours rather than employing an in-house department. "Long time no speak, how is it that we keep missing each other?" The pause at the other end defined his confusion. "I'm Maya Badruddin from Edits & More."

"Oh, yes. How can I help you?"

"By asking your agent…" I read his name from the email, "Asim Roy…to enroll in an ESL course. You know, English as a Secondary Language? We can actually help with that."

"I don't understand." His tone became sterner.

"Of course, you don't. Because if you did, you would obviously be more sensitive to damaging the reputation of your company."

"Excuse me?"

"You obviously have a much stronger command over all sorts of languages, I'm sure. Especially, the English language?"

"Well, of course."

"There's this atrocious tagline that Mister Roy is constantly pushing for, which isn't only grammatically wrong but conceptually laughable too. I mean the flaw is obvious as day."

"Which tagline?"

I read Roy's incorrect version from the email along with our editor's corrected one. "We can, of course, go with Mister Roy's hysterical suggestion. It won't harm us to regurgitate whatever."

"No, *don't* regurgitate. I mean I want the best, most correct work as I'm sure you know—"

"Yes, we do. We're professionally trained to know. Isn't that why you hired us?"

"Yes!"

"Good. Should we send the final drafts directly to you or should Mister Roy be involved?" I didn't want Roy totally sacked, just cautioned. "We do enjoy working with him. But we'll enjoy it more if he lets us do our job." I paused for just a second before continuing in a sweeter tone. "I so appreciate your time, sir. It was kind of you to listen. Thank you."

"Oh, not at all, I, uhm, send me the…or to Roy," he was fumbling, "either way is fine, I'll tell Asim to work with your writer, and please, call again. I mean if there's anything else."

"Have a nice day." I hung up and punched a digit on the phone handset to connect with the copywriter in charge to tell her she could toss this project off her workload.

"You have no idea what this means to me!" she cried. "I can be free of The Roy. I don't have to talk to him anymore!"

"I'm glad." I smiled at her through the glass wall of my cubicle and glanced at the ladies on the floor. They were writers, editors, proofreaders, formatters, website designers, ad concept creators, and one receptionist who wouldn't take a single call before she chugged down a large coffee.

All women.

All busy doing work they were so good at.

An alert from Meera, the boss's secretary, said that the boss was already on her way up. I gathered the bundle of folders she needed to see that morning and went to her office. Seconds later, Kulsom Sabih entered with a burst of colour and energy. She wore Pakistani clothing with pride, flaunting traditional cuts, embroidery, and jewels. Her stance not only pandered to societal norms, but she also made it cool.

"I heard you took care of the Gill account," she said, dumping her bag and other belongings in Meera's arms and walking to her chair. "I got his confirmation email for the go-ahead."

"Yes, a breeze," I said, pushing a yellow paper folder to her. "Here's that report on occult sciences. The client is fussing over certain myths for no reason."

"Have you seen the paper?"

"No." I hoped she wouldn't ask me to take a look at it. I had zero interest in the subject. "But I'll handle it if you want me to."

She started to look through the folder, but her attention was diverted as Meera placed a small covered breakfast tray in front of her: the usual hot serving of omelette and coffee.

"He added cheese again," Kulsom said as soon as Meera uncovered the tray.

"I specifically told him not to." Meera frowned.

"I'd find a new bistro if Zafar wasn't so nice." Kulsom hated cheese, which meant that Zafar – the bistro manager – had to pay special attention to her order and have his chef hold the cheese. She had been a loyal customer of the business since it opened down the street three years ago. It had benefitted a lot from her reviews and the free PR that she helped generate by occasionally sending some celebrity client or other to the tiny nondescript place. However, its new chef seemed stubborn about making meals to order. This was the second time he'd fallen short of good service in a month.

"I'll take care of it." I dialled Zafar's number using Kulsom's office landline. He knew who was calling. "Yes, we got the delivery." He sounded so excited I thought a second before destroying him. "What exactly is your idea of good customer service, Mister Zafar? The cheese, Mister Zafar. Hold it *off* please…yes, she *is* a valuable patron…yes, that'll be nice. Thank you." I hung up and looked at my audience of two. "He'll be here in ten minutes with a replacement meal."

"He's a sweet guy," Kulsom said sheepishly. "Maybe you were a little harsh?"

"Just doing my job." I smiled and took away the breakfast tray that nobody wanted.

I had a few minutes to spare before the next meeting, so I walked back to my cubicle. It was in sharp contrast to Kulsom's larger office that Meera kept spotless. She was the most serious person I knew. An inch shorter than me, she never wore heels, had her hair pulled up in a tight bun and was always dressed in some variation of beige.

"Maya!" her voice echoed over the intercom. "The new client is here. Drop by the conference room please."

He had arrived early. I checked my reflection in the glass wall: a slim brown girl with glossy raven hair in a thick ponytail, orange tunic, black leggings, and heels. *Not bad,* I thought. On my way over, I saw Nina frowning into the phone, a brochure in one hand and gesturing intensely with the other. It must be that travel agency that wasn't too happy with their brochure layout but also too stubborn to take any advice from the editor they'd hired to work on it. Nina and I went way back to college. I made a mental note to check with her later.

In the conference room, Kulsom stood in front of a long table, smiling at a man sitting in a chair with his back to me. He turned around slowly to greet me and stood up to his full height, all six feet, baring a perfect set of pearly whites in a boyish grin that I knew so well.

"Jazib?" The surprise in my voice was loud.

"You know each other?" Kulsom asked, looking from his face to mine.

"Yes," I said quickly. "He's my cousin."

"Just cousins?" He smiled with an extra ounce of mischief. "Maya is my—"

"*Cousin.*" I narrowed my eyes, giving him a subtle warning to behave. I would've kicked him in the shin instead if we weren't at my workplace. "Why are you here?" I asked with a stiff smile. All the reasons I could think of were terrible.

"I have a project for you." He royally eased back into his chair and looked at Kulsom as if prompting her to explain.

She obliged with a smile. Apparently Jazib received a ton of mail from clients that needed to be replied to promptly that he simply didn't have the time for. "He would like to entrust us with that job," Kulsom said. "And what a small world. You're related?"

"Yes, my mother and his father are siblings." I hoped it would put her queries on that topic to rest and focus more on the project. "What kind of clients are we talking about?"

"I'm a lawyer. Remember?" He furrowed his brow.

I bit my lip. I didn't want to indulge in details of whether

Jazib was a lawyer. Truth to tell, he wasn't. You can't term a law school drop-out a lawyer. He quit in his final year just because! I didn't want to remind him of it in front of my boss, especially when he was talking about potential profits.

My continued stare tempted him to explain more.

"A few months ago, I decided to help out a friend by funding his dying practice. A partnership. I bring the money and he does the work. But I didn't want to be lazy, so I thought I'll help with the correspondence. But it's so boring. All these letters and so many! Somebody has to answer them."

It sounded like a profitable opportunity for Kulsom's firm. Knowing Jazib, he'd probably dump his entire paperwork on Kulsom's shoulders and pay good money to make it worth her while.

"It wouldn't hurt looking into," I told her. "Check if it's worth your time."

"Perfect." Jazib smiled. "I'll have the papers sent over here first thing tomorrow morning." He stood up and shook Kulsom's hand. "It was very nice to meet you."

"Likewise," she replied.

Once the courteous farewell was over, I walked him out to the elevator where he suddenly decided he wanted to take me out to lunch. "Just a burger or sandwiches or something, nothing fancy," he pleaded. "Come on! We rarely see each other."

That was true. He lived in the country with his family and farms and flocks and acres upon acres of land that would one day all be his. He was a landlord like so many before him who reigned as kings over vast territories handed to them through generations. His little kingdom was called Gurhkot, known for its sugarcane fields, molasses shops and sugar mills. He rarely came down from there to visit my urban world.

"You're right. It has been a while," I said and pushed the elevator button.

2

"I HAVEN'T HAD THIS in years!" Jazib stuffed his mouth with yet another piece of pani puri.

"The gol gappa you have in South Punjab is not the same," I said, fondly eyeing the round hollows of crispy crepe served with chickpeas and spicy tamarind water.

"Yes, the yogurt in that makes it a whole new dish." He tossed his empty plate in a nearby trashcan and wiped his mouth with a single-ply napkin. His sunglasses gleamed against his light skin, a blue slim-fit dress shirt contoured his torso favourably, and dark trousers flaunted his long legs. He'd sensibly left his suit jacket in the car considering the hot sun and sticky breeze of a Karachi beach. His mass of dark hair was tousled and adoringly fringed his forehead. It had been two years since I'd seen him, and his boyish charm had only increased over that time.

"You never should've broken our engagement." He smiled at me.

"We were never engaged, Jazib." I threw away my leftover pani puri. The spice was irritating my throat.

"Not in the true 'will you marry me' sense, of course, but we were spoken for since birth," he argued.

"And you agree with that?"

"We make sense."

"No, we don't."

"Maya…" he hesitated. "I need to get married. That's the only way Baba Saeen will ever let me have my share of the land or I'll just die living on allowances."

"Oh please, that is a pathetic excuse." I wanted to laugh. His weekly allowance was probably more than what I made in an entire year. I saw zero issues with his life.

"I want independence," he argued. "*And* they want me to settle down. That's also a thing."

"Then, find yourself a nice girl. One you could make a case for. One you'd *want* to marry."

He sighed and gave me a tired look. Jazib wanting to marry anyone? We both knew that was a lost cause. He could flirt, had a long list of girlfriends he'd conveniently ditched and jilted without much, if any, consequence for him and had quite a reputation for it too, but he would never want to settle down. Unless he fell in love.

That was my theory for him.

Jazib hadn't been in love, ever. Naturally, whenever he was confronted with the question of settling down, it led him to me – his fiancée in the eyes of our parents, a girl he didn't have to either love or make a case for but still could marry with fanfare and zero objection from anyone.

But we didn't want that.

I was too independent for him.

He was too much of a *Vadera Saeen* for me.

"So, it's a no?" he asked, as though he already knew the answer but was just making sure.

I wrinkled my nose. "I'm sorry. I can't marry you. I can help you find a nice girl though."

"I've got a list of nice girls, thank you very much."

I chuckled at his mock retort and we walked back to his car. The brand-new metallic silver Benz went well with his taste for shiny things. This was probably the flavour of the year. I didn't ask what he'd been driving last year. All I knew was that he'd had an intimidating black SUV the last time he'd visited and he didn't drive any car for more than a year.

"You should visit the haveli, Maya." He revved up the engine. "Phupo misses you," he said, referring to my mother, his paternal aunt.

"Twice in a year is good enough, Jazib. I was there this winter. You were away at college, which reminds me…" I turned to him in my seat, "*Why* would you quit? How could you?"

"Oh, for heaven's sake, don't start that again."

"You would've been a lawyer."

"I don't need to be one, okay?" He rolled his eyes. "I'm a zamindar. I got acres to my name. I'm rich already."

"Education isn't a means to get rich, Jazib. It's about becoming a better you. And by the way, didn't you say you wanted financial independence? A job could miraculously do that."

"Or a wife." He snickered.

"Oh yes, that's why I'm so valuable to you, isn't it?" I frowned at him.

"Don't be silly. You know I love you. You're like a sister to me."

"A sister you just proposed to."

He made a face as if his insides would hurl all over him. "Okay, we're never speaking of it again. I've no idea what our parents were thinking."

"They weren't." I scoffed and then a thought crossed my mind. "Why did you really come here? To propose? All that business talk with Kulsom was…?"

"That was genuine," he assured me. "I was looking for someone like you guys and your dad directed me to it. It's a big project, really." He delved into details that weren't particularly interesting but as I listened, I realised Kulsom might want to hire interns. This workload would need extra help.

"Well, I'm glad you're doing something," I said. "Are you coming to Abba's for dinner tonight?"

"Your dad's fancy dinners are so boring," he said, rolling the car into my office parking lot. "And your stepmom hates me."

"Arju is like that with everyone. Don't worry about her."

"But I don't want to stay the night in Karachi. I could be home by the time that dinner starts."

"Please?" I made puppy eyes. "I don't want to be alone there. I won't know anyone except Abba and Arju and they'd want me to make friends with her all-American sister."

"Is she pretty?"

"How would I know? No one's ever met her."

"You should invite that professor of yours." He winked. "What's his name? Arhaan?"

My heart skipped a beat. I don't know why it always did that every time I heard his name or saw him or – I mean, we weren't romantically involved or anything. He was just very drop-dead-OMG-gorgeous, and I liked to look at him. A lot. "We're just friends," I said seriously.

"Oh, sure." Jazib chuckled but when I frowned, he promised to behave. "Okay fine, I'll come. I'll pick you up."

"I'll come myself. You just be at the party."

"No, I'll pick you up. I'm here now." And there it was, in his tone, that unspoken sense of control. His style was subtle so I wasn't infuriated but I couldn't shake off a long-lost memory where Jazib, handsome as he was with all his boyish charm, had barked orders at me to wear a bigger chador in public so that I could be more like a *respectable* woman.

It was an eventful summer at Gurhkot. Those were the good days when Ammi and Abba were together, and I lived in a blissful bubble where I ruled. Ten years of age and born in the city, I'd hardly ever worn the traditional shalwar kamiz, let alone a chador. Besides, the heat of the plains turned every cloth to sandpaper that scratched my skin. Jazib, three years my senior, had offered to give me a ride in his father's new four-wheeler with a retractable roof around the green acres that exhibited the extravagant wealth of both our families. Ammi had given me a cotton scarf to cover my head with, but it kept slipping off in the fresh morning breeze as I stuck my head out through the sunroof, enjoying the landscape, loving the wind in my hair.

"Cover your head," Jazib warned, standing beside me.

"I don't want to," I said, shrugging my shoulders so that the scarf slipped even further.

"Hey!" suddenly he growled. "Cover yourself. Didn't your mother teach you anything? Why didn't she give you a bigger chador? You're a *girl*."

My eyes widened at the outburst. Nobody had ever talked to me like that. How dared he? Scary as he'd hoped his reddened face might've been, I wasn't frightened. I was offended. "Don't talk about my mother. And don't tell me what to do." I pointed a stern finger at his face. When he tried to grab it, I pushed him away, nearly knocking him off his feet. The shock on his face was dramatic.

Upon arriving at the haveli, he marched straight to his father and announced that he no longer wished to be my beau.

My beau?

That was the weirdest thing I'd ever heard and weirder still was Ammi's confirmation of it. "Don't worry about it," she said. "It won't happen until you're older."

Was she serious?

I'd run to Jazib later that night to tell him that I couldn't be his fiancée, to which he strongly agreed, and we shook on it. And thus began our awkward – but cemented in time – friendship.

Later that same year, Jazib was sent off to Karachi to stay with us and to go to the same school I went to. He discovered a whole new world outside of his bubble and I found a new friend. After high school and a half-hearted attempt at college, he went back to his acres in Gurhkot. Tensions between Ammi and Abba mounted beyond reconciliation. Abba finally married Arjumand and brought her home, and Ammi permanently moved to our haveli in Kesar, a smaller village in Gurhkot's neighbourhood.

This had happened years ago. Jazib and I had both grown much since then. We both had a lot of memories between us. I'd become better with the ways of the haveli, accepted my conservative feudal roots and its norms of Vadera Shahi. Jazib had become civilised, more tactful. But I wasn't certain if the raw landlord in him was fully tamed, for that beast, once within, was hardly ever put to sleep.

3

WHEN I REACHED HOME, Aya-Ji was already waiting in the car porch as usual, rolling her tasbih beads, a tiny billowing white dot against the glistening red exterior of my house. It blended well with the rest of the cookie-cutter bungalows that looked like giant blocks of colourful Lego from a distance. Soft streetlamps and palms trees dancing in the sea breeze added to the charm of this gated neighbourhood.

"You are late. I hope you didn't forget about the dinner at Saeen's house." Aya-Ji fixed her chador and followed me inside, picking up after me as I kicked off my shoes, flung my bag on a chair, slipped off my jacket and crashed on the couch. She poured out some ice water in a tall glass and handed it to me. "Arju brought some new outfits for you. I put the bags in your room."

"That's nice of her." I took a sip. "Could you make some chai?"

"But you have a dinner to go to." She furrowed her brow, reaching for a kettle and tea-leaves.

Aya-Ji was my nanny, my surrogate mother since the day I was born and more when Abba and Ammi decided to split. They never divorced though. Ammi, popularly known as Bano Bibi, moved to acres of rural beauty and boundless skies and ruled her feudal kingdom in peace. Meanwhile, Abba lived his big city life in Karachi with his lovely city wife. And I, their only child, ping-ponged between them until I got a job and moved out.

I didn't complain. Life happened in all sorts of ways.

I critically eyed my reflection in the long mirror. A boat-neck knee-length kamiz of mint chiffon sparkling with gold thread embroidery, and a pair of ivory silk trousers. It accentuated my curves and flaunted my dusky skin. I admired Arjumand's choice for sending it over for me. There was no dupatta with the suit, so I didn't bother matching one. I pulled my hair into a low messy bun, strapped on a pair of glittery stilettos, and headed downstairs.

"You're waiting for someone?" Aya-Ji asked as she saw me standing by the living room window that overlooked the street.

"Jazib is picking me up," I replied.

"He's in town?"

"Just came today. I asked him to stay for dinner."

"Acha…" she sighed, sitting down in a nearby chair. "I wish you'd make up your mind about one of these boys. Do it while you're still young."

I looked at her, thinking if I should tell her about Jazib's proposal. She knew about the childhood engagement, but she also knew that neither Jazib nor I honoured it. "One of these boys?" I asked instead.

"I like Sahib," she said like she had a million other times.

Sahib – her fond nickname for Arhaan seemed to fit him to the tee. It spoke to the grace with which he did everything, the elegance that was so seductive. I liked Sahib too, because, who wouldn't? But Sahib couldn't care less about that. I'd invited him for this dinner, but he'd politely refused because "work".

I looked back at the street. A pair of headlights swerved by the curb and stopped. Jazib was on time. I bid a quick Khuda-hafiz to Aya-Ji and headed outside.

Abba lived about fifteen minutes away from me. It suited him. He could come calling whenever he pleased, and it was easier to keep tabs on me that way. I didn't mind. It was fun having him over. We played video games, listened to music, and he would cook for me. He would get to know tiny details about my life that were important to me for various silly reasons – my unusual job, the assortment of crazy clients I dealt with, and my knack for taking pictures. The days that Abba came over were a little window into my carefreeness that I'd lost quickly to shouting matches between my parents and then the awkward inclusion of Arjumand in my life.

Abba was a construction business mogul and his house, a sparkling jewel at the end of a dark cove, was testament of his skills. The sprawling structure sat on a four-acre lot surrounded by an intimidating boundary wall and a guarded entrance. I remembered every corner, every pillar, and every event that was ever hosted there.

Arjumand hadn't changed the décor even though her modern minimalistic tastes were vastly different from the intricate traditional themes that spoke more to Ammi. Everything from the faux finished walls, original oils that adorned them, delicate vases that sparkled in niches, carved Chinioti wooden furniture with gleaming damask upholstery, crystal chandeliers hanging from vaulted ceilings, to the authentic Persian rugs that graced the marble floors; it was a mansion of rich hues.

Past the long foyer was the main lounge that spilled into an expansive formal living area. There were a few dozen less people there than I expected. I spotted Abba but before I could head his way, Arjumand called to me from the other end. She was standing in a group of four women, one of whom looked like her younger self.

That must be the sister.

"Come with me," I said to Jazib and grabbed his arm.

After briefly introducing us to her friends, Arjumand presented her sister with an affectionate flare. "This is Ranya, my baby sister. This is her first time in Pakistan in more than fifteen years. Maya, I'm sure the two of you will hit it off."

I gave Jazib a quick *told-you-so* look that he registered with a grin. Then we both smiled politely at Ranya. She was tall, slim, and fair with a mass of glossy chestnut hair that spilled over her delicate shoulders to her tiny waist, her flawless makeup accentuated her hazel eyes and plumped her otherwise thin lips. She wore a long, shimmery wrap dress that complemented her elegant frame. I noticed that Arjumand was wearing something similar in bold blue, but it was tailored to her stouter physique. My stepmom with her dark hair and charming smile set her own standards that never backfired.

"You know, Ranya," Jazib spoke first, adding a sexy lilt to his voice. "I wasn't keen on coming tonight but…I'm beginning to think this evening may not be a total waste after all."

"Jazib." I arched a warning brow. "It's her first time in Pakistan. We want her to *like* it here?"

"I'll make sure of that." He smiled at her. "How long will you be staying?"

I looked at Arjumand to find any warning bells going off in her corner, but she had already moved on to other guests. Jazib, looking dashing in his suit, had turned on his charm and was totally engaging the new girl. So much for bringing him to keep *me* company.

I rolled my eyes and went in search of Abba.

Several people, some of whom I knew and some I couldn't recall having ever met, greeted me, trying to hold a decent conversation about the weather and what else was new. I stepped away every time with a quick hello and a smile. Abba was in the same spot I'd seen him previously, animatedly talking to his small audience who had forgotten to even blink.

His large frame, draped in a loose grey suit, dominated the space. His peppered hair was ever so thick and matched his bushy moustache, and his face had the healthy glow of a life well lived.

"There's no need for exhibition," he was saying. "Charity, uplifting the disenfranchised, these are noble deeds. They require sobriety and grace. Not loud, disruptive activism."

"Oh, yes, very true," everyone agreed unanimously.

"I think it's important to lend a loud and clear voice to those who can't speak for themselves." My objection had everyone staring at me. "We should use our privilege to draw attention, not just help in silence."

Abba's face broke into a big smile and he pulled me into a hug. "This is my daughter. She has some very strong opinions." He went on to introduce his friends, relating their names and careers as though he was reading out their business cards. After a few minutes of polite talk, the group dispersed into the larger party crowd, leaving Abba all to me.

"I'm so glad you came," he said. "I was worried I might miss you."

"You're going somewhere?"

"Have to meet a new team we employed for this new project and, oh, just some boring business."

"Will you eat with them?" I tried not to sound disappointed. This was a long-entertained habit of his. He would sneak out of his own parties for business meetings, leaving Ammi extremely annoyed. However, Arjumand didn't seem to mind much.

"I already sneaked in a few bites from the kitchen." He winked at me and chuckled, including me in his secret. "But I want you to eat properly and enjoy, okay? And try and make friends with Ranya. She doesn't know anyone here."

"I will," I said, stretching my lips into a smile that promised nothing.

I found my way back to Ranya after Abba left for his meeting. "How are you liking it so far?" I asked her. "You must've met a lot of people tonight."

She looked at Jazib with something like gratitude in her smile. "Jazib has been nice enough to keep me company. I don't really know anyone but my sister here."

"The pleasure is all mine, of course," he said, staring boldly into her big brown eyes. "Why else would I be here?"

"Because I invited you?" I glared at him, hoping he'd take the cue and stop ogling my stepmom's baby sister. There was a truckload of reasons why she would eat us alive if she got wind of him flirting with Ranya, and I expected Jazib to know that. "Oh, look, Arju is coming our way."

Jazib's gaze shifted from a very blushing Ranya to her sister. "Arjumand-Ji," he said. "Ranya let us in on a secret about you."

"Really?" Her plastic smile froze on her face. "What secret?"

"She says you haven't aged a day in fifteen years."

"Oh!" She broke into giggles, shaking her head and announced that dinner was served. Ranya threw us another one of her sugar-sweet smiles and followed her sister.

"You're so cheesy." I pinched Jazib's arm.

"It's the truth," he said. "Did you know how incredibly older she is than Ranya?"

"Yes, they have like half a dozen siblings in between."

"Yeah, so for someone her age, she's hot."

"You're ogling my stepmom now?"

"She just *is*."

I lost him again to the food options at the long, white-clothed buffet tables. The displays were appetizing and enviably Pinterest-y. The cuisine featured all the party favourites including biryani, korma, tikka, simple salads and raita, desi desserts of halva and kheer, and chai. I was told Ranya had decided the menu but Arjumand had added her signature twists in taste and presentation to every dish. I helped myself to a plateful of rice and kebabs, then made my way to a vacant table that filled up quickly with guests who expected me to make conversation.

Remember me?

Are you married?

Engaged, then?

See there, that's my son, you're the same age!

I quickly gobbled up as much as I could and excused myself. Handing a waiter my plate, I grabbed some soda and made my way out of the dinner area. Jazib was nowhere to be seen but I did spot Arjumand introducing Ranya to a horde of fashionable socialites – the formidable Rishta Aunties who were indefinitely stuck in a matchmaking mode, eyeing every young person of marriageable age and prospects with care and ranking them on a mental scale of suitability, desirability, and possibility. I'd endured that onslaught many times. My childhood engagement to Jazib was never announced, hence I was still a catch, presumably at the top of the charts given my family background and my father's wealth and my grandfather's fame. The only part I played in scoring high were my "dusky, yet good looks". Not my education, not my goals, certainly not my opinions. In fact, I was told if I smiled more and talked less, I'd do better.

Now, it was Ranya's turn through the grind. She was looking at all the faces, her smile forced and confused and head nodding as words failed to make it to her lips at appropriate times, or maybe it was her heavily accented Urdu that made her consciously not talk much.

I was about to slip away before any of them saw me when a masculine voice startled me. "I'm Amir," he said. He was young, dark suit, similar to the dozen men already around me. "My dad is friends with yours. It's funny we've never met..." he rambled on, but I was only listening for a pause in his speech.

"Excuse me, I have to go," I said the first chance I got and walked away.

He wasn't the first person to ever walk up to me like that. I'd always been dragged into conversations I never wanted to have. That was why I didn't enjoy Abba's large gatherings. That was why I'd asked Jazib to come along, so he'd be by my side.

I switched on my phone and sent a brief text:

SOS! I'm dying!

I didn't expect a prompt reply, but it was worth a try.

Out on the patio, it was quieter. Only a few people hung out there and they were all too involved with each other to notice me. I went to an empty bench in a corner, kicked off my heels and put up my feet. The night breeze rustled through the palms and carried their leafy scent to me. This was my favourite spot in the backyard. I closed my eyes and listened to the night.

"Why the SOS? You look mighty fine to me." His voice, I could've recognised it in a million others. My eyes popped open and I found him standing in front of me.

"Arhaan! You really came."

He smiled and sat beside me. He wore a white shirt underneath a black jacket over matching trousers, no tie. "It was easier since I was already here." He smelled deliciously of something citrusy.

"What do you mean?"

"I was in a meeting with your dad."

"You're the new team on the project?"

He nodded. "I didn't realise it was him we were preparing the research for. I just finished presenting to him."

"Have you eaten anything?" I looked over at the buffet tables that were still laden. "I could get you something."

"Not hungry." He rubbed his eyes; his lashes were a mile long. "It's been a long day. How about you?"

"Okay, so…" I started to sing like a canary, delving into every detail from how I'd got up in the morning to my "accomplishments" in the workplace to Jazib's visit. "That reminds me, Kulsom would need interns. Do you know anyone?"

"Nobody I can think of right now…" he paused, then, shaking his head, turned to me, "why are you still there?"

"Where?"

"It's not a real job, Maya." He took a long serious look at my face. "It never should've gone beyond an internship unless you took up writing there or editing or anything substantial." His tone became firmer when I pulled a face and threw back my head in protest. "I'm serious. You're wasting your time. What exactly is your job? Telling people off for your boss?"

"It takes a lot more skill than you think."

"You have so much potential," he argued. "Join your father. His new construction project could really use a fresh mind like yours. Like you did with Green Point, only you'd be more involved this time."

Green Point was my neighbourhood and an experiment for Abba who had many traditionally fancy projects under his belt. I remembered how those bungalows were once drab and beige until I meddled with the project. I coaxed him to let me decide the colour palette and as a result, all homes in the colony were painted bright. A yellow house here, a teal there, an apple green tucked in between, and an orange structure flaunting a corner lot somewhere. I picked a red one for me and after months of arguing, he finally agreed to let me move there.

"But I'm not interested in construction or buildings or business," I said.

"You're a business graduate."

"Only because Abba thought it was the coolest thing and I didn't have a better idea."

"Nonsense, Maya, I taught you. You were one of my best students."

"So of course, I must become a business star and head some Fortune 500 something because Arhaan Mahyar was my teacher," I said teasingly.

He stared at me. "It's not impossible."

"Fine. Would you smile if I promised to think about it?" His frown lines melted to give way to a warm smile that made everything better. "I'll see you more now that you're working with Abba."

"And you'd like that?"

"Of course."

He looked at me for a long moment, then shaking his head, leaned back in the bench. "You're just a kid," he said.

I didn't know what that sad tinge to his tone meant and I didn't ask. I also killed an urge to snuggle too scandalously close to him because stepping out of the friend-zone for a guy I'd crushed on forever would be just the worst because…what if he didn't like it…?

He could be very stern if he wanted to. I recalled our first interaction at my business school. I'd walked in late and seen him standing at the podium with a list, checking off names.

"And you are?" He cast a cursory glance over me.

"Are you the class monitor?" I joked, and everyone else broke into laughter that quickly died as he looked up sharply. Tall, chiselled, tan, warm brown eyes; he could've just walked out of a designer's business-casual catalogue.

"Arhaan Mahyar," he said. "You only get one tardy so I'm guessing you picked today. A second occurrence will mean you're not serious about this course."

He was my teacher?! I'd spent the rest of the class figuring this mess out. *Was I allowed to crush on him or was that an instant demerit?*

I decided I was an adult, this was college, he was part of visiting faculty, I only had him for the one course, and it was just infatuation that nobody would ever know about because I wouldn't ever tell. Except by the end of our semester, all my girlfriends knew. Maybe the bazillion pictures I'd taken of him (and shared with them) while stalking him all over campus were a huge giveaway. And the fact that he and I became friends didn't help either. He even recommended me for an internship that quickly turned into my first job at Edite & More.

"You worship him!" my friends would say. "You two should so be together!"

"I've friend-zoned him and you can't go back from there," I'd explain.

Honestly, it was he who'd friend-zoned me, but it didn't matter who did it first.

It was done.

There was a distinct click-clack of heels on the concrete and I saw Arjumand standing in front of us. "I was wondering where you went," she said to me and then smiled at Arhaan, her eyes tactfully taking in his every detail. "I don't believe we've met. I'm Arjumand Badruddin."

"Arhaan Mahyar." He stood up. "I'm the research head for Mister Badr's new project."

"Oh, yes." She tucked her hand under her chin, the jewels on her wrist sparkled brilliantly. "I've heard of you. Badr seems extremely impressed. You must've done something right."

"That's very kind of him."

They talked some more. Arjumand insisted that he try some of her favourite dishes on that night's menu, and then, graciously extended another invitation to him to feel free to drop by anytime he liked. That was huge since I'd known her to hardly entertain anyone like that, not even family. She had never exactly invited Jazib over nor did she spend much time with him even when he visited. Not that I faulted her for it. That man could get insufferable without even trying.

"Have you met my sister, Ranya?" She gave Arhaan a wide smile. "I hosted this dinner just so she'd meet people and make new friends, get the feel of Pakistan."

"I hope she likes it here," he replied gently, stuffing his hands in his pockets.

I knew that gesture. Arjumand couldn't tell but behind that polite demeanor, he was blocking her off. He was tired and wanted to go home and the only reason he was still standing there was because of me.

"Arhaan was just heading home," I intervened. "He stopped by when he saw me."

"Oh, I'm sorry. I won't detain you any longer," she said and held out her hand to him. "It was very nice meeting you, Arhaan."

He delicately took her hand but didn't kiss it. Then, he turned to me. "I can give you a ride."

"Oh, no. I'll go with Jazib. It'll be a while for us. You should go. It's late."

"Okay," he said, and with a final farewell nod, walked away.

Arjumand kept staring after him until he disappeared. "Such a nice boy." She turned to me. "You never told me you knew such a nice boy."

"I've known him since college…" I waited for her to ask more but she just smiled with a peculiar glint in her eyes. "And whatever are you thinking?"

"You should quit that job thing and settle down. Arhaan leaves a nice impression. Badr was all praises."

"No Arju, it's nothing like that. I'm not ready for marriage anyway."

"But he's so much better than Jazib," she argued.

"Jazib is a non-issue. Nobody even remembers the engagement. It's like, ancient history."

"True. So, you're sure you're just friends? Arhaan and you?" She sighed when I nodded. "Did you eat properly? I think you should stay the night. It's late for you to go."

"It's only midnight, and I won't be alone. Jazib will drive me home." Distant sounds of loud laughter caught our attention. It was Jazib with a group of young men and women, perhaps cracking jokes, having a good time and certainly not looking in the mood to call it a night. I saw Arjumand purse her lips. "I think you'd want him to leave now," I said.

"You're not going with him. He looks high."

"He was sober when we came in."

"These *vaderas*." She sounded agitated, glaring at Jazib who was now busy taking selfies.

"Yeah, we'll leave now," I said and turned on my heel to grab a certain someone by the ear and head home.

4

"WHAT THE HELL HAPPENED here?" I stared at the mess of papers and brown boxes in my cubicle.

"This is all the stuff Mister Sultan wants us to work with," Meera explained. "I literally had no other place to put it in."

"Where's my chair?" I couldn't see the desk either to be honest.

"Oh, it's in there somewhere," Jazib said with his face fresh as the morning sun. He stood clad in a cotton button-down and jeans, casually sipping coffee from a café paper cup. I wished he'd choke on it and die.

"How many letters do you want us to write in a day?" I frowned. "This looks like it's been piling up for years."

"Oh, everything," he said. "Rewrite all the office documents. There are many grammatical mistakes in the old ones."

"You can't rewrite old documents. That's not even legal. Does Kulsom know about this?"

"Not in so many words…" Meera mumbled. Even she couldn't believe what she'd done by letting Jazib in with the boxes. "I can arrange for a chair and table for you in Kulsom's room," she said in a conciliatory tone.

"No." I examined the stacks for another second, then,

pushed them all off. The taped cubes fell to the floor with a thud, clearing off my chair and a section of the table. "We definitely need interns now. Do we have any applications from last year's interviews? Some of them might come if still available."

"I'll check," she said, and turning on her heel, left.

"I already hired someone to help out," Jazib told me.

"How kind," I deadpanned. "Anyone from last night?" I expected an eye-roll from him at my jibe but instead he started grinning. "What?"

"Ranya," he said, putting a hand over his heart.

"Ranya?" I blinked.

"Did you know she's doing something in human resources with some correspondence something as one of her majors? She'll be brilliant for this job." He had shot off into praising her many attributes, but I was still stuck on the first word he'd uttered.

"*Ranya?*"

He stopped in mid-sentence and stared. "Yes," he said. "You remember Ranya? We met her last night."

I closed my eyes and started rubbing my temples, thinking of less violent ways of making him disappear from my life. I came up with none. "She's Arju's sister, Jazib," I said seriously. "You cannot possibly swing her around the way you do your other—"

"Of course not." He frowned. "Did you even hear her résumé? She isn't experienced but good enough to intern."

He was probably right for once. If she was studying correspondence, she just might come in handy. And if Jazib hired her, it would mean less workload for our office, and consequently, less boxes in my cubicle.

"But she's just one person," I said. "This work is too much for one person."

"I'll help her," he said.

"If you can hire her, you can hire a few other people too," I suggested. "That way you won't have to outsource all of your correspondence and rewriting."

"I would hire more but…" he paused, making his way through the boxes to me, "but I don't have an office. Not a concrete one where I can sit and, you know, work."

"What about your friend's?"

"He doesn't live in Karachi. He lives near Gurhkot."

"But you hired Ranya."

"For you," he said. "I'll recommend her to your boss and then she'll hire her."

"But you said you would help her…" I narrowed my eyes and stared at his face. Something of a bilious annoyance rising from my gut told me that my first instinct about the way he mentioned Ranya was on point. To Jazib, women were either hot or forgettable. There was nothing in between.

"Yeah so, I'll drop by every day. You know we did hit it off last night."

Before I could respond, the dull ring of an elevator and the voices that followed interrupted me. In a matter of minutes, the ladies of Edita & More were in and another workday had officially kicked off.

Jazib let out a soft whistle as he eyed all the women on the floor. "Think I'll go say hi."

Ugh!

I grabbed him by the sleeve and pulled him down to the floor, crouching between the towering stacks of boxes so nobody could see us. I couldn't let him loose among my colleagues before setting some ground rules. He protested but I fiercely shushed him. "This is my office and if you step even a hair out of line, I swear to God, I'll kill you."

"I understand that," he said innocently. "Perfectly."

"And don't you for one second think I don't see through your

Ranya ruse. She's my stepmother's baby sister for goodness sake. You can't toy with her, I won't let you."

"I swear, Maya, I'm not."

"Don't you shit with me, Jazib." I pointed a stern finger in his face. "I saw you ogling her last night, charming her and talking and what not. I know how you play. I've seen it all before and that's none of my concern, but you cannot do this to Ranya. Especially in my office."

"Maya, I honestly think she'll be a great help. She really will. And I'm not toying with her...I..." he stopped.

Something hard sank to the pit of my stomach in a whiff of premonition. "You what?"

"I think I'm in love with her."

"Oh, for fuck's sake, you just met her!"

"I know right, it's crazy." he chuckled.

The number of times Jazib had professed to falling in love was too many for me to remember. He was a poster boy for the rich and the flirtatious. It was the same story every time and even those instances hadn't been as outrageous as this one. He'd known those other girls for at least a few days. What was worse, I'd seen Ranya return Jazib's attention.

And she was Arjumand's *sister*.

Arjumand had no children of her own and always talked of Ranya as one. There was a reason she had smilingly entertained all the Rishta Aunties at the party. Being an older, more established sibling, she would have a say in making a match for Ranya. And she couldn't stand Jazib. Knowing her, she wouldn't even let something as harmless as a prolonged conversation between them slide, let alone a romantic connection. It was a miracle she hadn't noticed anything last night.

There was no way in hell I could allow anything to happen between Jazib and Ranya, on my watch, at least.

"You need to un-hire her," I told him. "There's no way she can work here. You're not going to recommend her to anyone."

"But I—"

"Maya?" It was Kulsom who interrupted us, knocking softly at the door frame. "Are you in here?"

I stood up instantly, causing my head to spin a little. Jazib caught me in time so now the two of us stood face to face, his hands on my waist and mine on his shoulders.

"Yes, I'm here," I said, quickly detaching myself from him.

"We weren't doing anything bad," he said.

I silently cursed him as my boss stood there blinking, clutching a clipboard to her breast. "Well, I'm glad you could join us this morning, Mister Sultan," she finally said. "I'm especially thankful for your recommendation. I do have a few other names on my list. I'm sure we'll beat all deadlines."

My ears pricked like a cat's. "What recommendation?"

She looked at her clipboard and read, "Ranya Raees. Mister Sultan sent her name in an email last night."

"And you've hired her?" It wasn't really a question.

"She seems qualified. I've called her in for an interview today. And Maya, I'm sorry for this mess. I wish we had more space."

"It's fine," I said. What choice did I have?

Although Jazib initially offered to help sort out the numerous boxes and their contents, he only lasted in there for twenty minutes. Tossing a particularly stinky-looking file at me, he hopped out of the cubicle and made his way to the kitchenette. I hoped he'd get really bored and leave but emerging giggles all over the floor told another story altogether.

"Jazib looks really good." Nina came up to me. "Did he always look this good?"

"Is Kulsom not in to enforce some discipline?" I frowned.

"Discipline?" She laughed. "She's our boss, not our principal. This isn't a school."

"But nobody is working!" I threw up my hands, gesturing towards the room full of women, only few of whom were sitting at their desks, heads bent and working. The rest were either hovering over Jazib or sitting in their seats with eyes pinned on him, listening as if he was some deity imparting great knowledge. "He's not even that good looking." I rolled my eyes and turned away.

"Are you kidding?" Nina followed me in. "He's totally attractive. Like one of those hotties in a fragrance commercial by the ocean."

"No, that would be Arhaan," I said without thinking, but Nina's smile told me I was about to regret it when she commenced with her teasing. I held up a hand to warn her. "I'm totally not in that mood."

"I was just going to agree with you," she said, leaning against the edge of my desk. "Only he's not the one by the ocean. He's the one with the city lights and night life and expensive cars."

I couldn't help smiling at that. "Wearing sharp suits and walking with a swagger."

"So suave." She winked and we both laughed. "You still got pictures of him?"

Of course, I did!

I grabbed my phone and started scrolling through the photo library. They were all there. A wholly different life preserved in pictures, our years in college, and an entire album of Arhaan's close-ups and shots that I'd stolen of him on numerous occasions during his days with us as a teacher – undeniable evidence of my extreme crush on him.

"Look at him." Nina was totally ogling. "And he's not even in makeup."

"Right? This is his everyday face," I added.

"By the way, Maya…" she took the phone from me, scrutinising the pictures with a different expression. "These pictures are really good. You have a knack for photography."

"You think so?"

"I think this is your talent."

I wanted to continue that conversation when I caught a glimpse of a slim figure walking towards Kulsom's office. My heart sank. Ranya was there for an interview, which I believed was just a formality since a hefty client had recommended her. If she met even half the requirements, Kulsom would hire her because we really were in dire need of extra hands to help with the editing.

I filled Nina in.

"Are you serious?" she gasped. "Girl, you should stay as far away from this drama as possible. Your stepmom will not like this."

I knew that.

It was evident I had to concoct a plan to either not have Ranya work here or to keep Jazib away. He was still in the kitchenette and chatting. I assumed he hadn't noticed Ranya walk in.

"Hey!" I went and stood next to him, smiling sweetly. "Don't you have anywhere to be?"

"Such as?"

"I thought you were going back to Gurhkot today."

He shook his head. "No, I've decided to stay. And I realised my beach condo needs a makeover. The ladies here have such wonderful ideas."

It was impossible. Jazib didn't pick up on tones or subtle hints. You had to either hit him with a hammer or trick him. I opted for the latter.

"So, Mamu-Jaan called. Something important he wanted to talk to you about," I lied with a straight face, invoking his father. "I think you better leave."

I saw his smile give way to a concerned expression. He stood up and took out his phone. "Why didn't he call me?"

"Maybe he couldn't get through to you. You know, signals. You should talk to him on your way."

"Okay, but I was just waiting for Ranya—"

"I'll let her know you asked." I looped my arm around his and started leading towards the elevator. "It was really nice of you to recommend her."

"Really? You don't mind?" He looked relieved.

"Not at all." I gave him a big smile as I pushed the elevator button. The doors opened instantly. "Call me when you get there, okay?" I said softly, giving his hand a gentle squeeze.

He looked slightly taken aback but didn't say anything. Instead, he stepped into the elevator and pressed to go down. I stood there until the doors closed. Then, I got back to my cubicle with some peace of mind.

The office atmosphere also returned to normal. Everyone was back to work; nobody was suddenly craving coffee or chai or juice or snacks anymore. A glimpse of Kulsom's room showed Ranya's interview was still in progress. She sat there talking to her, making an impression.

"So, Maya…" Kareena, a web editor who spoke with a toxically sugared lilt, stabbed my thoughts. That woman could give anyone diabetes if she tried. "You know the new client?"

"Yes," I said and picked up a file from my desk. I had much work to do to clear my room.

She hung by the doorway, smiling her signature condescending smile. "He's your mother's brother's son? Your cousin?"

"Yes."

"He was waiting for that new girl, what's her name – Ranya. You didn't tell him she was here?"

I slapped shut the file and stared at her instead. "Oh yes, I weeded out the competition because he's mine. In my family, we still believe in cousin marriages. Got a problem with that?"

"Oh?" She was surprised. "I see," she said faintly, and then walked away.

I watched the space she was occupying a second ago and shook my head, wondering what it was about handsome men that made women act so weird.

Obviously, Jazib found out I'd lied to him about the phone call. It took him fifteen minutes to get to talk to Mamu-Jaan but by then he was already driving.

"This isn't funny." He growled at me over the phone.

"I'm sorry but you had to leave," I said.

"I'm coming right back, okay," he threatened. "And I'm going to sit there and help Ranya and work with her."

"If you come back, I'll have you tossed out on your behind."

"Maya!" His tone was incredulous and a little amused. "What's your beef with Ranya, man? Are you jealous?"

"I literally threw up a little in my mouth," I said dryly. "This is an office. *My* office. I won't have you whoring around in my office. You want to date that girl? Do it on your own time when she's not working here or living at my father's house."

"I don't take orders from you."

"Oh, I think you will, or I'll tell Mamu-Jaan all about what you're up to, lover boy."

This was one threat that had stood the test of time. In Mamu-Jaan's eyes – as much I hated to admit it – I was Jazib's fiancée, the only one who had a right to all his attention, all his love. If I told on Jazib about Ranya, it would have grave consequences for him.

Jazib and I had often wondered how his father (and my mother) would react when either one of us tied the knot with someone else. We'd hoped there wouldn't be blood.

"You know what, Maya?" he huffed over the line. "One of these days, I'll marry you and lock you up in a dungeon and *then* I'll whore around all I want."

"Don't be silly. You don't have a dungeon."

"I'll have one built just for you!"

"Bye, Jazib," I said and hung up.

I hoped this would take care of things at least for the day. Hopefully, Jazib would act smart and not come back. I had tons to do in my office. I was about to get back to the files when Meera walked in with Ranya. Her face lit up as she saw me, and I was sure there was nothing reciprocal on mine. This girl had just become such a red flag from the moment we'd met. To top that, Meera gave me glad tidings that the intern would assist me. Only me. Nobody else.

Joy.

I managed a smile as Ranya expressed her excitement over her new job. I didn't understand why she needed one to begin with. Wasn't she on vacation? Shouldn't she just enjoy the city rather than being tied up with a work schedule?

"This experience would look good on my résumé," she said. "I'm here for some time so might as well not waste it."

"Does Arju know you're here?" I was suspicious. How'd she even let her out? She'd only landed a little more than seventy-two hours ago.

"I'm not used to her lifestyle. I need to keep busy," Ranya explained. "This internship was just too good of an opportunity to pass up."

"So, you made this decision yourself?"

"Of course." She looked at me as if I'd asked her the dumbest question ever.

Okay, so she wasn't as much under Arjumand's thumb as I thought.

We tidied up my office, and it took us the entire day. Ranya already had her work cut out for her so she didn't just sort and categorise, she made a stack of documents that she was to work on first. She wasn't a bad companion either to be honest. She liked to talk. By the end of the day, I pretty much knew everything about her life: youngest of five siblings, born and bred in the US, rich parents, sheltered lifestyle, mom was conservative but dad was too busy to care, and the brothers were off to college having fun with their own adulthood, Arjumand was the star of the family with her own established lifestyle and fame she'd earned for being a rich man's wife, and Ranya had just hatched and was new to the whole phenomenon called world. She was only nineteen.

I almost choked on my tea when she told me that.

Did Jazib know?

"You're a child," I said it like I was accusing her of a crime. "You should be in school, not looking for a job. Wait – Jazib said you were doing a correspondence major, right?"

"I'm in college," she said proudly. "And yes, that's one of my courses but now I'm here and I thought some experience would be nice."

*Hmm...*I shrugged my shoulders and got back to packing my stuff to leave. We were the only two left on the floor and I wanted to head home on time for once. "I can give you a ride," I offered her.

"Jazib said he'll pick me up," she said, her face beaming like a thousand-volt bulb. "He said he'll be waiting for me."

"He left." I smiled. "I'll drop you off."

"He left?" Her face was suddenly drained of all joy.

"Yeah." I crushed any pangs of guilt and looked at her with a straight face. "Let's go."

We'd just reached the reception desk when I froze in my tracks and stared at a couch in the small waiting lounge. Jazib was sitting there. He saw us approach and stood up, his face decorated with his usual boyish smirk while his gaze was pinned on me. His expression became drastically more pleasant when he looked at Ranya.

"I told you I'd wait," he said to her, a soft lilt in his voice that had sharp sirens ringing in my ears.

Ranya stood there, smiling up at him like a total fan girl. She had that explicit bright-eyed look about her that came with being smacked by cupid's entire arsenal on the head.

This had to stop!

"We're getting late, Ranya," I interrupted, trying to sound as firm as I could.

"Don't let us hold you back." Jazib shot me a burning look and returned his doting stare to Ranya. "The lady has alternate transportation."

She went pink! Her lips curled into a shy smile and her eyes became heavy with an emotion that could best be defined as enchantment.

"Fine," I said and started punching keys on my smartphone. "Let me tell Arju you'll be escorting her precious little sister for the evening."

"You don't have to tell her anything," Jazib said quickly.

"Really? Why?"

"Because she doesn't understand a thing!" He started off sharply, but immediately stopped as his gaze shifted to Ranya whose smile had faded slightly. "I mean she won't…understand why I went out of my way to…" he left the sentence incomplete, hoping it would fix itself.

"Is it out of your way? My sister's house?"

"Yes, but it isn't out of mine," I replied before Jazib could and held up my phone for him to kill another protest. "Or you can talk to Arju."

He held up his palms and stepped back. This was resignation. I bid him farewell, urged a visibly disappointed Ranya towards the elevator, and we were out of the building in no time.

5

"YOU. ARE. EVIL!" JAZIB was pacing my living room and fuming.

"Popcorn?" I offered him the large bowl I was eating from, curled up in my pyjamas in my comfy chair in front of the flat screen.

"Chai?" Aya-Ji hollered from the kitchen, dialling up Jazib's frustration a few more notches.

"No!" he shouted at both of us and slumped down on a couch next to me, holding his head in his hands. He'd been screaming at me for nearly the entire ten minutes he'd been in my house.

I dusted my hands, punched the remote and scrolled down a long list of pay-per-view movies. "What do you want to watch?" I asked him.

"Nothing!"

"I think you're overreacting."

"Are you insane?" He was riled up again. "You just ruined my life. Snatched away the one girl that I finally loved, and you really think I want to watch a movie? I don't want a movie!"

"You want banana shake?" Aya-Ji yelled from the kitchen. "I can make some."

Jazib clipped the bridge of his nose and shut his eyes. "Aya-Ji, *please.*"

"Banana shake sounds good, Aya-Ji," I told her, then looked at Jazib. "There are a million girls in this city and hundreds more where you live. Pick one of those."

"What's your beef with Ranya?"

"It's not her, it's *you*. You'll ditch her in seconds because you always do and she's Arju's sister and do you have any idea how much that'll complicate the already tricky situation between Ammi and Abba?"

"Oh, so this is all about you?"

"Yes."

"Maya, I swear I've never felt this way about anyone as I do about Ranya."

"She's nineteen years old," I informed him. "Did you know that?" His shocked face said he didn't. "And you're like three years away from the big Three-O. You and her – that's literally child abuse."

"Child?" Jazib found his words. "Legally, she's an adult. Also, she looks older. Like twenty-four."

"Oh, how charming. And wait till she's swept off her feet by a younger guy and sees you for the old man that you are. She'll dump you like a hot steel tumbler."

"Then...that'll be her choice."

What?

I peered at his face to make sure it was really him. Since when did Jazib Sultan become so mature about letting go of things he wanted? He was the kind of guy who was never denied anything and if he were, he'd find ways to own it. And he always won. In this material world, everything came with a price tag and Jazib was a tactful buyer. For him to talk about respecting someone else's choice was like saying the world didn't turn anymore.

"Banana shake," Aya-Ji announced as she came in with a tray holding two tall glasses. She set them on the small coffee table and lingered, as though she was holding back something she wanted to say.

"What is it, Aya-Ji?" I asked.

"Bano Bibi called again today," she said. "I think she's right. Why don't you two marry each other?"

"Aya-Ji…" Jazib looked at her, holding up his glass. "This is delicious but that's all I want from you. Not relationship advice."

"Hey!" I admonished him but Aya-Ji held up her hand to stop me.

She sat down in a nearby chair and stared at him square in the eye. "This is what your father wants too. If you really want to break off this engagement officially and finally, you need to settle down with someone who'll earn his favour just as much as Maya has."

"That's why Ranya—"

"Ranya won't do." She shook her head. "You need a girl with a feudal background like yours but better. Besides, Ranya has a million issues of her own. Her sister is one to begin with. If you ask me, you better get serious and find a suitable girl soon. Or you'll have to marry Maya. And Maya will not have a choice either." She looked at me with a warning in her eyes. "This is the vibe I got from your mother. You both are running out of time."

Jazib and I looked at each other and slumped back into our seats. Aya-Ji went back into the kitchen. This entire deal with a promise that our parents had made to each other in another age with neither our consent nor knowledge just stank.

"I'll have to talk to Ammi," I thought aloud. "I'll have to go to Kesar to talk to her in person."

"I'll come with you," Jazib said.

"You don't have to."

"No, I insist," he said. "If I'm there and I tell her I refuse this proposal and that I stand by you in not marrying me then she'll – you know – she'll get it. The two of us can convince her. Together."

"You think so?"

"I know that she'll be easier to convince than my father, and once she's convinced, she'll convince him." He sat back with his hands spread out as if he'd just played out a winning hand.

My gut told me he was right. Even if I couldn't persuade Ammi, I knew that Jazib could. Ammi doted on him and if he told her that *he* was backing out, she'd have to accept it. Although, the mere thought that my mother, a powerful woman in her own right, attached more value to a man's word than she did to her own daughter's was just – betrayal.

Who said women weren't complicit in enabling patriarchy?

"Okay," I said. "Let me talk to Kulsom to see if she can give me a couple of days off. Or we can wait till the weekend."

He shrugged to indicate either was okay with him, and got back to sipping his milkshake.

6

MY OFFICE SCHEDULE BOASTED of a full day. I was so not in the mood to work and had just come in to ask Kulsom for a few days off but…!

"Okay, so this travel brochure guy finally decided to come in. I was meaning to talk to Nina about this anyway…wait, what is this? Why do we have a meeting with a studio team?" I pointed to an item on the sheet Meera had given me. "We don't do photography. And why is Asim Roy coming in? I thought I took care of the Gill account."

"He didn't say," Meera said. "I'm guessing he's coming in with another brief. Kulsom thought if you're there this time, he'll behave."

"And the studio?"

"They just want to pitch in a new possibility. Kulsom wants to look into it."

"Oh, like what we did with Jazib?" I'd begun to regret my advice to Kulsom to consider Jazib's project for various reasons since.

"It even smells like cardboard in there," Meera said, wrinkling her nose.

"It's fine." I sighed and walked back to my desk. "Let me know if anything else comes up." Ranya sat in my cubicle, diligently working on and sorting through the documents. "I know this is not what you thought you'd be doing when you decided to intern here," I said to her apologetically. "This is neither editing nor correspondence."

"But it's part of interning," she replied cheerfully. "I don't mind. It's all work."

I had the strangest feeling that she was just happy to be there because it gave her an excuse to step out of the house, away from her overbearing sister who'd undoubtedly parade her in front of the mothers of all potential suitors and introduce her to as many matchmaking aunties as could promise to grab a good proposal.

"Good then." I smiled. "Any interesting plans for today other than filing?" I asked casually, getting back to a file with information on Nina's travel brochure assignment.

"Oh, yes. We're doing lunch," she said, all but clasping her hands with joy. "Jazib is taking me to this amazing place that serves sushi. I didn't even know they had sushi in Pakistan."

"Jazib?" I didn't even care for the rest of her statement.

"Yes!"

"Ranya, you're nineteen, right? Don't you think you should be going out with someone your own age? I mean, don't get me wrong, I have nothing against you and Jazib being together—"

"Together?" Her eyes widened as she blinked in surprise. "We're just friends. Why? Did Jazib say anything?"

"Yes, well…I thought you two were…" I was not prepared for this. How could she not know with Jazib so visibly pouring his heart out every time he even mentioned her name? And what with her going pink at every line he threw at her? Had I misread or was she playing dumb?

"I really like him though," she said. "You know, he's very sweet."

"Indeed." I wanted to bury my head in the file I was pretending to read.

"In fact!" she sounded as if a light bulb had gone off in her head. "I *do* like him a lot and if he feels the same way, that's wonderful."

"Oh, I don't know about that," I said quickly. "How would Arju feel? I mean she doesn't particularly approve of Jazib – or anyone."

"She's tough that way," Ranya agreed. "But she has taken a fancy to this guy she met at the dinner."

"Fancy?"

"She's been talking about him since. About him, then my wedding, then him, then my wedding. I'm not stupid. I know she wants me to have a favourable view of him when she invites him over. I know she's thinking of matchmaking the two of us."

"Who is he?"

"Arhaan something. I haven't met him yet."

"Arhaan Mahyar?"

"You know him?"

Yes! He's brilliant and amazing and gorgeous, and wait – he can't be Little Miss Nineteen's beau!

"Yes, we're *very* good friends," I said with a little more emphasis than necessary. "He's a true gentleman." And suddenly, it was my turn to have a light bulb brighten my brain. Maybe it wasn't such a bad idea – egging her on to think about Arhaan rather than Jazib. It was sure to get her mind off him, which meant they wouldn't be together, which meant no fear of him ever dumping her and causing a feud between my trio of parents. As for Arhaan, he was too mature for Ranya. He wouldn't even consider her beyond a polite social invitation that Arjumand might extend to him. He might accept it and show up, eat, talk, and then leave. He wouldn't care to court Ranya beyond that. She wasn't his type either.

I smiled, switched on my phone, picked out a lovely close-up of Arhaan, and sent it to Ranya. Her phone rang out a mangled tune of some famous song. "That's him," I informed her as she read my text. "Let me send you a few more." This time I added his character profile too: name, age, height, job title, favourite food, a few taglines. I could've gone on but this much was enough. I wasn't really matchmaking them.

"Oh, wow!" Ranya's eyes popped. "He doesn't look old at all."

Excuse me? He isn't old. It doesn't make you old *to be beyond your teenage years!*

I checked myself before anything rolled off my tongue and smiled at her instead.

I was on my way to my first meeting when I saw Sana engaged in a passionate discussion with a familiar face. She was our book editor and had the most interesting clients. I went straight to those two instead of the conference room.

"Dilavar Sahib! Asalam Alaykum," I greeted the elderly man adorned in a dark olive safari suit, thick, black-rimmed glasses resting on the nose bridge, a canopy of wavy grey hair, a pen in one hand and a big, hearty infectious grin on his clean-shaven face. "How are you? Long time no see."

"Oh, Maya! Walaykum Asalam," He stood up and patted me on my shoulder. "How wonderful to see you again."

He was the only client who never had any issues, never had a bone to pick with anyone at the firm, and he made sense – a rare trait. Sana was lucky to be tasked with editing his manuscript. They spent hours together because he was just so much fun to talk to. He was writing a memoir exploring his spiritual journey, the way he perceived life, his opinions on controversial religious and political issues arising every now and then in the country, his commentary on recent events, and such.

"Sana thinks my book will get me into trouble." He told me. "But all I've done is be honest."

"That usually gets people into trouble," I said.

"He's advocating for equality, for feminism, for science," Sana said pointing to a thick printout on her desk. "There's not one topic in here that won't rub the religious lot the wrong way."

"See now, why you would say the *religious* lot?" he spoke in his usual soft tone. "I'm a man of God, and I regard myself a very staunch believer, deeply religious. When you generalise the religious lot, you yank me in with the extremists. It is this divide that I'm trying to bridge."

"Yes, I know you wrote about it at length in here, but it still doesn't totally negate what I said," Sana argued.

"I sort of agree with her," I said. "The generalisations are not just in how we portray a certain stratum of society but also in how a certain topic is perceived by many in the general population. For instance, science is generally perceived to be at war with religion."

"But it isn't," he replied passionately. "The way I see it, religion and science work on two separate planes. Religion is finality, and science is curiosity. Religion says this is what happened or what was or wasn't done. Science tries to find out the how and when and where and why of it all. And none of that is forbidden. Pursuit of knowledge is not forbidden."

"Yes, it is," Sana said. "Scholars will tell you of instances where God stopped people from seeking knowledge beyond what they were meant to."

"Then, let Him stop again. We stop each other before He stops anyone. Why do we play God? The human mind is designed to think. That's an essential function. We stop thinking, stop seeking, stop being curious, we stop being human." He leaned back in his chair and took turns to look at us both. "That's the real sin in my book."

"Yeah, he'll get into trouble," I looked at Sana and issued my verdict. "Maybe if you grow a beard, your ideas won't come off as so dangerous."

"I do have a beard!" he gasped, rubbing his face. "It's just under my skin. But it's there." We all laughed at that. Then he became quiet, with only a smile playing on his lips, his eyes cast down, deep in thought as if staring at something in the abyss of the earth beneath us. When he spoke again, his voice had a far-off, dreamlike quality. "Out beyond the ideas of wrong-doing and right-doing, there is a field. I'll meet you there…Maulana Rumi wrote this. My great-great-grandfather was a Sufi of the Chishti order. I am a follower too, as was my father and his father, as I hope my children will be. We go looking for God as if He's the one who is lost. We look for Him in structures of brick and stone, in the wilderness, in the deafening din of pulpit sermons, we try to establish peace by forcing laws on people who do not understand them." He shook his head. "You just keep your door open, your heart open. And you don't judge anyone but yourself. That's what I live by."

His words were profound, and he was a good man. But I could foresee the hate mail he'd soon be getting just by sharing the rules he lived by with the world around him. *May God protect him and his kind.* I made a silent prayer for him, wished him all the best for his book and moved on to the conference room.

My two seconds of Zen were over.

Nina was waiting for me; her arms full of two large binders, an angry nerve graced her brow and she generally looked paler than she usually was. She looked at me and let out a loud, annoyed sigh. "If we lose this account, I'll be the happiest person on earth."

Kulsom had already sent me a text earlier saying that if I couldn't talk sense into the client, it'd be fine to let him go. "What's going on?" I asked Nina as I took a seat.

She spread out some glossy 12x18-inch template posters on the table and glared at them in silence. They depicted a very vibrant rural and urban Pakistan – its people, its ancient and contemporary architecture, its unique landscape. The most captivating were images of the people: a close-up of an old Kalash woman wearing her traditional threadwork cap and a hundred colourful bead necklaces against a breathtaking backdrop of the snowcapped Himalayas; a rippling golden desert surrounding a slender woman with piercing kohl-rimmed eyes and white bangles, dressed in a voluminous patchwork maxi skirt and chunri billowing in the wind; a man with long hair and embroidered glossy green silks dancing at a local fair; a young guitarist sitting by the beach, his jeans a combination of light and dark contrasting blues, feet digging in the sand, and a young girl, dressed similarly, standing in the distance with her hands in the air and hair flying in the breeze.

"Nina…" I sighed in admiration. "These are beautiful. Perfect for a travel brochure. I'd love to visit a country with so much culture."

"Yeah, well, he hates them all," she said, collecting all the posters in one dull pile. "The brief was 'We want all pictures, very few words', so I gave them pictures. I mean you can do so much with people in pictures, can capture so many angles of the culture. But he said he didn't want the human element, especially women and dancing, and that guitar just really riled him up. I said, how about the food? We can do food and camel rides and such – but no. No people anywhere! Okay, let's do landscapes. But no, no run of the mill Nanga Parbat or Lake Saif-ul-Maluk or the Arabian Sea blah blah. Not even the city shots. Okay, how about architecture? We have ruins, we have preserved history, we have new stuff. But no. He doesn't want temples or shrines, nothing from the British Raj because it wasn't us who built it, nothing from the Mughal era either, no ruins of the Indus Valley Civilisation because I don't know…" she looked at me, threw her hands in the air and cried, "I don't know what he wants."

"He sounds very difficult," I agreed. "And he's late."

Just then, our receptionist showed in a stocky middle-aged man carrying a leather briefcase. He wore a brown three-piece suit that seemed a size too tight; his tie was a repugnant shade of ochre. He was dark-skinned, had a short beard that framed the entire lower half of his face, and beady eyes that were too shifty. He stood by the door a second, looking around the room, then without a word, he took a seat at the far end that was some six chairs away from us. He put his briefcase on the table, folded his hands in front of him and then stared at me.

"This is Maya. Maya, meet Mister Fazal," Nina quickly introduced us. "Maya is part of the admin team and will stay for our meeting."

"Asalam Alaykum, Fazal Sahib," I said. "Thank you for coming in today."

"Walaykum Asalam," he finally said to us both, then reached for his briefcase, clicked it open and took out a smooth, red plastic file that he held out for Nina. "This is what I have in mind."

Nina walked over and took the file.

I realised if we sat at two opposite ends, it might take more time just to get the documents to one another. Hence, I gathered the posters in my arms, walked over to his side of the table and placed them near him.

"This is a new template?" Nina took out an A1 size sheet that was printed on one side with images and some text. "I have prepared a few templates already according to the previous brief."

Mister Fazal made a negating gesture with one hand. "No, no," he said. "I've seen the emails you sent me. I didn't like those. This is what I want."

"You want more mosques." She looked at the printout again. "We can do that. We have some stunning images of some of our famous mosques." She reached over to the posters and took one that was studded with vibrant pictures of the Badshahi Masjid, Faisal Mosque and Masjid Wazir Khan. "These are the staples, of course, but we can pin images of neighbourhood mosques, something of a rustic mystery, simple beauty, of diamond-in-the-rough quality that speaks to the aesthetic senses of your tourists."

"I've seen this," he said, glancing at it with an uninterested eye. "What you're proposing is from an architectural point of interest."

"Yes…" she looked confused. "Architecture is a strong point to draw tourists. Every tourist loves a good guided tour in the ancient history and buildings of the country they're visiting."

"That's all fine. But I want to feature the school too," he said. "That's very important."

"Is it an ancient construction? Any other touristy salient feature?" She placed the paper on the table so I could see the image in the print-out too. It was of a classroom at a religious seminary. A couple of dozen boys sat on jute mats and appeared to be reciting from open books in front of them, their white skull-caps neatly secured on their heads, a teacher with a long, black beard wearing a pastel-coloured shalwar kamiz stood in their midst, supervising the class.

"This is our madrassah, the only school in the entire area covering three villages," he said proudly. "I want it to be advertised too."

"That's wonderful. We can do a whole other pamphlet for it, complete with information on your curriculum. But I'm afraid this has no place in a travel brochure."

"It's important to show people in the brochure too."

"I agree, but people who depict our culture."

"This *is* our culture. Not those dancers at the fair or guitar-playing youths." His face turned a shade darker as he frowned. "We are a Muslim country. None of your slides show that."

"The mosques do that plenty," Nina insisted. "We have a proud legacy of those and of Sufi shrines and colourful fakirs that grace every dargah from the Indian Ocean to the Himalayas. We can show all that and grab anyone's attention who happens to look at it."

"Shrines and dargah." He scoffed. "That may be your culture, but I won't have it. That's blasphemous content."

Nina's mouth hung open as she clearly searched for words that wouldn't come to her. She looked at me, and I knew it was time I stepped in.

"Fazal Sahib," I said calmly. "We appreciate your input and concerns about depicting Pakistan's identity to the outside world, but, sir, we are designing a travel brochure. A seminary is not culture. It is a system of education, and it is not the only system prevalent in Pakistan. We have schools based on Western education, schools that run on the local matriculation system, and a few others. A travel brochure is just not the right place for any of these, I'm afraid."

He was about to speak when a knock at the door made us all look up. It was Kareena.

"So sorry to bother you, but Maya, Asim Roy will be here shortly. Kulsom just wanted to let you know," she said with an apologetic face, before leaving after I nodded to confirm I'd heard her. Mister Fazal stared at the door long after she was gone and only looked back our way after I coughed to grab his attention.

"We don't have to put in any human element like we discussed before," Nina carried on the conversation. "We can do landscapes or buildings or any other interesting non-human sights."

"I have issues with your language too," he said. "You don't use words like 'Mashallah' or expressions like 'by the Grace of Allah' or similar. Why don't you?"

"Your brief was for a simple travel brochure. It didn't call for a brochure to attract people to a religious or spiritual cleansing experience. We can work on that angle if you give a different brief."

"Isn't travelling a spiritual experience?" He frowned again. "And besides, we must talk and write like Muslims."

My head started to spin. I could only imagine what Nina had gone through for weeks with him dictating to her. Good thing Kulsom had already given me carte blanche over this one. It was time we had a heart to heart.

"Mister Fazal," I said, casually sliding in a chair near his. "A quick fact check will tell you that while Muslims are predominant in Pakistan, we aren't the only religion here. Also, I understand you didn't have a problem with the copy before this exact moment in time?" I knew this because neither Nina nor Kulsom had mentioned it. Usually that would be the first thing a client would criticise and the first thing the editors would look at and worry about. Images came last when everything else was in top shape.

"That is my mistake," he confessed. "But now that I look at it, I don't like it."

"The language of a travel brochure is kept neutral on purpose so you can attract a variety of tourists," I explained. "However, there can be a sidebar on Pakistan's demographics to highlight the Muslim population and other statistics."

"Sidebar? It should be at the forefront!" He was upset again. "I knew it was a mistake to trust an agency run only by women, *Westernised* women. Maya, is it? Sounds like a Hindu name to me. Nina. Kareena. These aren't Islamic names. Maybe that's why you're not getting my point."

Dafuq!

I glared at our soon-to-be-*not*-client. He was suddenly unsightlier than he had been at the beginning of our meeting.

"What a bigoted thing to say, Mister Fazal," I said flatly. "These women are professionals, experts in their field, and it was this reputation that brought you here, not their declaration of faith. And the reason they're not getting your *point* is because a travel brochure shouldn't look like an ad for a pilgrimage to a seminary in a remote village of the travel agent's choice."

He stared at me quietly for a second before standing up. He collected the papers he'd brought and stuffed them back in his briefcase, snapping it shut tight. "So, you won't employ my ideas even though it is my brochure and I am paying you to make it?"

"Any printing press can do that for you," I said. "May I suggest a few good ones?"

"Very well, I can't say it has been a pleasure working with you, Miss Maya and Miss Nina."

"Oh, Fazal Sahib," I cooed. "The feelings are remarkably mutual."

His face twisted into a confused expression that bordered on anger, and without another word, he was gone. Nina and I looked at each other and broke into a tired laugh.

"You have The Roy next," she reminded me. "Go get him, girl. Let him have it!"

Truth was I didn't want to go get anyone anymore. It was tiring and toxic and had begun to stress me out of late. I didn't particularly enjoy letting people have it. It was just that it came naturally to me, and most people made it easy for me to trash them. Like that Fazal had. Like Asim Roy usually did. But it gave me no pleasure.

I grabbed a quick cup of tea from the kitchenette and walked back to the second conference room. I could see Kulsom and the copywriter assigned to the Gill account, Sabine, standing by the glass door talking to a man. He seemed slightly taller than me, but I suspected his heavily gelled and combed-over hair added to his height. He wore a silver-grey suit with a neon-green tie that went well with his tweezed face and manicured aura. He looked at me and asked for an introduction.

"Maya Badruddin," I said. "I believe you're Asim Roy?" His eyes widened with a sparkle and he nodded slowly. It satisfied me to know that he knew who I was and what I'd done. That meant I could hope to expect less idiocy from him this time.

After everyone had taken their seats, Roy stood at the head of the table, animatedly issuing a brief from a new client that his ad agency was quite excited about. "*Power ties.*" He made a fist and lightly punched the air in front of him. "Or business ties, as we know them, are the new product we're dealing with. I'm wearing one right now." He caressed it with two fingers like a seasoned salesman. "The ad concept will be to link this clothing accessory to the success of the wearer."

"There are a number of ways we can do that," Sabine started to say but he put up a finger to silence her.

"I already have an idea of what the ad will be," he said. "I just need the copy for the print ad. We'll do the graphics and images ourselves."

"What's the ad?"

"Okay, picture a businessman wearing a great suit but missing a tie. Nobody notices him, people walk past him but one day he shows up with this power tie – the product of our client – and all the women in the office surround him, swooning and crushing, and now he's popular and the credit goes to the power tie."

Kulsom and Sabine exchanged glances, then Sabine sat up straighter and cleared her throat. "So, you're saying, his entire success is tied to women swooning over him?"

"No, it's linked to the tie."

"Yes, but the measure of success, the tangible outcome that shows the tie works is when women swoon over him. Right?"

"Yes."

"It's somewhat…cliché," Kulsom said. "A businessman's success is when he succeeds in business. Showing women swooning over him isn't exactly what success looks like in the real world."

"Exactly," Sabine agreed. "Show him in a boardroom meeting. Maybe show a successful businessman from the start and make him wear a different tie for every shot. Show that this successful man chooses this particular brand of tie because this brand speaks to him – the guy who is so successful."

"But how does that credit the tie for his success?" he asked.

"Because he chose that tie so it's the brand of successful people."

"I don't see what's wrong with my original concept?" He creased his forehead.

"It's sexist, Mister Roy," I said bluntly. "Swooning women might have been the measure of a man's success in the 1960s, but we don't live there anymore."

"What happened to 'dress for success'?" He curled his lips into a lopsided smile, flattened his palms on the table and leaned forward, staring straight into my eyes. "Wouldn't *you* fall for a guy in a nice suit and tie?"

"I haven't fallen for your neon tie yet." I stared back. "Isn't that the product you're trying to push? I don't see anyone swooning."

"Well…" he blinked, apparently registering the jab and searching for words. He stuffed his hands in his pockets and breathed deeply. "That idea came from the client himself," he confessed to the air in front of him.

"The ad world is changing, Mister Roy," Kulsom spoke calmly. "Hyperbole doesn't often work well. I suggest we brainstorm this, see what the creatives come up with and we'll get back to you. You can always reject and send us back to the drawing board if you don't like what we present."

He took a few more seconds to mumble an affirmative, and then went on to emphasise how any concept must only go through him, as he would be the last word on any decision and blah blah, and then headed out. He did turn back once to give me a stern glance before he resumed walking to the elevator and disappeared.

I felt edgy.

I needed to get out of a place where I made random people hate me…

"Kulsom," I said, following her into her office. "I need a day off. A few, actually. I have to go to my mother's."

"Hmm…it is going to be busy around here but okay. And oh, I stole something from you today," she said, settling in her large swivel chair. "You remember you sent me a few pictures of our office picnic?"

I remembered. Kulsom had secured her first big profit of the quarter and that called for a celebration. So she'd rented a hut at the beach and taken us all on a picnic. Soft sands, playful breeze, a sparkling blue sky, and the rhythmic ocean waves sprawling forever into the horizon – it was paradise for a day. The girls had brought food and drinks and their dance moves. I'd brought my camera.

"I took those for you," I said.

"I showed them to this photo studio team. I've seen their work and it's dynamic!" She broke into vivid details of how the enterprise worked. It was a husband and wife firm that needed help with captioning photographs for their clients. "They were also thinking of hiring another photographer down the line and you were just the perfect choice that came to mind when they asked me if I knew someone."

"So…" I wasn't sure of what to say. "You want me to leave?"

"No," she said warmly as she slightly leaned forward. "You're more valuable to me than you'll ever know. But, Maya, this isn't a real job."

Wait a second…

"Have you been talking to Arhaan?" I eyed her suspiciously. "He said the exact same thing to me the other day."

"Well, he wouldn't be wrong." She eased back into her chair and smiled. "But no, this was my idea. You have a real talent for photography."

"I'm an amateur. I do it for fun. A professional studio would need a professional."

"Then you become one. Get a degree in the field or learn on the job. I know you'll be great."

Right.

Clearly, now I had professional things to think about on top of my personal mess.

7

"WHY? WHY WOULD SHE invite you? And why do I have to come?" I was home, stuffing my clothes into a small travel bag and getting upset with Arhaan over the phone at the same time.

Arjumand had invited him to dinner. *Why?* He didn't know. All he knew was that when he got back to his office after dealing with some smart-ass client on the other end of town, a message was waiting for him from Mrs and Mr Badruddin, specifically Mrs Badruddin, earnestly requesting the pleasure of his company etcetera.

"But why drag me along?" I rolled another shirt into a ball and tossed it in the bag as well. "And why are you going anyway? As far as I know, you don't entertain clients outside of office hours."

"I wouldn't go if he wasn't your father. Didn't you say we'd see more of each other now that I worked with him?" he said, then there was a slight pause before he added softly, "Maya, please come."

Ooh…!

I all but melted. Sank onto my bed amid the clothes strewn all over.

"What time?" I asked.

I was just about done scrunching and brushing my hair with my fingers so the loose ends would seem naturally curled when the doorbell rang.

Arhaan was already here!

I spritzed myself with a subtle fragrance and gave myself a final once-over in the mirror. Yes, red became me like a charm. I hurried downstairs and found him standing in the living room, looking dreamy in white and navy blue. He was talking to Aya-Ji and smiled when he heard me. His gaze rested on me long enough to let me know he liked what he saw but before it could turn into a moment of any kind, he blinked.

"Aya-Ji thinks I should ditch dinner and have tea here instead," he said. "Because she makes the best tea."

"She does," I smiled back.

Minutes later, sitting in his car, I was filling him in on everything in my life, from Jazib being such a pain and my sudden upcoming trip to Kesar, to how everyone thought I had a knack for photography. Could he believe that?

"From a business graduate to photography?" He furrowed his brow slightly. "It's a jump but if you think you should then you should."

"I don't know the first thing about professional photography."

"It's still a better option than what you have right now."

"Could we talk about something else, please?" I rolled my eyes. "Like you could tell me how pretty I look because, honestly, I dressed up just for you. I would've gone in my jammies if it was just me. I mean, it is my father's house."

He suddenly slowed the car to a halt.

I looked at him questioningly.

"We're here," he said. "At your father's house."

So soon? But we hadn't finished talking. I had so much to tell him and…be with him a little longer…I frowned, flipped open the visor mirror and took stock of my face. My makeup was intact, but I involuntarily started fixing the black-lined edges of my eyes even though nothing was smudged. I fluffed up my hair, viewed my face this way and that way and smiled faintly for the mirror. I really looked okay; I didn't know why I was bothering. I flipped the visor shut and turned to Arhaan, only to find him smiling at me. "What?" I asked.

He turned in his seat so that he faced me completely. The car interior lights had long faded away and only the moonlight shone through the sunroof, lending Arhaan's face a soft glow. His eyes harboured a warm glint as he studied me. I couldn't decipher the expression, but it made my skin tingly.

"You never wore makeup when you were in college," he said.

"Because it was college," I said, trying to understand the intensity of the moment. Even his voice sounded more molasses-y than usual. "I didn't have the time." I wondered why he asked. "You don't like it?"

"No, that's not what I meant."

"Then, what *did* you mean?" I felt my heart race, but I kept my gaze steadily on his face. I didn't know what I expected him to say, but I had a feeling about what I wanted to hear.

"That you've always looked beautiful," he said softly, his face inches away from mine made everything else seem blurry. Suddenly, there was a loud tap at his window, and a set of gleaming white teeth in a bearded face stood grinning at us. Arhaan instantly pulled away from me as I tried to catch my breath.

"Oh, it's you, Maya Bibi?" our trusted gatekeeper, who'd been with Abba since the dinosaurs, asked me. "Everything okay?"

"Yes, Khan," I said with a stiff smile. Thanks to him, Arhaan hadn't kissed me, and now I could never be sure if he ever wanted to or ever would!

"I didn't mean to scare, but you were sitting in the car so long after turning it off, I thought maybe something was wrong," he explained, glancing curiously at Arhaan. "I didn't know it was you in the car, Maya Bibi."

"This is Abba's project manager," I said. "Learn his face. You'll see a lot more of him in the coming days."

Khan grinned again and stepped away.

I took stock of the cars in the driveway as we walked towards the main door. There was just one other besides Arhaan's, and I was a little surprised to see it. I didn't think Arjumand would ever invite Jazib, but maybe Abba had. I shrugged and joined Arhaan on the front steps where he was holding the door open for me.

I could recognise Abba's laugh, Jazib's banter and another delicate giggle that was unmistakably Ranya's flowing in from the family room. I led Arhaan there through the winding hallway, past the formal drawing and dining areas. We were greeted with a loud welcome. Arjumand appeared from some corner of the house, relating her tales of culinary adventures in the kitchen and horrors of the hopeless domestic help. She was especially attentive to Arhaan, snatching her sister away from every other conversation to engage with him, much to Jazib's dismay.

"Why is *he* here?" Jazib whispered crossly to me.

"He was specifically invited by the Lady of the House. Why are *you* here?"

"Ranya invited me."

"You didn't listen to a word I said to you, did you? You don't care." I frowned at him, only to have him roll his eyes all the way back in his head. "You will cause war to happen in this family."

"Relax," he said and went back to Ranya. Her smile dimpled even more and her curls bounced with joy.

Ranya was a pretty girl, but this shade of crimson beauty that her face lit up with every time she looked at Jazib was something else. His eyes turned a warm hue of honey that seemed to melt her as she stared back into them. She didn't even care for the murderous look her big sister gave her as she stood holding Arhaan hostage.

"Okay, let's have dinner," Arjumand announced rather loudly, and all but hassled everyone to get moving. Arhaan looked at me from the far distance of the room where she'd cornered him, possibly asking to be rescued, but I just helplessly smiled back.

The formal dining room boasted of a large oak table and a dozen richly tufted chairs. It was laid with fine food served in expensive china and silver. Arjumand, the perfect hostess that she was, urged her guests to try every dish on the menu, passed the gravies and salads and made sure that no dinner plate went unnoticed.

"Arhaan, you must try this chicken, it's my own recipe, very different." She passed the bowl to him and smilingly watched him take a spoonful out onto his plate. "I cooked everything myself today."

"It's all very delicious," he complimented her.

Arjumand's smile widened a few more miles across her face and she looked at Ranya, who quickly got busy with her own food. The girl obviously didn't feel too comfortable sitting right next to a man she'd maybe never talked to beyond a formal hello and a discussion of the weather. Oh yes, the seating at the table was deliberate. Abba and Arjumand of course occupied their respective seats at the two heads of the table. To Abba's right, I sat with Jazib. Ranya and Arhaan sat across from us.

"Did we really have to sit at such a large table?" I said. "We could've eaten off the kitchen island."

"That's what I suggested," Abba agreed, digging his fork in a thick drumstick that wouldn't behave.

"It is decorum," Arjumand insisted calmly. "Next time when Arhaan comes over, I'll make it less formal and let you all eat in the kitchen."

"Next time?" I raised a suspicious brow and looked at him. "And what would the occasion be next time?" He returned my stare for a lingering moment as he took a sip of his water. In that moment, I forgot I was at a dinner table at my father's house…

"The occasion could be our return to the city from the rural inlands," Jazib casually suggested.

"Rural inlands?" Ranya's eyes sparkled with interest.

"We're going to Kesar and Gurhkot for a few days, Maya and I."

"I didn't know you were going together," Arjumand said, stressing the word "together" for some reason.

"Oh, how exciting!" Ranya clasped her hands. "Can I come?"

"No!"

"Yes!"

It was hard to say who'd spoken first – Jazib or me? But our voices had echoed loud and put a momentary hush over the room.

"Of course you can come," Jazib said to her. "Of course she can!" He turned to me, making a case for her right there at the dinner table.

"No, she can't," I said firmly. "It's a total strange land with weird customs that are scary and possibly fatal."

"Excuse me?" Abba frowned. "You are going to visit your mother. I see no harm in Ranya visiting her."

"But Badr—" Arjumand tried to protest but Abba shook his head.

"It'll be a chance for her to see more of this country," he said, wiping his mouth with a cloth napkin.

"My sentiments exactly," Jazib said, then turned to Ranya. "We leave early morning by the way. You should pack."

Arjumand looked from one face to another and then quietly glared at Abba, too well bred to publicly lash out at her husband. She pushed away her half-eaten plate and asked to be excused so she could order for tea. "Please, carry on," she said with a stiff smile, and we all heard her heels clack against the marble as she left the room and disappeared.

Ranya ran up to her room to pack and the men vanished somewhere within the house, I traced my steps to the kitchen and found Arjumand standing by her vast island, sprinkling some slivered almonds on a decorated terracotta bowl of kheer and issuing orders to her two maids to set the tea trolley.

"I'm so glad you made this." I ogled the rice pudding. She smiled and told one of her maids to pack some for me to take home. "Everything was great, Arju," I told her honestly. The tensed lines on her face eased some more, but I could see the shadows of worry hiding in her eyes. "I'm sorry for crashing the party though."

"Absolutely not. This is your house. What are you talking about?" Then a vein in her forehead popped a little. "I just had no idea Jazib was coming."

"Ranya invited him. And now she'll be taking this trip with us."

Arjumand stopped working, told her maids to wheel the tea trolley into the living room where we all had been before dinner. Once they were gone and it was just the two of us left in the kitchen, she looked at me. Her face colouring a little with an emotion I could define in the vicinity of annoyance. "That's exactly what's making me nervous," she said. "Bano hates me. I'm sorry, I know she's your mother, but…Ranya is my sister. I don't think it's appropriate for her to be a guest at Bano's house. It's very awkward."

"But…you're not worried about Jazib?" I couldn't help asking. Surely she must've seen the two of them together, acting like they desperately needed a room. How was she not worried about Ranya going on a trip with him more than she worried about her being a guest at my mother's house?

"Why would I be worried about him?" She blinked. "He's your fiancé, has nothing to do with Ranya." That was shocking. She'd never referred to him as my fiancé before. In fact, she had always sympathised with me on the subject on whatever rare occasion it had come up. But now, it was suddenly *your fiancé*? "Face it, Maya, it is what it is," she said. "You've been attached to his name since birth and these promises aren't meant to be broken. I suggest you accept that too."

I stared at her, trying to decide how to react. Fortunately for her, her opinion on the subject, especially if it wasn't in my favour, didn't matter. Therefore I saw no need of lashing out. "Do you know where might Abba be?" I asked instead.

"His library, I think," she said, trying to engage my gaze, but I turned on my heels and left.

Arjumand's words did trouble me though. Was she deliberately playing the scenario out this way so she could pull her sister out by pushing me in? I wasn't even sure if Ranya knew about Jazib and me. If she didn't, this piece of information could very well destroy her budding emotions for him. But then, if I explained things to her and she stayed with Jazib, it would free me…

"Maya…" it was Jazib coming out of the library. I was so deep in thought I hadn't realised I was there. "We have to talk," he said, and led me to a nearby nook that housed two giant planters and a great oil portrait of an old man and his odd collection of candles, work of an unknown artist.

"What is it?" I asked.

"Ssh, softly." He put a finger to his lips and whispered, "I'm begging you to not create any trouble for us."

"Us?"

"Ranya and me. You'll try and talk your dad out of letting her go on this trip, wouldn't you?"

"Yes," I said and turned to leave, but he grabbed my arm. My heel slipped on the marble floor and I fell against him. "Ow, Jazib, are you insane?"

"I'm sorry, are you hurt?" He let me use him like a crutch, helping my balance. "I'm sorry. But seriously, promise me you won't ruin it."

"How heartless of you. I probably broke my ankle!"

"Oh please, you're fine!"

A sharp sound of footsteps died right outside where we were. Arjumand stood there looking at us, pinned against each other. Jazib let me go like I'd suddenly grown thorns that stabbed him, but she had seen all that was wrong with the picture. Her face went from raised eyebrows to a meaningful smile. "Chai is ready. Please, tell your father too," she said, and casting a lingering look at me from head to toe, turned and left.

"What's wrong with her?" Jazib asked.

"She thinks we were fornicating in public and she approves," I deadpanned, but the way Jazib's face contorted as if he were about to puke made me laugh. "I wouldn't say it's totally inappropriate since everyone thinks we're as good as married."

"We're not," he protested. "And we won't ever be and that's why you need to let Ranya come along."

"You're taking her to meet the parents?" I'd meant it as a joke, but when he looked at me as if I'd read his mind, I was a little surprised. "You can't be serious."

"I am."

"You're moving way too fast! You guys hardly know each other. Have you told her about us?" His silence told me he hadn't. "And how do you think she'll react when Arju tells her what she saw?"

"She saw us talking." He frowned. "We're cousins. Cousins can talk."

"Just cousins?" I couldn't help teasing him the same way he so often had done to me before he met Ranya. "You're my *fiancé*."

"It's not funny." He turned to walk away, but I pulled him from behind, lassoing his shoulders with my arms.

"Oh no, Jazib, don't leave me! Whatever shall I do?" I cried in my best damsel-in-distress voice.

"Stop it, Maya, let go."

"You should remember all the times that you grabbed and dragged me, like the time that was, oh, five seconds ago?"

"Okay, okay!" He leaned to one side, still trying to get away from me, but he wasn't frowning anymore. "Let go," he chuckled. "Maya!"

"Say I'm stronger!"

"You're Hercules!"

We were still laughing like silly kids when I saw Arhaan standing by the library door. I didn't know for how long he'd been there or what the expression on his face meant. Unlike Jazib, he wasn't an open book that I could easily read.

"We were just talking," I said, even though I didn't owe him an explanation.

"And chai is ready," Jazib said. "We were just going to inform you guys."

"Oh no, thank you," Arhaan replied, regarding Jazib with eyes that narrowed curiously for a split second before going blank. "I was just leaving."

"You are the star guest tonight. You can't leave." Abba had joined us too by then and was shaking his head at Arhaan. "Don't ask me why, I never question my wife's motives. That's wise, I'm told. Wouldn't you agree?"

"I wouldn't know." Arhaan smiled. "I'm not exactly suited for that life."

"No man is, Arhaan, but we all try." Abba roared with laughter. He looked at me and pointed towards Arhaan with his cigar that wasn't yet lit. "I like him. He's sensible."

I smiled but didn't say anything. I didn't know what all that meant – that exchange between Abba and Arhaan, this invitation that Arjumand had so unusually extended to him, and the way he wasn't looking at me anymore…

8

THE VILLAGES OF KESAR and Gurhkot, tucked away amidst bountiful sugarcane fields, mango trees, and green pastures of where the province of Sindh met Punjab under vast sunny skies and starry nights, were two tiny kingdoms to my family's name, some eight hours away from my city life.

The roads leading to these havens were paved with speed bumps, dust, dirt, occasional potholes, and unruly traffic. There wasn't a thing that could ever make me enjoy that car ride, least of all the idea of a stopover at a horrendous roadside café, gas station, or a rest area, all boasting of suspicious foods and dimly lit, unhygienic restrooms you could smell from miles away.

"Yes, I *can* hold it." I frowned at Jazib, while Ranya pranced around like a kitten out in a garden full of butterflies, her chador all but flailing behind her in the wind like a long, wild scarf that she stopped every now and then to wear correctly.

"We have three more hours." Jazib seriously looked like his hair would be on fire soon. "Please, *please* go! It's not that bad. It's clean. I checked it myself."

"No."

"You can't pee in my car!"

"This is what real Pakistani countryside looks like?" Ranya could be heard screaming from a distance as she looked over a pasture off the road. "This is so full of life! You can stop anywhere on the interstate, there are literally zero rules here!"

"I don't think that's a very proud commentary for this country right now," I said, staring at her with one eyebrow raised with judgement to high heaven, knowing she couldn't hear me. "Your girlfriend is such a firangi," I said to Jazib.

"You need to pee." Jazib frowned. I think he was more annoyed by not being able to reel Ranya in than my not using the restroom. If I knew any better, and I did, it must've taken every ounce of self-control in his being not to tell her to zip it, cover her head and sit all ladylike in the car.

Jazib's shiny little dinky of a Benz was parked at a gas station, located over what would be an extension of the interstate shoulder over a sandy stretch of land that merged into the farms beyond the borders of the highway. That's how rest areas were established along our freeways: a little off the highway, to the curb, by the roadside. There were no proper exits. The freeway itself was usually a two-way street permitting fast traffic at unchecked speeds, even though there was a legal limit. Trucks, oversized loads, public buses, private vehicles, and bikes all shared all lanes and zoomed past each other. To add to this mix, a free-spirited cow would saunter over from a nearby barn and try to cross the highway to get to the other side. It would be fortunate if it was just the one cow. Often, it was an entire herd led by a skilled farmer.

The stopover spots came in a variety of their own. It could be an exposed brick and beam café, offering a variety of fried and baked goods with complimentary seating at a table in Western style or on a charpoy to cater to your more desi taste; a plain old solitary gas station; a row of shops and kiosks selling snacks, meals, general household and travel items; or it could be a combination of all that as part of an accidental downtown established by the roadside, because the freeway sometimes curved and flowed through towns rather than around them. That's how you met Pakistan – raw, blunt, untamed, daring with all her beauty and blemish, and accepting what she may at her own terms.

We'd left Karachi a little after sunup and made a quick stop at a nice rest area where we snacked, got gas, and were back on the road shortly after. I slept for most of the first three hours that Jazib raced his car over a newly carpeted highway that took us to the city of Hyderabad. After that, it was the old-fashioned freeway serving its travellers with all its regular flaws and bad restrooms. With just the three of us in the car – Ranya in front next to Jazib and me sprawled all over the backseat – it had been a comfortable trip so far. I was glad he hadn't brought his usual army of bodyguards and servants to escort him from and back to Gurhkot because Jazib, when not bogged down by the pressures of his vadera protocol, could be very sensible.

And fun.

The last time he'd come alone to Karachi, he'd talked me into sneaking out one early morning to take a day trip to a nearby lake, famous for its mystical powers and folklore that featured a centuries-old shrine built by its banks. We'd spent the day exploring a small town whose economy depended on whatever tourists the lake and its shrine pulled in, and a bazaar that overflowed with its merchandise of clothes, beads, spices, tinselly fabrics and rose garlands for the shrine, terracotta pottery, glass bangles and bejewelled ropey hair extensions that hung like curtains on display. The people were tough, tanned by desert suns, and draped in interesting palettes of burgundy folds of ajrak over shalwar kamiz in faded pastels for men and thickly embroidered chunri and floral tunics for women. Their eyes were lined with kohl, hair oiled, and lips rouged against miswak-white teeth, sure-footed and at home. In our jeans and sunglasses, Jazib and I were a stark contrast to those enchanting people. But we shared their respect for the Auliya of Allah.

The saint that graced the shrine had quite a legacy to his name – a rogue warrior stung by lost love, a vagabond looking to lay his head, a sinner saved by God. The lake, it was said, was all the tears he shed, first pining for his love, and then in prayer. The winds of that town were his unsung songs that died in silence when he turned his back on the world. The shrine itself was a dainty gazebo of white stone erected over his grave. He'd died on that spot bowed in prayer. The locals revered his memory by tying colourful threads onto the trellis surrounding the shrine, and asked God for their dearest wish to come true.

"What did you wish for?" Jazib had asked me.

"For you to fall in love so you'll be a better man," I told him honestly, only to have him laugh out loud and shake his head.

All that was so long ago…

I braced myself, tightening my dark blue chador. I wore a decent matching shalwar kamiz underneath and had braided my hair too. After all, this wasn't a sprint to a long-lost shrine. This time we were on our way to where all patriarchy was birthed.

I pinned my thighs together as the pressure on my bladder increased. Next, I was shaking my leg for distraction.

"I cannot believe you." Jazib glared at me. "Ranya went. If it's good enough for her, it's good enough for you. She's from *America*."

"That's so racist."

"Maya!"

"You remember that time when we went up north to the mountains that summer? And we got lost in the woods and couldn't get to the hotel in time?"

"Yeah, and we just…" He stopped abruptly and stared at me, his eyes widening with recollection of a memory from eons ago. "We were *fifteen*."

"You were fifteen, I was twelve. Hey, there's a song like that."

"That was in the *woods*. With plenty of trees and trunks and boulders to hide behind and this is all flatland."

"There are those cornfields," I said, pointing in the distance.

"No." He shook his head. "No!"

Ten minutes later, down the side of the busy highway, we were trekking through thick stalks of spring maize, standing tall and ready for harvest. I wasn't going to go in the cornfield. No, I had my mind set on the brick kiln ahead in the distance. The tall kiln with mounds of dirt around it looked perfect. A cluster of trees would've been better though, and I wondered if I could find any nearby.

"This is completely inappropriate!" Jazib was protesting. Holding onto Ranya's hand in an aggressively protective grip, he walked close behind me, keeping an eye on the surroundings as well as the women he accompanied. "I don't even have my gun with me!"

"Will you relax? We're not going hunting," I said. "And stop shouting or you'll attract attention."

"Imagine if somebody walks in on us when you're…" He stopped and pursed his lips. "Maya, let's go back to the gas station. Please!"

"Didn't you tell me people in your village do this because they have no toilets inside the house?" I asked.

"They are people of my kōt." He gritted his teeth. "*You* are family."

"But they are people. And they have dignity just like us. They have honour just like us."

"Blah, blah, blah!" Jazib mocked me in his most annoyed voice. "You don't even have wipes."

"I'm always prepared." I held up my tote bag in both hands and boasted.

We were almost at the kiln when Ranya spotted a cluster of wild shrubs and small trees a few yards away, behind a wall marking the yonder boundary of the kiln area. It was a good healthy patch, probably riddled with critters, but the foliage promised more privacy compared to the brick kiln. I rushed to it, amid Jazib's fresh barrage of protests, and found a nice spot at the foot of a large rock fringed with leafy hedge. It was secluded and apt. I handed Ranya my chador and instructed Jazib to stand watch.

"I know that!" he yelled back as he directed Ranya to stay close to me.

It only took a few minutes and I was done. I was about to wrap my chador again when we heard distant sounds. Someone was shouting something. Then there were gunshots. The first one wasn't close. The second one seemed to ricochet off the tree trunks around us.

"Run!" Jazib barked and we all bolted instantaneously.

"Why is he shooting at us?" I gasped.

"What is he yelling?" Ranya asked as she staggered behind us.

Jazib was in the lead at first but then he stopped for us. I had slowed down to give Ranya a hand. She had her chador in one hand by now and her sandals were full of dirt and slowing her down. She took a moment to take them off and then she was like a cheetah dashing through the landscape. I was behind her and now Jazib was behind me. If this were the Olympics, Ranya would have won gold – except she abruptly stopped and shrieked. I stopped too, following her lead, but Jazib stumbled and fell into what lay before us – a generous pile of poop. His hands broke his fall and saved his face, but the rest of him lay deep in cow dung.

There were running footsteps behind us that came to a halt just then as well. I turned around to find two shooters – an old man with peppered hair, moustache and a thick stubble on his chin, and a boy who couldn't have been more than twelve, both dressed in dusty-grey shalwar kamiz, their hunting rifles smoking but pointing up in the air.

"Who are you?" the man asked us.

"Why were you shooting at us?" I asked him instead.

"I thought it was that jackal again," he said, hesitating as his eyes shifted back and forth from me to Jazib. "Is he shot? We were only firing in the air."

"I don't know how to get up." Jazib growled this time. He was lying very still, doing the plank to be precise. The shooters rushed to his aid and helped him up.

"You should wash up," I suggested. "You'll stink up the car."

"No shit." He glared at me but that only amused me more.

"Is there a river nearby?" I asked the man. "Saeen would like to bathe."

"I live right there at the edge of this farm," he replied. "Please, come with me."

The three of us looked at each other quietly before Jazib asked him to lead. Ranya edged towards me and, whispering, asked if it was at all a good idea to trust someone who'd been trying to kill us just a few minutes ago.

"They were hunting jackals," I said. "Let's go."

Karam Din was a farmer who lived with his wife and son by the highway on his few acres of land that he cultivated for his own use and to sell. He also herded cows, churned butter, and made other dairy products for his family, and had a chicken coop that yielded enough eggs to make his family's breakfast a happy one. All in all, he was a fortunate man.

"But recently, this darn jackal has been a nuisance," he was singing his woes now after counting his blessings to us. "It's been ruining my crops this season. It was that darn dog I was trying to scare away."

We sat on roped cot beds in a red-brick courtyard in the centre of Karam Din's single-story brick house. He and his son helped Jazib wash up under an outdoor hand-pump while his wife served us sherbet. It was a burning afternoon, somewhere in the vicinity of a hundred degrees Fahrenheit and the idea of a sweet beverage, even when not ice cold, refreshed me to the bones. I emptied my glass, but Ranya hesitated. "You're in rural country," I told her. "Don't wait for everything to be sterilised now." She cast a second glance at her drink and then glugged it all down in one go.

"Get them something to eat," Karam Din told his wife as he peeled Jazib's shirt off his back and threw it in a corner on the concrete floor below. Jazib was standing up to his full height and offering an unobstructed view of his ripped body. He was a fine specimen of his gender. His sun-kissed chest was gleaming clean and contrasted well with the coral pink towel over his shoulders. Usually he was happy to flaunt, but just then he looked uncomfortable and conscious. Perhaps it was the irritation carried over from his unflattering fall. Or perhaps it was the unfamiliar vibe of modest surroundings. I glanced at Ranya to gauge her reaction and she didn't disappoint me. She was trying hard to not stare, kept averting her eyes, but her gaze kept returning to the man she was so obviously smitten by.

I studied her face.

There was a kind of maturity about her. The depth of her eyes didn't spell teen years. And her delicate looks completely checked off our societal beauty standards. She wore a pale lemon shalwar kamiz underneath a large white chador that she elegantly wrapped herself with. She'd dusted off her sandals and slipped them on again in her pedicured feet. She was exactly the sort of girl, dressed exactly the way that Jazib preferred.

I, in contrast, just sat there with my chador hanging from one shoulder while the rest of it piled up in my lap. My sneakers were well-worn, and my messy braid screamed for a redo.

"I'll have your shirt washed in no time," Karam Din was saying to Jazib.

"No, I won't wear it," Jazib said, looking with disgust at that tiny pile of ick. "I'll just get another...but the car is parked far away."

"Baba," Karam Din's son addressed his father, "The general store down the lane sells undershirts. Some with sleeves too. I'll go get one."

"How much will it be?" Jazib asked.

"Oh, don't worry, Saeen, it's on me," Karam Din insisted, shaking his head decidedly. "You're our guest, Saeen." He then excused himself, only to return minutes later with a tray of steaming food.

"Where's your wife? She wouldn't eat with us?" Ranya asked him.

"You please start," he said. "Please eat. It's simple food, nothing fancy, but it's all from my farm."

Jazib and I obliged him without delay as I made a mental note to explain the ways of our rural folk to Ranya later. Rural families usually ate twice a day, brunch and dinner, and traditional hospitality dictated that you fed the guest first, because guests were considered a blessing from God and to tend to them properly was a matter of honour. Even though we were treated to a simple serving of chapatti and potato curry slow-cooked in a clay pot, it tasted like manna from heaven.

"That cornfield is yours?" I asked Karam Din.

"Yes, and I have wheat and fodder that I also sell in the market. The potatoes and other vegetables and bit of sugarcane I grow just for myself," he replied, casting his eyes down. He hadn't looked at Ranya or me directly ever since we'd entered his house. That's how most rural men talked to women they weren't related to but regarded with respect.

"Sugarcane?" Jazib said. "I didn't know there were any sugarcane fields here by this leg of the highway."

"There aren't. The rich landlords don't allow it."

"What do you mean?" Ranya asked. "If there are no government restrictions, how can a landlord control what you do or do not grow on your own land?"

"There's not much government control when it comes to powerful feudal lords," I said.

"I had a sizeable sugarcane field," Karam Din said, "but the vadera of my area didn't approve. He warned me one year, but I didn't listen, so the next year, he had my fields burned. I stopped growing sugarcane to sell after that."

"You didn't go to the police?" Ranya asked.

Karam Din laughed. "He has the superintendent on his payroll. Of course I didn't go. We bow our heads and keep at it. It's better that way." He looked up at us and, as if recalling from memory, said, "I did go to Shah Sultan for help. He lent me money and guaranteed security. He's a powerful man so my farms have been safe since."

"He helped you with money instead of helping you report that bully? What good is his power then?" Ranya couldn't appreciate the complexities of our feudal culture. She turned to Jazib. "You're a powerful landlord. Are you this way as well?"

Jazib stared at her, not looking too impressed with her blunt interrogation, then turned to Karam Din. "Thank you for your hospitality. I'll convey to my father how highly you speak of him." He paused with a deliberate air of grandiosity that came so naturally to him, then said, "Shah Sultan is my father."

"Shah Saeen?" Karam Din stood up in reverence. "I had no idea! How blind of me to not recongise you!"

"It's okay." Jazib smiled. "You've been good to us."

Karam Din's transformation from gracious host to grateful servant, who now stood with his hands together was comical, sad, yet expected. Ranya eyed one face after another and I hoped she would simply take heart from the fact that it was Jazib's father who helped the poor farmer when nobody else would.

After spending a relaxing afternoon at Karam Din's, we hit the road again. I took the wheel while Jazib lay sleeping in the backseat.

"He snores?" Ranya eyed him from her seat in the front.

"I guess," I said. It was the first time I'd heard it too.

"We talked all night." She smiled. "Well, not all night, only till four in the morning. It's remarkable, isn't it? To think that a few weeks ago, I didn't even know he existed."

"Uhm, Ranya," I said. "You do know how Arju feels about him, right? Not to mention the unsettling age gap between the two of you that…" I stopped abruptly. "I'm so sorry. It's none of my business."

"It's not that," she spoke softly. "I'm not that young."

Eh?

"How young?"

"I'm not nineteen. I'm twenty-two."

I looked at her so fast the car swerved a tiny fraction. "But you told me," I said. "Arju told everyone. Why? Does Jazib know?"

"He does," she answered with an amused smile. "When I called to invite him for dinner, he refused. Said I was a child and he just couldn't. I told him then."

So he did take it to heart the way he should have. I knew many wouldn't lose sleep over this issue, but to me – it was a bit icky. But I was still suspicious. "You told him you're twenty-two so he would come?"

"No, of course not."

"Then, why'd you lie before?"

"Arju said it was customary."

"No, it isn't!" I knew we had a truckload of cultural craziness, but this wasn't part of it.

Ranya looked uneasy. She glanced back at Jazib and I could sense her body tense up a little. "I'll tell you, I promise, but at another time. Please?"

I sighed. She wasn't going anywhere, and neither was I. We had plenty of time to talk about things. "We're going to Kesar, to my mother's," I told her. "You and I will stay there and Jazib will head off to Gurhkot alone."

The surprise in her eyes told me this wasn't the plan she had in mind. She was perhaps planning out an entire weekend with him, but of course, that couldn't happen. Jazib couldn't bring home a girl he liked to meet his family because *one*, he was already engaged as far as they were concerned, so how inappropriate would that be, and *two*, what a blatant breach of decorum it would be to bring home a girl that he liked?

I glanced at Ranya's fallen face and felt sorry for her.

She had so much to learn.

9

ABBA'S HAVELI, IN CONTRAST to his city mansion, seemed to be in perpetual ruin every time I saw it. It wasn't, of course. It just looked that way to me, perhaps because of its old-fashioned architecture. That, however, was no deterrent for any visitor to be in awe of it.

I'd given Jazib control of the car a mile before we entered the haveli grounds. After draping my chador around me so that nothing but my eyes were visible and instructing Ranya to do the same, I sat in front with Jazib while Ranya moved to the backseat.

It was time to be proper.

The driveway to the haveli was long and winding and, once you hit the gated boundary wall, a horde of gunmen jumped you. Unless you were family. Then, they'd salute you, remove the heavy chains from the giant iron gates and let you in. Acres away, sitting on green grassy lots flaunted by ancient trees, was the haveli. The pale-yellow stucco walls with extravagant floral patterns and turquoise murals drew you in even before you stepped out of your vehicle. You'd park the car in a covered carport, hand the keys to the armed attendant and walk through an expansive courtyard that merged into a long, roofed veranda decorated with cane furniture. This was where Abba had entertained his farmers who came in crying, pleading, loaded with their everyday problems, seeking advice of their trusted feudal lord – their Saeen. His word was the law of his land. Whatever he decided, stayed.

Now, Ammi had taken up that responsibility.

The long veranda ended at a heavy, intricately carved dark wooden door that led to an indoor checkered terrazzo courtyard and a garden of potted plants. Our expansive haveli with its many columns and rooms, imposing archways, riddling hallways, and stained-glass windows was built around that courtyard.

Zaytun, the head housekeeper with her army of under-maids, was waiting there to receive us. She locked me in a tight embrace as soon as she saw me, respectfully acknowledged Ranya, and slightly bowed her head for Jazib as per custom. When Jazib asked for a drink of water, she immediately directed one of the under-maids to go fetch, another to prepare for tea and snacks, and two others to make sure our luggage reached our rooms.

"Bibi is on the patio," she said. "Maya Bibi, you'll be in your old bedroom and your friend has the room next to it and Jazib Saeen—"

"I'm not staying," he said. "Get me some ginger tea. My throat is itching."

"Saeen, joshanda will be better?" She referred to an herbal concoction that was super good for colds but tasted horrid.

Jazib scrunched his nose in disgust, shook his head, and went towards the patio. I peeled off my chador, handed it to Zaytun, and followed him into a long, arched hallway. It led to a sunlit red-brick covered patio spilling into a large vegetable garden with fruit trees and lush grass.

Ammi occupied one of the two charpoys on the patio. I stopped in my tracks to take in her glory and wondered why nobody had ever painted a portrait of the most royal woman I knew.

She was Gohar Bano, the only daughter of the Sultan household of Gurhkot, the first wife of Mir Badruddin, and the rightful vaderani of Kesar. The regal elegance and demeanour that came with it made up her aura. She wore pastels with a hint of embroidery made from the finest fabric, and her jewellery, from her thick bangles and bell-shaped earrings to her rings and nose-pin, was pure gold. The summer heat was sweltering, but she had her dupatta steadfastly over her head, draping her torso gracefully.

I remembered a time from long ago, when Abba, Ammi and I lived together. Ammi wasn't quite the feudal lady I saw before me. Back then, Ammi liked to wear her hair in stylish hairdos, lead the latest fashion trends. She had good, healthy hair and I got that from her. But her light complexion, thin lips, hazel eyes, and high forehead seemed more in line with…Ranya.

Ranya, who was a replica of Arjumand.

Was Abba aware he'd married the same sort of beauty twice?

"Zindagi!" Ammi stood up with her arms wide open, saying my childhood nickname. "I was expecting you earlier. It took so long. Jazib told me what happened." Then her gaze went to Ranya who stood behind me. "Badr told me you'd come too."

Ranya stepped forward and offered her salutations. She didn't bow her head as per custom to receive an affectionate pat on her head. Just stood there, tall and straight, draped in her chador from head to toe.

Zaytun entered with two maids pushing a tea trolley heavy with cookies, cakes, gram flour fritters, beef samosa, and, of course, chai. One of the maids handed Jazib a steaming cup of his ginger tea. Another offered Ranya an empty plate.

"No, I'm not hungry," she said. Her smile, as polite as it was, looked forced. "Just tired."

"Take Bibi to her room," Ammi ordered Zaytun and watched Ranya go until she was out of sight.

It felt awkward. Jazib watched Ranya leave without a proper goodbye, which I'm sure was him being instinctively careful in Ammi's presence. Then he announced he was leaving as well. Ammi protested, but he shook his head firmly. "I'll visit later," he said, and smiled at me, "soon."

But of course! You're supposed to convince Ammi to break off our engagement.

I smiled back.

Besides, I needed him to not be near Ranya lest Ammi suspected anything between them and became more obstinate than ever to save Jazib from the Evil Other Woman by throwing me at him full throttle.

It was summer and that meant mango season. The orchard was pregnant with green fruit that hung like heavy oval pendants from bowing branches. Most of it would drop, if not picked, with a gust of wind. I could see large baskets on the ground amidst the trees to collect the fruit, whereupon it will turn a bright, ripe yellow and be ready for consumption. The orchard only had about ten or less trees and took only a day to harvest, but while that hadn't happened and the baskets were empty, the view of the mature green foliage provided a spectacular view.

I could see it from Ammi's favourite room in the haveli, a small library lounge decorated purely with Sindhi furniture and aesthetics. There was a large divan by a tall window wall where she sat every morning reciting her Quran. There were two other living rooms in the haveli: one was decorated exactly like Abba's at his Karachi residence and was meant to entertain esteemed guests, while the other was a den used for religious ceremonies like the annual Milad or Ashur as well as the various Khatam, Dars and Durood events.

I went and stood by the window. The silence of the winds outside and the way each tree stood still and yet rustled softly calmed my nerves several notches. *I'll go for a walk there tomorrow*, I decided.

"Maya," Ammi called me from her divan, getting her legs and feet massaged by one of the maids. "Is that girl really good friends with you?" she asked.

"Which girl?"

"Ranya."

"No," I replied honestly. "She just wanted to see the countryside and Abba thought it was a good idea."

"Your Abba has gone senile. Even more."

There she goes, I sighed. "It's just for a few days, Ammi, nothing drastic."

"It's improper." She frowned. "To let a young, unmarried girl travel and take trips to unfamiliar places, un-chaperoned, with strangers."

"I'm young and unmarried and I travelled un-chaperoned."

"You were with your fiancé."

"Ammi," I said, taking a deep breath, "you need to lay off this engagement bit."

"Why? You're of age, done with college. I think it's the perfect time."

"I'm still not ready," I said, stiffening my back just so I'd look more determined. "And I don't think Jazib is ready either."

"Of course he isn't. Looking at you the way you are right now, hair all tousled and dry, no shine at all. Complexion all thrown to the sun and burned, and what are you wearing? No dupatta, dirty sneakers, nothing that will speak to the ways of this family." She gave me a stern onceover, her forehead crumpling. "And look at that girl, what's her name? Ranya. So fresh, so fair, and so properly dressed. Looking like exactly the kind of woman Jazib would want to marry."

"Oh, for heaven's sake, you sound so primitive."

"Man is primitive. Your father is a prime example of that. He ditched me for a girl half his age simply because she had a prettier face, she could dress more to his taste. She smiled more!"

"You know that's not why he did it." I was annoyed. I'd heard this rant a gazillion times before. And I'd heard Abba's side of the story too. He didn't marry Arjumand because she was prettier. She wasn't. She may have been on par with Ammi, but she wasn't *more* in looks or stature or education. She was younger, yes, but Abba wasn't a womaniser. He married Arjumand because he was in love with her.

Badr and Gohar – the two children of two powerful feudal lords, arranged to be married since forever by their elders. Badr secretly loved someone else, but nobody knew, and when they did, they didn't care or tell Gohar because the elders had spoken, and when you are part of that system, you do not object. You just obey. Badr obeyed and made good on his first commitment to Gohar, but he never forgot Arjumand. In this love triangle, in the eyes of the two lovers, Gohar was the other woman. Not Arjumand.

I knew all this and yet it never seemed to help. I couldn't ignore the fact that my father had cheated on my mother. But was he really to blame?

I stood up.

"I have to shower," I said firmly as a way of excusing myself, and without waiting for her response, marched out of the room.

10

THERE WAS LITTLE CHANGE to my old bedroom. Ever since I'd had those atrocious princess-pink drapes and bedding removed that were remnants of my eight-year-old self, it was mostly wood furniture and terrazzo floors that ran throughout the haveli. The four-poster bed was covered with white bedding that added a certain coolness to the room and made the scorching daylight of the plains bearable.

My luggage was already unpacked; clothes hanging in the wardrobe and shoes lined neatly on shoe racks in the dressing room. I picked out an ajrak-print kurta with white shalwar and changed into it after a satisfying warm shower. The geometric patterns in deep burgundy and blues on the loose shirt went well with my mood. My hair was glossy again after rigorous shampooing, but my skin – much to Ammi's horror – was still dusky. I found a couple of new tubes of the country's number-one skin-whitening cream in my drawer and tossed them in the trashcan.

"The world craves for my kind of complexion!" I'd tried educating her on various occasions. "White people in the West pay good money to tan like me, but no, it's my own mother who's forever propagating her colonised complex of how superior white skin tones are."

"Haw." She'd object. "I say this for your own good."

She wasn't that wrong given the premise of our society. We were a people brought up in a culture of colonisation, of discrimination, of constant reminders that we weren't good enough for anyone, including ourselves, simply by being who we were. The colour of our skin, the most identifying trait about us, was also the most targeted one, the one that gave us a reason to hate that reflection in the mirror, because life was just so hard because of that dark skin. Consequently, the fairer ones among us were revered, because they looked less like "Darkies" and more like Gora Sahib. Skin-lightening products made up a billion-dollar industry in the country. It targeted every brown girl, promising her most cherished dreams that could only come true if she were fair and lovely. And she would be lovely only if she were fair.

She'd get the man of her dreams if she were fair.

She'd ace that test, nail that interview, win over that client, get that promotion, impress her boss (evidently male), and get ahead of all competition if she were fair.

She'd win hearts of everyone around her if she were fair.

She wouldn't ever be bullied, passed over, looked down upon and disrespected if she were fair.

The world would be hers, its treasures strewn at her feet, if only she were fair.

A fair complexion was synonymous to success. Use the cream, the soap, and the lotion and betray your natural skin tone, become fair and fairer, learn to hate the way you are. The complex was centuries old. Entrenched too deep to be uprooted. People like me could protest and declare to not care but not escape it. It was a constant battle.

I looked at my window, out to the horizon streaked with dull pinks and a vanishing glimmer of sunshine. Summer days were long, and sunsets came late into the night. I decided to go check on Ranya and see if she wasn't too uncomfortable with her new surroundings. Her room was right next to mine. I knocked softly at her door. "Come in," her tiny voice echoed from within. I turned the handle and went in. She sat on the bed, showered and changed from one pastel suit into another. Her damp, loose hair fell around her like a shiny, heavy cloak, wrapping her up like she was a delicate china doll.

"Hey," I said. "Just wanted to check how you were." There was a sense of hesitation about her, as if she wanted to say something but didn't know how. "You probably didn't think we'd be staying at my mother's place?"

"Jazib said he'd take me to Gurhkot with him," she confessed. "And I don't think your mother is comfortable with me here either."

"She'll be fine. Are you hungry? You haven't eaten anything since lunch."

"This is a beautiful house," she said instead, her eyes appreciating the room around her that wasn't so different from mine.

"Come on, I'll give you a tour of the haveli. It's worth seeing," I said, delighted to see her jump at my offer. It was hard to pass up on the many murals and architectural designs and wonders of this almost-a-century-old structure that seemed more inspiring and curious as time passed by.

The region of Kesar and Gurhkot was thousands of years old. Historically it was part of a province that was once ruled by Rajas and royals of old, later divided into districts under the British Raj, and then handed over to local feudal families, who were either loyal to the colonisers or had enough political power to matter. I'm not sure which category my ancestors fell in. All I knew was they had lands, thousands of acres. And they had tales of rebellion and revolutionary bravery decorating their personal histories, erasing all suspicion of them ever being cordial to their English masters.

I never doubted them.

For what it was worth, Abba had sold off most of his land to the farmers and peasants who'd worked on it for generations. All he was left with was the haveli and a few acres of agricultural land that he legally transferred to Ammi's name. Abba's property was in the city – his house, his construction business, his life. Apparently this was bound to happen, as everyone from his family and Ammi's would always tell me, "Badr just doesn't have the acumen to farm the land or even possess it or even act like he respects the feudal lifestyle."

This was fascinating history that made for engaging conversation.

The haveli décor captured Ranya's interest just as much. The floral murals replicated the bright flowerbeds outside. The same theme was carried on in stained-glass windows. The arches, wooden beams and doors were artworks of artisans who'd often graced royal palaces with their craft. The carved wood panels and shutters and handles and hinges and everything – it was unique. The furniture told various tales as well: a swing that was built to order as a gift for my grandmother's wedding, a table that was acquired from a Raja's clan, a cupboard that was bought at an auction managed by the outgoing officers of the British Raj. There were few portraits, but many paintings, as Ammi was an ardent fan of oils, mostly landscapes or slices of rural life, usually of Kesar.

"Who painted these?" Ranya asked, lightly touching the vague initials on one canvas.

"No idea," I said. "I think there was a local boy who painted. Maybe him."

Even the floors of the haveli were something quite new to her. She was more used to stone or porcelain tile, nothing like the colourful patterns of terrazzo or *chips* that was used in our part of the world since forever.

"We used to play chess on this," I told her about the floor in the foyer and skipped a few squares to demonstrate. "Hopscotch, four corners, 'the floor is lava', tag. Every game that could be played outdoors, Jazib and I played here when the weather was too hot or too wet."

She giggled as she imagined my childhood through my descriptions. I realised we could be friends. She wasn't some unintelligent, ignorant foreigner who needed constant babysitting – like I'd imagined initially and now prayed she'd never find out.

"And this is the formal dining room that we rarely use now." It was a large room decorated royally with modern furniture, a deviation from the traditional décor of the haveli. "We eat in the other one."

"How many are there? This house is a labyrinth of mammoth proportions."

I chuckled. That's how havelis were constructed. In fact, that's how most old houses were built. An average traditional home would usually be single storey, built room after room, linked through hallways and doors opening into one lounge and another. The reason was that owners bought the land first, then constructed on it as time went by, according to their familial needs. It was easy to get lost in such homes if one wasn't familiar with the floorplan.

We turned a corner and ended up in the second dining room. It was tucked away in one of the many corners of a vast red-brick kitchen that seemed to span some half an acre itself, lit by rustic lantern-style light fixtures.

"This is the biggest kitchen I've ever seen!" Ranya gawked at the expanse. "You can't even see it entirely from standing here."

"I'll show you around later," I promised.

Ammi sat at the head of the table, slicing some apples on a blue pottery platter. She looked up and smiled. "Dinner is cold now."

"I'm not hungry," I said, taking my seat near her and picking an apple slice. "But Ranya hasn't eaten anything since lunch time."

"Oh, I'm not hungry either," Ranya replied quickly in a low tone and slipped into a chair beside mine, sitting with her hands folded in her lap. Everything about her timid behaviour suggested she didn't want to offend her hostess.

"Tani, peel some mangoes for Ranya Bibi. Would you like a mango shake?" Ammi asked Ranya, but she shook her head. I wondered if she was that scared of Ammi to be essentially tongue-tied. "Dice it," Ammi instructed the maid, "and don't forget the forks."

Ranya stared back at her hands, sitting so still as if trying not to breathe too much.

I stood up, cradling the heavy apple platter in one arm. "I'm giving Ranya a tour of the haveli. I want her to see the roof. We'll eat our mangoes upstairs," I told Ammi and gestured at Ranya with a lift of my eyebrow to get up too. She instantly obeyed like I'd thrown her a lifeline. I walked her through the kitchen. "This is the bigger, dirty kitchen for heavy cooking, and that is the smaller one that's in use twenty-four-seven for small stuff like snacks and chai and such. This is the tandoor for fresh naan, but nobody eats naan anymore so…that is the wet area for all the dishwashing and that's the pantry."

"You could go shopping in that pantry!" Ranya could hardly keep her mouth from falling off its hinges as she looked on.

We entered a hallway that led to a staircase leading upward to a vast roof and its garden.

Flat rooftops – an outdoor space where people lounged, hung out, stargazed, flew kites, slept through hot summer nights, partied, hung clothes-lines, dined, enjoyed the monsoons, studied for that dreaded test in the morning, chatted in peace (and in secret) with their hot crush over the phone, and just lived their lives – were a unique feature of the homes in my world. Those who never knew it didn't know what they'd been missing until they saw it. And then there was no going back.

"I've never seen anything like this." Ranya scanned the area with curious eyes, drinking in every detail of the roof terrace: a great expanse of endless concrete and balustrades of varying heights, a roof garden complete with a gazebo that housed a large swing and some chairs. By day, it was a grand display of dazzling colours of the cacti and flowers, but by night, it was another mystic world of soft glowing lanterns and fairy lights. "Houses back home don't have such interesting rooftops," she said. "Roof gardens are for skyscrapers and city buildings, but none this large. And normal houses? Not a chance. I wish I had this."

"I have it," I boasted. "It's tiny, way tinier than this, but I have one."

"Really? But even Arju's house doesn't have one."

"I know, that's so tragic, isn't it?" I mused. "Abba had his house built to resemble a Victorian castle or whatever because that's what Ammi liked. All sloped roofs."

Suddenly, the air around Ranya seemed to weigh heavier, as her beaming face lost a little bit of its shine. "Maya," she said, hesitating. "Did my sister really wreck your mother's marriage?"

How was I supposed to answer that?

Yes. No. It's complicated…

"It wasn't like that," I finally said. "Whatever happened was so long ago and everyone involved has moved on. You needn't burden yourself with any of it."

She seemed to understand, sighing and nodding her head slowly. "I know that feudal families value their relationships and commitments. If Jazib was spoken for, I never would've looked at him twice."

If?

We were engaged. But we didn't acknowledge it, hence it made sense Jazib wouldn't tell her about it. But we were *engaged*, even if we didn't acknowledge it, hence he should've told her.

Should I?

"Maya Bibi, Saeen is here," the mango maid interrupted us like a reporter breaking important news.

"Which saeen, Tani?" I asked, taking a bite of the apple slice in my hand. "They're all saeen here. Is Jazib back?"

"No, Bibi. It's Mir Saeen."

"Abba?" I stopped chewing. "He's here?" That was highly unusual. Abba only visited once a year and he'd already done that.

"He's sitting in the big drawing room."

I looked at Ranya, handed the apple platter to Tani and headed downstairs.

11

ABBA SAT ON THE largest of the four gilded ivory couches placed
on a hand-woven rug that anchored the room's colour palette of
teal, ivory and gold. Crystal chandeliers and candelabras studded
in the walls and high ceiling added to the sparkle of an already
rich décor. Ammi sat on a smaller settee, looking displeased.

"What a surprise, Abba!" I exclaimed as we entered. "I didn't
know you had plans of coming too."

"Of course, he did," Ammi replied instead. "He had to make
sure I wasn't a total witch to his sister-in-law."

I sensed Ranya stiffen as she took her seat next to me. I truly
wished that Ammi would just, for one second, practise some
restraint over her own speech.

"I came because I had time and I thought I'd spend it here,"
Abba said.

Zaytun brought in a tray carrying fruit bowls of diced mango,
java plum and peach wedges, and set it on the coffee table.

"What is that?" Ranya asked me, pointing to the java plums.

"Jamun," I said and offered her some. She popped one in
her mouth and chewed. I could tell her tongue was rolling in
her mouth, separating the seed from the flesh of the fruit, and
experiencing its astringent taste of a sweet and sour combination.

"This is the best thing I've tasted," she declared, holding the jamun pit between her thumb and forefinger. "And it colours everything purple."

"Yes." I laughed. "Especially the tongue."

Ranya smiled at me, and even though it was the same sweet smile I'd seen so many times before, it didn't look fake to me this time. Her interest in her new surroundings was genuine and endearing. It even made Ammi smile when she admired something as simple as a jamun.

"You should try them with salt next time," I told her. "You take a plate and fill it with jamun, sprinkle salt, then cover with another plate and shake it."

"Shake it?"

"Shake it! That breaks the fruit and softens it and gets it nicely salted. The sweetness with the salt is to die for."

"Nothing beats mangoes," Abba said, then sighed at the platter of diced mango in front of him, "but definitely not diced ones. You cannot essentially taste a mango unless you eat it the way it is meant to be eaten. Forks and knives are insulting to that fruit."

"I understand nothing in this conversation," Ranya confessed honestly, making us all laugh.

Even Ammi.

"He means, you cut it into wedges and eat it by scraping the flesh off the peel with your teeth," she was finally talking to Ranya. "Or you hold a small mango upright in your hand and roll it, using your fingers and thumb. Purée it in its skin, then peel off the dried stalk, make a tiny hole and drink it from there, as if it's a juice box."

Ranya was amazed. "You'll have to show me that!"

"Wait till you taste falsay," Abba suggested, forking the last of his diced mango.

"What's falsay?"

"You don't know falsay either?" I cried. "What kind of boring land do you come from? It's like a blueberry but smaller and tastier, and purple. By the way, what's English for falsay, Abba?"

"There's no falsay in English," he said, "because the English never had falsay."

We roared with another round of laughter. It was true that Abba's presence brightened up any environment. He'd done the same for the haveli. Didn't Ammi miss him?

My smile froze on my lips with a strange realisation.

Ammi missed him.

Of course she did!

I eyed them as they sat talking, her face twisted into an expression of joyous disbelief while Abba told her he'd stay at the haveli for a few days. She stood up with energy that was so lacking in her until now, shouting orders to prepare for Abba's stay. How strange was that? Just one assurance from him had her dancing around with joy.

I felt a tug at my heart. Were all women so hopeless in love?

Every morning at the haveli woke up to a soothing recitation of the Quran in Ammi's melodious voice. She sat on the divan after her Fajr prayers until a soft sun rose high and filled the universe with light and the birds woke up and chirped to greet the new day with their song.

I yawned, stretched to get all sleep out of my system and hopped out of bed, brushed my teeth, showered, changed into a mustard-yellow-and-green-printed lawn kamiz shalwar and knocked on Ranya's door to see if she was up. It was a bright day, yet cool for summer, which meant we could venture outdoors after breakfast.

"I didn't know what you'd like," Ammi said to Ranya. "If there's anything else you want, just tell Zaytun to make it for you."

Ranya looked at the various food items that lay dished out across the wide expanse of the dining table: bread, butter, jams, cheese spread, paratha, omelette, fried eggs, French toast, tea… what was missing?

"Pancakes," I said. "Or maybe waffles. And where's the cereal?"

"No, not for me," Ranya said quickly, sitting even more upright than before, clearly looking in every mood to please her hostess. "This is already…too much, a lot! I usually only have some cornflakes in the morning."

"What?" Ammi stared at her as if she couldn't disapprove of the idea enough. "That is not breakfast. That is birdfeed. Have some French toast. Or would you like pancakes? I'll send someone later to get your cereal. You can have it tomorrow morning, although I do not see why you should eat that unhealthy boxed thing."

"No, please, this is perfect," Ranya said. "I don't want cereal. This is fine. Thank you."

"You're too easy," I teased her. "But yes, rural settings call for a rural breakfast. Have some desi butter. It's to die for, seriously." She eyed the snowy-white ball in a small round dish and scooped out a spoonful. I guess she liked its creamy, somewhat tangy texture because her next move was to butter her toast with it.

Abba had taken his breakfast earlier and was outside with the farmers and locals who'd heard of his coming and had dropped by to pay Mir Saeen a visit. "He'll join us for lunch," Ammi said as she got off her chair. "I have a very busy day ahead. Maya, make sure you take good care of our guest."

I knew she'd be busy cooking. She rarely cooked, but she cooked for Abba every chance she got. That was something as obvious to expect as oxygen for breathing. And when she cooked, it was detailed, from scratch, a worship that she revered, and enough to feed an entire village.

"Can we make requests?" I asked her. "I'd like biryani. Ranya, what would you like? Ammi makes the *best* biryani in the world."

"Biryani is fine," she replied quickly, and got back to buttering her already buttered toast.

"Quick question," I said to her. "How much butter does one piece of toast need?" She looked up at me sheepishly, the same pleading eyes that were becoming quite her hall-mark. "Eat it," I said. "Then I'll take you around the haveli for a walk in the orchard."

"Outside?" Ammi objected. "I don't think so."

"I'm going," I said, sipping my tea to the finish and setting the cup down. "And I'm not covering up or anything. You can tell all the haveli men to go wear their own chadors and look away."

Ammi stared at me much the same way she used to when I was a child and I'd done something extremely out of line and she wanted to spank me. She never did spank me even then. And now I was too grown up for it. So she simply sighed and walked away with a tart, "Acha!"

I smiled.

It was nice to have my own way.

If you've ever walked in a mango orchard, you'll notice the immense foliage that completely shades you, piles of yellowing green oval fruit on the ground in season, its sweet scent, and the cooing mynah filling the air with her haunting song.

"I can hear it!" Ranya exclaimed. "It's so musical."

There was a gentle wind and the cool green canopy of leaves let the sunlight drench us in soft rays, not bold shards. I walked Ranya all the way to the edge of the orchard where a large boundary wall stood, cordoning haveli gardens off from the main pastures. Another path from there led out to a pool house that served no purpose ever since Ammi had the pool filled in when Abba permanently moved to Karachi.

"There's also a secret garden here." I took her behind the neglected pool house to a secluded patch of overgrown shrubs, dandelions, and untrimmed trees, fenced in by a rotted iron gate. It creaked as I pushed it open and leaves crunched beneath our feet as we entered. What lay ahead were ruins of an old wood shack that sat in the middle of a forgotten garden.

"What's that?"

"Our clubhouse," I said. "Jazib and mine's." I pushed the door open and it moaned in protest. A single unfurnished room, big enough to accommodate two adults, was what welcomed us, alongside cobwebs, dust, a possible termite or some other insect infestation, a magic portal leading to an alternate universe – I expected to encounter all sorts of things there. "Nobody comes here anymore," I said to the walls, caressing them with my fingers, remembering a million memories that I shared with the place.

It had never occurred to Jazib or me to ever furnish our empty clubhouse. We just spent hours there, lying on the floor, reading, or making caricatures of each other or of things around us, or playing house. I'd be the wife, cooking dinner on an imaginary fire in imaginary pots, while he, the good husband, went out into the gardens and orchard to hunt me some food to cook. Why I cooked while he was out hunting was something that never occurred to either of us. We never had any children. I'm not sure if that decision was mutual. We never talked about it. We just didn't have any. One day, I decided I didn't want to cook anymore. It was boring work. Waiting all day for him to return. It was also silly that I had no pots and pans to cook in, no fire to cook on either and no dining table and chairs to sit on to eat it. He argued that I never cleaned house. How absurd really, I mean what was there to clean? We had nothing! So I stormed out on our marriage and he never came after me, his wife. He did come after his friend though, and we never played house again.

"How silly we were!" I chuckled. My voice echoed in the void.

Ranya stood looking at me intently. "You and Jazib have a lot of memories together," she said. "He's very fond of you." There was a strange longing in her voice. It wasn't exactly jealousy, but envy that recongised the different places we held in his life and the different stages we'd entered it in.

I wanted her to know I wasn't a threat, that I never could be one. If I were to have an honest relationship with her, I had to start by never pretending. "He is fond of me, but not in the same way as he's fond of you," I said. "You two have something really special."

"I know," she said in a low voice, staring down at the floor and slowly scuffing it with her toe. "You know I lied about my age, and Jazib knows that too, right?"

"Yes."

"Arju thought it was a good idea. Just say it once or twice and word travels fast on the gossip vine. Nobody would even care to confirm what was said a year or so ago. In fact, people would simply assume from memory that I was a teenager when I came and would add years to that and bam! I'd still be in the list of most sought-after bachelorettes. Young, fresh." She stopped and looked at me.

I still didn't understand. If snagging the best catch and pinning him down with marriage was the point of it all, then why not take the plunge head on? Plenty of twenty-something women had come and instantly conquered unsuspecting and suspecting suitors that way. Why wait?

"Because…" Ranya scratched her forehead and began, "I was dating someone, but it ended and I didn't want to marry, but then…" she bit her lip, "I met Jazib."

Excuse me?!

"He's your *rebound* guy?"

"It's not like that."

"Oh, please." I glared at her. "You came here pining for someone else, not even ready for a relationship, but now you're standing here telling me you *met* Jazib? Oh no, missy, this is *exactly* like that!"

"No, Maya, please. Please, listen." She took my hand in hers and looked desperate. "The boy I was dating was my senior. Somebody I'd met at a friend's house. I didn't even like him much, but I just agreed when he asked me out to a movie. Then to a private dance party and a few basketball games."

"Oh really? All this with a boy you didn't even like much?"

"Because I just wanted to break loose! There were too many rules. Too many walls. My parents were too much!"

"I highly doubt that, Ranya, judging by what I personally know of your sister's love life." I was not even trying to be civil. "You do share the same parents, don't you?"

"You don't understand. She was here. I was there."

"What does that mean?"

She sighed. "Desi parents, no matter how liberal they pretend to be while in Pakistan, get all crazy once abroad, especially in a country like America. There are just too many things they're scared of. Their urge to not betray their roots runs stronger and deeper than ever, and all that is manifested in how they control their children. Arju probably had more freedom than I did because she was in Pakistan. Our parents had that useless but perceived peace of mind that comes from familiar surroundings. Yes, she loved an older married man, but at least he was a *Muslim*, and rich. And well, look at how well she's done for herself!"

"While you're just a confused Desi kid trying to live the American dream?"

She nodded. "For me, rules must change. What if I stray? What if I choose a white boy? Or worse, *not even* a white boy? What if he's a convert? He must be Muslim by birth. A Pakistani by descent. Good family. Single. Settled. Not a fresh-off-the-boat struggling immigrant who's the only one out there from his clan. I'm not allowed to stray so I must marry young. They don't even realise how hard it is to make marriage your focus in a land where it is a part of life but not life itself. Nobody wants to think of getting married at eighteen." She faintly smiled at me. "College to me was a way out, a permission I could give myself to grow up. To see the kind of person I was inside. I wasn't doing anything wrong. I wasn't sleeping around or hooking up. I just wanted to stand at the edge of all that was forbidden and observe. A date isn't bad if it's for companionship, is it?"

"I'm not sure that's even a date."

She laughed softly and this time, I joined her too.

I understood her. I could imagine the countless nights she might've spent in frustration over a birthday party she'd had to miss because her parents didn't approve of the friend who'd invited her, the school trip she couldn't take because they had concerns, the foods she couldn't eat, the outfits she couldn't wear, the sports she couldn't play, and so many other rules she had to abide by that set her apart from her crowd, and there's nothing scarier for an already conflicted teenager than something that puts her in the spotlight. The list in my head was very generalised, and I didn't know Ranya well enough to chalk out her past life exactly. Maybe she really was such a wayward child that even her very liberal parents had trouble pinning down and so they shipped her off to a land far, far away from them. But still, I got her.

Perhaps it was that broken and sad inner child in me that connected with the broken and sad inner child in her.

"So they sent you here to be corrected?" I asked her. We were now sitting on the floor. The old, wide wood planks were still strong and felt just as comfortable as they used to decades ago to my much younger limbs and butt.

"In a way," she admitted. "That subtraction in age was so that I'd still be young enough to be desirable even after four years, if I took that long. Smart plan, isn't it?"

"Deceptively."

"But I met Jazib…"

We fell silent at that. It was as if we'd used up all our words.

The sun was showering down heat, so we made our way back indoors. Ammi ordered for a pitcher of icy lemonade the instant she saw us come in. Ranya looked spent. She asked to be excused right after she emptied her glass and was escorted back to her bedroom. I lingered on in the kitchen, not trying to help at all, but chatting away with everyone there and chewing fresh vegetables.

"Make yourself useful." Ammi slapped a big woven platter of potatoes in front of me and handed me a peeler.

"All of these?" I was horrified.

"Maya Bibi, I'll help you," said a young, petite maid slipping in the chair beside mine.

"Why are you cooking all this food anyway?" I asked Ammi. "Abba doesn't even like potatoes."

"Jazib is coming over," she said and looked at me with intrigue. "Bhai-Jaan and Bhabi are coming too."

I stopped peeling and looked at her just as curiously. "Why?"

"I'm not sure, but I have an inkling," she said with a smile that only a desi mother could be capable of when hinting at her daughter regarding a potential marriage proposal.

But I knew she was wrong. I knew exactly why Jazib was coming over. "I wouldn't count on that inkling if I were you."

Ammi's face lost a bit of its mirth. "Leave us," she ordered the petite maid. Then, planting herself in that same chair, stared at me like I was a criminal about to undergo some acute interrogation. "Maya," she said, lifting an eyebrow, "Bhai-Jaan is coming over to formally propose."

"And I'm saying no. Formally."

"Maya…!"

"We don't want it. Jazib doesn't want it. I don't want it. In fact, that's exactly why I came here this time. To tell you to stop pushing for this marriage that nobody wants."

"If Jazib isn't interested, why are his parents coming over?"

"They told you they're coming for this reason?"

"No, but I have my hunch. And besides, it's time," she said decisively. "And it's time you started treating Jazib with the respect and decorum he deserves."

"Respect?" I laughed. "You're saying as though he's a prize to be had."

"Isn't he?"

"No. He literally has no qualifications other than being a rich man's son. Besides, this is about me, Ammi. About what I want. Why won't you understand?"

"Of course, it's always me who has to understand." Her lower lip started to quiver. "Your father did whatever he wanted to and now you're free to do the same."

I just couldn't ever with her emotional meltdown. I hated tears. I hated the pity party that my mother so conveniently kept throwing herself every time things didn't go her way. Yes, her life had been tough, but none of that was my fault! Why was I made to feel I had to right every wrong in her life? Who in their right mind ever expects that of their children? And what was worse, I couldn't fight my way out of this trap. I couldn't stand my ground on anything when my mother cried.

I just…caved.

So of course, I held her hand and begged her to stop crying.

To add to the drama, Zaytun came and announced that Jazib had arrived early, ahead of his parents. That sounded like bad news to me, but Ammi forgot she'd been crying after being so badly hurt emotionally at the hands of her utterly evil disobedient daughter, and stood up in an instant, smiling wide like sunshine. She sent Zaytun out with a host of new instructions on how to serve and host Jazib, then she looked at me. Top to bottom and back again. "Go change. Wear something nice, you have so many clothes. And put on some jewellery, you have a drawer full of it. Bangles, earrings, necklaces, rings, everything. Look at how Ranya dresses up. She's always sparkling and fresh. Did you use the creams I left for you in your dresser?"

"I threw those out," I said. "I am naturally tan and I actually like myself that way."

She glared at me for a second, then ordered me again to go change.

I mused, scrutinising myself in the mirror. The embroidered strawberry-pink kamiz and plain shalwar fit me perfectly, accentuating all the right curves. My hair was thick and glossy, and my skin was smooth. But I was still many shades darker than the *preferred* complexion. As I stared at my reflection, a faint memory of an old remark made its way back to me.

Jazib had told me something once.

I was fifteen, sitting in a stubborn huff on the beach, refusing to go back inside the hut, ranting about how Ammi wanted to drag me out from under the sun and lather me with layers of gunky creams so my skin wouldn't tan. I already wore sunblock, what more did she want? But yes, I wished I could be fair like her. Why did I have to be so dark when she was so pretty? Why couldn't I be lovely like her? Then I began to cry. That's when he took my face in his hands, looked me in the eye and said, "You're gorgeous, Maya. And if we hadn't known each other, I might even be attracted to you."

That felt good.

Any other day and my feminist self would've demanded that the universe rule in favour of brains over looks, but I didn't mind his endorsement just then. There was a feeble corner of my teenaged heart that did want to hear praises sung to my physical beauty. And hearing a heartthrob like Jazib say just that had meant everything…

I smiled. And posed for the mirror some more, loving my reflection. Then, putting on some pink lip gloss, adjusting my dupatta and slipping on a pair of sandals, I went knocking on Ranya's door to wake her up. When she didn't answer, I called her name and went inside. The room was empty. Her bed was made up and everything else was tidy, which meant she hadn't slept. The bathroom was vacant too. I was about to leave when faint voices floating in on air from the window caught my ear. Ranya's room faced the backyard, the part where my old shack was, and that's where the voices were coming from. I pressed my nose against the glass, then opened the window altogether, and leaned out to get a better glimpse. Two people, a man dressed in a white shalwar kamiz and a girl in familiar pastels, stood near the iron fence. Holding hands.

I couldn't hear what they were saying, but maybe it wasn't necessary. Their body language said tons. Jazib's bold gaze on Ranya's face and her shy giggle said tons. And then, like a climax to a very intense movie, Jazib did something I never expected from him. In one swift move, he took something out of his pocket and slipped it on Ranya's finger. She beheld it, hand over her heart, gasping for words. Jazib held her, lifted her chin up, and softly kissed her on the mouth.

Meanwhile, I was hanging halfway out the window, trying to not drop dead. Literally!

Was he out of his fucking mind?

I instantly pulled myself back from the window. I wasn't sure what I needed to do, but it had something to do with knocking him over the head with some sense.

He had proposed to her!

He had...*proposed*...

The oddity of that gesture hit me yet again with damning force. He wasn't the kind to propose. Ever. He was the kind to kiss, yes. I'd seen that before. That was the move I expected from him, but that ring...so he was serious when he told me he was in love with Ranya? My heart was racing, and I wasn't sure of how I felt about that entire episode.

Was I jealous?

No.

Was I hurt?

No.

Then why the palpitations?

I didn't know.

I went back to my room and called him.

"Hey, Maya," he said. "I'm already here."

"Yes." I hissed. "I *saw*."

"What?"

"I saw you, Jazib. Outside the shack."

"Oh..." there was a pause before he spoke again. "Are you mad?"

"Have you lost your mind?" I was trying not to scream his head off and it was making me sound hoarse. "You're *rushing in*. It's too fast. Too soon. Not to mention Ammi is breathing down my neck about *our* engagement and your parents are coming over. Plus, you hardly know Ranya and Arju hates you. Don't you see, there are just too many issues with this."

"I love her, Maya," he said softly.

"Okay...but does she love you back the same way? I mean, are you sure?" I had the strongest urge to ask him about Ranya's ex-boyfriend. I didn't know if he knew about it. I didn't know how he would react if he found out. Probably unfavourably. Most of all, I didn't know why I wanted him to know about something from her past when his own wasn't spotless. Did Ranya know about how many girls he'd been with? Did she know about *us?*

I cringed.

"Maya, I need you," he was saying. "I need my friend by my side in this. More than ever."

"I'm here. Can't have you mess it up with the *one* girl you actually fell for."

"I knew you loved me." He chuckled.

"But Jazib, does she know about us? I tried telling her but chickened out every time. Besides, I think it should be you who breaks that news to her."

"I haven't," he said. "But I mean, it's so inconsequential and once everyone gets to know about her and me…that'll be the more important thing to talk about, right?"

I hoped so. I got off the phone and heaved a deep sigh. There was no room for doubts anymore. Jazib's mind was made up and I had promised to stand by him.

And that was all there was to it.

12

SAEEN FARID SHAH SULTAN – aka Bhai-Jaan – aka Mamu-Jaan – was the jagirdar of Gurhkot, indisputably one of the richest landlords in the country, and consequently, one of the most politically influential people as well. He was Ammi's brother, my uncle, Jazib's father, and the most ardent advocate of mine and Jazib's engagement.

Jazib was the only heir to Gurhkot's throne. Although Gurhkot wasn't a princely state, it wasn't anything less either. My maternal grandfather was a huge name in politics, like his father before him. He had tried to push his son into it as well and Mamu-Jaan obeyed for as long as his father was alive, but after his death, he pulled himself out. He was more comfortable with funding campaigns and propping up candidates than being the racehorse himself. He was an emperor who excelled at the art of king-making. His political power, which came from thousands of peasants who lived and worked on his lands and depended on him for their bread and butter, was unchallenged and limitless. He reaped the profits of their toils while they took home small shares. He invested in factories that provided more employment opportunities for the locals and he hired them for small salaries while he took home huge profits. To the people, he was the provider of their livelihoods. To the elite, he was a capitalist who funded their projects. To the governments, he was an endorsement to be had because his validations came with cash offerings and vote banks.

That much power could not possibly be humble.

Mamu-Jaan was used to being revered, served, saluted, and obeyed. He travelled with his own entourage of gunmen and servants. His haveli was palatial. His lands sprawled over thousands of acres and beyond. His wife was the queen of his kingdom, bedazzling in gold, silks and jewels, but placed decoratively on a pedestal by her feudal lord husband. She could expect to be pampered, expect the royal treatment and reverence. She was the most cherished and expensive of all his possessions, but she was a possession nonetheless. Like a prized pedigree kitten.

This was the world that Jazib came from.

Gurhkot's pampered prince was entitled to an enormous inheritance of power and money that he hadn't worked a day for in his life. He was raised to claim it as his with all the rights but none of the responsibilities. He was laid back and uninterested in work. After high school, he'd enrolled in a business school, the same one that I went to three years later. He'd just about made it through the first year there when his Commercial Law course tickled his fancy and he quit business school to go to law school. He was shipped off to another grand institute in Lahore this time, because Mamu-Jaan had a friend whose son also studied there. Apparently he was supposed to be a good influence on Jazib. Instead Jazib turned him into an absolute party animal and the boy was suspended for an entire semester for showing up stoned out of his mind to one of his lectures.

Law school must've been fun for Jazib to stay there for as long as he did. I never understood why he quit. Said he got bored. That's how he was: non-serious attitude, no career path, no skillset. No interest in acquiring any either. He owned farmlands but he couldn't tell the difference between a sickle and a hoe, a seed and a grain. If all his farmers quit, his crop would die, and he wouldn't know what to do. To add to this, there was also his complex persona that changed with a difference of location. He was a liberal city boy in the city but a Vadera Saeen in his haveli. Any girl he took as his wife would have to replace his mother just as he would replace his father.

I wondered if Ranya understood all of that.

Evening approached the plains and the haveli sparkled like a jewel in its midst. All chandeliers were lit. All rooms were spotless. All domestic staff alert and ready. A rich home-cooked menu greeted the guests when they arrived.

Mamu-Jaan, clad in a crisp white cotton shalwar kamiz, an ironed ajrak over his shoulders, and feet snuggly encased in brown leather Peshawaris, presented a roadmap to what Jazib would look like decades down the road of age. His hair was thick and peppered and his dark moustache had a presence of its own, with its pointy ends turned slightly upward. He sat at the head of the formal dining table, being our guest of honour. His wife sat to his right. Dressed expensively in embroidered chiffon and gold jewellery, she looked like a portrait of a maharani come to life.

The seating at the table was quite segregated, as all the women sat on one side and all the men sat on the other. I looked at Ranya. She'd changed into a refreshing colour palette of lime and lilac.

"I love your lip colour," I whispered in her ear. "Where'd you get it?"

"From that new cosmetics shop at the mall I told you about," she whispered back. "I forget which brand. I'll tell you after dinner."

As we chatted, my gaze inadvertently travelled to Jazib and caught him staring at his new secret fiancée. He just sat there blatantly ogling her as if they were the only two people at the table. He was sitting opposite me and his long limbs were quite within range, so I kicked him in the shin. He looked up with a start and a quiet "Ouch."

"How's the korma, Jazib?" I glared at him, trying to warn him to not forget his manners around people who had zero idea about the hell he'd done. "*Look* at your plate, it's practically empty." He narrowed his eyes at me in response and would have said something too had his father not beaten him to it.

"The food is excellent," Mamu-Jaan announced in his deep, dominating voice. "I can tell that Gohar cooked everything herself today."

"She did," I said, taking a forkful of chicken pilaf. "I was there, peeling potatoes for the cutlets."

The audience chuckled in good humour. Ammi urged everyone to try more of her extensive menu, asking Zaytun to refill the dishes. Abba passed on the platters and bowls and helped everyone with second and third helpings.

After dinner, it was time to lounge and talk some more and have chai with dessert. Everyone took their seat in the formal living room while Abba excused himself and stepped outside to take a business call. Mamu-Jaan and his wife sat on the throne-like sofa that lay in the centre of the room, commanding all attention. Ranya sat with me and I realised that nobody had tried to engage with her in any meaningful conversation beyond a formal greeting all evening. They all knew who she was and their cold response towards her troubled me, especially given her relationship with Jazib.

Meanwhile, Jazib looked strangely unruffled.

He was smiling and talking with Ammi, getting plenty of smiles from his parents for his remarks, while Ranya sat practically shunned, looking lost. She did her best to appear social, chatting with me, answering all my queries about her lip colour and experience of rural Pakistan, but I could see it in her wandering eyes that her mind was elsewhere. She kept stealing glances of Jazib, clasping and unclasping her hands in her lap and trying desperately to keep a straight face with a fixed smile.

"You're trying too hard," I finally told her.

Her lips parted slightly and her eyes widened, baring her heart. She quickly recovered and swallowed. "He said he'll talk to them soon."

"Tonight?"

"I don't know." She shook her head, and I knew it was this that unnerved her. If I were her, I wouldn't want to be anywhere near when Jazib battled his parents for his right to choose his bride.

"Well, did he tell you to wear this colour?" I smiled at her, hoping to lighten the mood. "This is so far off from your pastels."

"Is it too much?" she asked. "The shade is too strong for me, but he said it's his favourite."

"It is. And it's perfect for you." I reassured her, thinking if there was even a way to calm her nerves just then.

"Gohar, I want to take this opportune moment to say something to you," Mamu-Jaan, the ever-ceremonious speaker, caught my attention as he spoke to Ammi. "I think it's time we strengthen our familial bond."

"Yes, Bhai-Jaan," she said eagerly.

"Where is Badr? He should be here for this, but he's run off to attend his business calls?" He shook his head. "But you are my sister and this subject not being anything new, I think we can discuss it without him."

A pit in my stomach hardened and I quickly looked at Jazib. He wasn't looking at me.

Fool!

"Yes, of course, Bhai-Jaan," Ammi said, grinning widely. "I'm sure Badr wouldn't mind."

"I think it's time we officiate Jazib and Maya's engagement. Don't you agree?"

"Oh, yes!" Ammi gasped with delight. "This is exactly what I want too."

I felt numb.

I couldn't decide whether I should jump to my feet and protest or sit there and wait for a visibly frozen Jazib to do the jumping and protesting instead.

And, of course, there was Ranya.

"Engagement?" she cried.

"Yes," Mamu-Jaan answered without looking at her, as if he didn't think she deserved either the attention or the information. But he was excited enough to go on and explain it to the air in front of him, "They've been spoken for each other since birth."

"Since...*birth*?" she looked at me and whispered because the shock of revelation wouldn't allow her to speak any louder. *What is this? How? Nobody told me!* Her questioning gaze made me want to die.

"I think we should set a date while we're at it," Jazib's mom was talking now.

"Whatever suits you. Maya is now part of your family, yours to take home whenever you wish to. We're ready."

That was a battle cry!

"No, we're not," I said, with my heart throbbing in my head. "I'm not. I'm not ready."

Ammi looked at me as if I were spouting gibberish. "If this is about your job, I think I've had enough of that excuse. You won't need a job once you're married."

"But I'm not getting married." I spoke louder this time. "I'm saying no. Jazib, tell them! *We* are saying no. It is off. I'm not going to marry Jazib."

"Maya!" Ammi looked horrified.

"And I told you about this. So many times, too many times to recall."

"Gohar? What is going on?" Mamu-Jaan looked surprised, but still maintained his benevolent smile as he looked at me kindly and asked, "Is our little Maya angry with us for some reason? What can I do to make it right, Beta-Ji?"

Why did he always talk to me like I was his favourite kitten or something? I wasn't quite sure of how to respond to him, but his words seemed to bring Jazib back to life. He stirred in his seat and softly addressed his father.

"Baba Saeen," he said, "this may not be the best time or way to address this issue. We should talk later."

Omg, what a mouse!

I glared at him, hoping he'd look at me, but he didn't. I couldn't believe his calm demeanor at a time when passion should've been his driving force. He'd just promised himself to a woman who sat right there in the room where his own father was making plans of marrying him off to another woman who also sat in that same room. He should've been standing there in the centre with a proverbial sword in hand, valiantly defending his forbidden love and declaring war. Or something!

"Why later?" Mamu-Jaan asked, looking a little concerned, then turned to his wife. "I don't understand what is happening."

"I think I do," Ammi said acidly, slowly turning her head to glare at Ranya. "I'll be damned if this isn't about her."

"Her?" Mamu-Jaan scoffed, again not even bothering to look at Ranya. "What about her?"

"Did your sister help you hatch this plan?" Ammi was talking directly to Ranya now. "Is this why you suddenly flew all the way from the States? Did you really think it'd be that easy to steal from me again?"

"Stop it, Ammi, this is ridiculous. Jazib, say something!" I cried.

"Baba Saeen," he said again in a measured tone, "I like Ranya.
I want to marry her."

The gasps following the scandalous confession were
legendary. They should've been noted in the archives of history
of shocked reactions. I wished I weren't part of this drama just
so I could watch it unfold from the sidelines, preferably with a
steady supply of popcorn.

And dear God, where was Abba?!

After a momentary lull, Jazib's parents pounced on him. *Are
you out of your mind? Are you drunk? This is a joke!*

"I will not allow it," Mamu-Jaan declared icily. "There is no
place in this family for another gold-digger. Not in my house. No!"

"You're insulting my choice, Baba Saeen. I promised this
girl—"

"*This* girl," Mamu-Jaan interrupted him with a scowl, "is the
sister of the woman who insulted my sister, wrecked her home.
This girl has the same dirty blood in her veins as that unrefined
woman with her inferior upbringing. This girl is not welcome!"

The hate in his words was too much to process in a single
moment. It required several moments, and while I felt stifled
and Jazib clenched his fists, Ranya stood up.

"How dare you?" she said, trying to sound stern but her
voice quivered. She looked paler than usual and I feared she
might faint, but she stood staring at Saeen Farid with her fists
clenched at her sides. "How dare you insult my family!"

"Your sister had an affair with a married man," Mamu-Jaan
replied, directly looking at her for the first time.

"And that married man had an affair with her. Why is she
the only one taking the blame?"

"Men are easily manipulated," Jazib's mom confronted her.
"It's up to a woman to know, respect, and enforce boundaries.
But of course, that requires strength of character that only a
woman of integrity and good breeding would have. What would

you know of such things? Your parents never taught you or your sister as much."

"I'm sorry you feel this way." Ranya suppressed a shiver, pressing her fingers into her palms until her knuckles were white. "How pitiful and regressive are your own ideals."

"This is your choice?" Jazib's mom turned her head to look at him and frowned. "These are her manners? Such disrespect."

"Ranya, please, don't escalate the situation," Jazib said, much to Ranya's surprise but not mine. I expected that. I expected worse.

"You're telling me?" She incredulously looked at him.

"I'm just saying there is no need to get upset and argue. Let's keep a cool head, okay?"

"You didn't say that while they insulted me and my family. You kept your mouth shut."

"Because what we said was the truth," his mom said coolly. "You and your family aren't respectable."

Ranya continued staring at Jazib. "Is that how you feel too?"

"That's irrelevant, Ranya," he said. "What's important is that we love each other and that we're in this together."

"Okay," she said, swallowing hard, stepping forward and putting an unsteady hand on his arm. "Marry me, then. Right now? Marry me."

"Ranya, please, be reasonable."

"Your father has made it clear I'm not allowed in his house nor this haveli. You just said we're in this together. You promised me—"

"I'm not breaking any promises, okay." He'd begun to sound frustrated. "There is a way of handling delicate issues, a respectable way. And this isn't that way."

"I came all the way here for you." Her voice was an echo of a heartbreak that I was afraid Jazib wasn't listening to. "Jazib?"

He looked back at her in a manner that was all dark and wrong. "So what?" he said. "You say that as though it does any damage to your reputation. *Nobody* knows you. You don't have a name to live up to."

"So that's it then," she said, her chin jerking upward, the delicate slope of her shoulders stiffening, "...*this* is what you think of me."

He must've comprehended the shock on her face because he didn't reply. But it didn't help. His arrogance had finally broken through the façade of his humility and exposed the true vadera in him.

Ranya stared at his face steadily for a quiet minute. Then she slipped his ring off her finger and dumped it in his palm like an undesirable object. "I wouldn't cry over this," she said. Her eyes were glistening, but her voice was determined.

"Be very sure about this, Ranya," he hissed, tightening his grip around the trinket. "I will not come after you."

"Goodbye, Jazib," she said, and walked out in a whiff of stunned silence.

"Jazib..." I was trembling. "Have you lost your mind? You let her go!"

"I didn't ask her to leave."

"You didn't ask her to stay either."

"I asked her to take it easy and think a little. What else was I supposed to do?"

"Grow a spine and fight for her, you moron! You just proposed to her this morning!"

"Maya, behave yourself, this is no way to talk," Ammi said, suddenly remembering all sorts of etiquettes again.

"Wonder why none of you remembered that like two seconds ago," I said.

"Oh, Gohar, don't shout at her," Mamu-Jaan said. "Maya dear, nobody is happy with what happened, but darling, this was inevitable."

"You insulted her. And her family. You had *no* right."

"Beta-Ji, truth always hurts no matter how you say it," he said, rolling his eyes slightly as if explaining the obvious to a dumb child. "Her sister did the same to your mother. And now she was trying to repeat the offence with you. We were merely protecting you."

"Jazib and you belong together, Maya," Jazib's mom said. "That girl has no place in this circle."

"Maya." Ammi glared at me. "Apologise to them for your outburst."

I stared at their faces. Cold. No remorse. Not a single after-thought about what they'd done to another person, how they'd stripped someone of her dignity and tossed it across the horizon in one swift move. They'd only thought of Ranya as a sharp pebble in their shoe and had discarded her just as scornfully, never once humanising her in their minds. They wanted her gone and now she was gone. They couldn't be bothered with the cruelty of their behaviour.

I stared at Jazib, who looked lost in a world of his own, staring at the trinket in his palm. I couldn't read his mind, nor did I care to. He was an utter disappointment and I wished him nothing good just then.

"I'm taking Ranya home," I said, commanding their attention one last time. "And I'm breaking off this engagement. Don't any of you *ever* talk to me about it again."

13

I DIDN'T WANT TO talk about my trip or of the silent-as-death ride back home. But my friends had questions. I finally decided to spill the beans as Nina, Sara, and Meera gathered round my desk in my cubicle. They listened with interest, and as my narrative ended, Meera's eyes widened and she looked quite uneasy.

"So, where does this leave us?" she asked.

"Us?"

"Ranya is our intern and Jazib is a client," she reminded me, rubbing her forehead. "Is Ranya coming back to work? What about Jazib's account?"

"What about his account? His account will stay," I reassured her, although I had no real basis to confirm it.

"And Ranya?"

"I don't know," I confessed. "Let me talk to her, okay?"

"You did the right thing, by the way," Nina said. "It'll work out, don't worry."

"Thanks." I smiled at her, then heavily sighed with my head in my hands as soon as they were out of my cubicle.

It sucked.

I pulled out my cellphone from under a million things stashed on my desk and punched in Ranya's number. The bell rang, she answered, but the moment she heard my voice, she hung up. After that, she didn't pick up again. I conceded after four attempts and decided to try Arjumand instead. She answered my call after the first ring.

"You have some nerve calling here!" she barked at me.

"Look, I just want to speak to Ranya about her internship at my firm. It's purely business."

"I don't think she'd want to continue at that company anymore. And if you think you can coax her to—"

"I will do no such thing," I replied just as crossly. "I'm not interested in reliving the Kesar visit, okay? None of what happened there was my doing. I didn't tell Ranya to rush head-on in a relationship with someone she'd known for three seconds or Jazib to treat her the way he did, so quit your attitude."

There was a grave silence at the other end of the line, and then Arjumand said slowly, "She'll send in her resignation as soon as she can."

"It's an internship, Arju. She can just call in to say she won't continue and that's all, okay? Bye."

"Maya!" she said, just in time to stop me from disconnecting. "I know it wasn't your fault, but whatever happened, whatever they said to her, I can never forgive that."

"Why are you telling me all this?"

"Because you'd want to know why Badr will never visit Kesar again."

"What?"

"He promised me he wouldn't go there. Ever."

"He can't do that! Ammi is still his wife. Kesar is still his home."

"Gohar Banu should have thought of all that before she insulted my sister." It sounded as if she was snickering, a sort of triumph danced in her voice. "It's too late now."

"You're enjoying this?" I asked. Ammi had always said that Arjumand wanted Abba all to herself, that she detested having to share him with Ammi even for a few days once a year. And now finally, she'd won. "You know what? Now I don't feel so bad about all the things my mother said about you." I didn't wait for her response and disconnected.

Okay, so Ranya wasn't coming back. We needed a new intern, maybe more than one. But before that, I had to make sure that Jazib's project would stay with us. That project was the reason we'd be hiring interns at all. I didn't want to call him, though. For one, I knew he'd be completely disagreeable and would give twisted answers to straight questions, and two, I just didn't want to talk to that spineless grub. I went over to Meera and asked her if she had any other contact regarding Jazib's project, but she shook her head.

"Any mention of his partner in the books whatsoever?" I was desperate.

She shook her head again, then asked me to follow her to Kulsom's office. Kulsom was out for the day, meeting clients. Meera slowly closed the glass door behind us and stood staring at the staff outside in the main area. "Sometimes I wish these walls weren't so transparent, so everyone couldn't see everything." Her face was weary.

"What is it, Meera?"

"I hope it's nothing big but…" she paused, "things being as they are on social media, anything can go viral. Anytime."

"What happened?"

"That brochure client, you remember him? He posted something about us on his Facebook page." She switched on her laptop and showed me; his status was written in Urdu informing everyone that Editz & More was a firm promoting indecency and un-Islamic values under the guise of a business, by employing only women who dealt with male clients and didn't observe proper dress code…

My gaze travelled to the floor where two of our expert formatters worked diligently at their laptops. Both those ladies covered their heads, one with a hijab and the other with a dupatta. Ninety percent of Edit2 & More staff wore shalwar kamiz to work because that's what Pakistani women wore. Some of us cared to pull off western apparel such as jeans, trousers, and long skirts, but nothing that showed skin, so where was the *indecency?*

"This is garbage." I rolled my eyes, dismissing the post. "He's not even coherent."

"People like it," Meera said.

"Like-minded bigots and moronic friends on his wall, I'm sure." I smiled at her. "It's just a stupid Facebook post, Meera, don't worry. I'm just surprised grown people rant this way. So petty."

"He's even mentioned yours and Nina's names as Hindu names."

"I know, such fake propaganda on his part. We're not even Hindus."

"But *I* am." Meera's anxious cry rang out in a hoarse whisper. Her cheeks reddened as she struggled to not tear up. I didn't know she felt so strongly about the issue. It was just a Facebook post. "You don't understand!" she insisted. "His post is public. Any fanatic can pick up on this post and drop by or stalk us as we move in and out of the office building. Don't you read the papers? Don't you know how many non-Muslims are targeted because of what someone wrote about them on social media or through some rumour that they're being anti-Islam?"

She had a point there.

There had been incidents in the recent past. People were beaten up and arrested or even killed by angry mobs over false charges of blasphemy, just because someone spoke about them or they shared something questionable or controversial on social media. This was a very real and constant threat, dished out especially to the members of non-Muslim minorities. Meera wasn't exactly being paranoid. She also wasn't the only non-Muslim at Edits & More.

Moreover, the information piece that Edits & More was an all-women workplace sounded like an open invitation for any lunatic of the proverbial Ghairat Brigade to harass us in the name of honour and propriety. What better way to teach modesty by being completely immodest and disrespectful to women and coercing them into submission, right?

"Bastard." I swore under my breath. "Does Kulsom know?"

"I don't think so."

I picked up the phone and dialled Kareena's extension. In a few seconds, she was standing at Kulsom's desk, peering over Meera's shoulder at the laptop screen and frowning.

"Can you handle this?" I asked her.

Kareena was our internet guru. She handled all editing projects pertaining to websites, social media profiles, and media presentations. She had a substantial following of her own on various social media platforms and was known for her sharp responses. Even though we weren't friends on Facebook or anything, I knew she must be an excellent troll. And trolling was what Mister Fazal needed actively.

"Hmm…" She tucked a hand under her chin and stared at the screen. "I'll have to rally a few contacts first. The more the merrier. Also, did you check his Twitter? People usually get more traction there for such posts."

"No," Meera replied nervously, but Kareena's confident smile seemed to calm her down a bit.

"It's okay," she said. "I'll look into it."

"I want him to delete his post," I told her.

"I can't guarantee that, he can make it private and block all those who bash him. But we can report him. Facebook can take his post down, but that only usually works when they get a lot of requests. Zuckerberg won't pay attention to just one complaint." She said it like she'd personally seen Mark Zuckerberg sitting in his office deleting people's unwise posts.

Classic Kareena. I suppressed a chuckle.

"We can all complain," Meera suggested.

"Yes, do that," Kareena said. "Also, if you have friends who like a little drama, tell them to jump in, okay?"

"Okay," Meera and I said in unison and watched Kareena march back to her desk like a girl on a mission.

"Better?" I asked Meera.

"Thank you." She smiled back, colour returning to her face.

"Don't thank me yet."

I instructed everyone else I encountered to do as Kareena had said, and then I was back to my own cubicle. I had a challenge of my own to scale. I had to talk to Jazib. I took a deep breath and punched in his number.

"What is it?" he snarled; his voice was thicker than usual, as if he'd just woken up from deep slumber. Or he was drunk.

"Are you drunk?" I frowned.

"What. Is. It?" he growled again.

"Just wanted to make sure my firm still gets to edit your firm's documents."

"Yeah, sure." He sniffed, then chuckled. "Tell them to double Ranya's salary. It might be hard for her to work for me after all that."

Son of a – I pursed my lips like I'd swallowed something bitter. "She quit," I informed him. "I think she'll be fine not thinking about you or having anything to do with you after *all that.*"

"She quit?" I could hear him stir, possibly sitting up in bed, as it sounded like sheets rustling. "When?"

"What does it matter to you? You go be drunk."

"I'm not drunk, Maya." He sniffed again.

"Oh? High on drugs, then."

"I was upset, okay? I was upset! She just walked out on me. Can't a guy get upset?"

"You're a fucking moron, Jazib." I hung up. But of course, he instantly called me back. "What do you want?"

"I need to talk to her," he said desperately. "I've called her several times, but she won't pick up. I just need to talk to her once."

"Why on earth? To apologise?" I highly doubted that.

"What do you mean why?" He sounded annoyed. "I proposed to her. We're engaged. She's my fiancée."

That gave me a moment's pause. Was he suffering from amnesia because of whatever he'd been snorting? "You two had a big fight. She gave you back the ring and walked out on you," I said. "Remember?"

"That doesn't mean a thing."

"She told you goodbye. Remember that?"

"It's not over just because she says it is."

"Dear God, Jazib, that's *exactly* why it's over." I grabbed the phone so tightly that my knuckles turned white. "And if you try your alpha-male-she's-mine-because-I-like-her psyche with this girl, she'll kick your ass to the moon. And I'll watch! With a big bucket of popcorn in my arms."

"So, you won't help me?"

"No!"

"Fine," he said slowly, "I'll deal with it myself."

"What is that supposed to mean? Jazib!"

But he'd already disconnected. I swore under my breath, then took a minute to think. Maybe I was overreacting. I'd never really known Jazib to go alpha-possessive-jerk on any of his previous girlfriends. But then, none of them had walked out on him or broken up with him. He'd always done the honour of that to *them*. He'd also never proposed to any of them either. I was the only one he'd ever really asked to marry, even just as a favour to him or a joke, and I'd truly been the only one to refuse him.

But it was different with me. I presented to him the image of a woman he knew not to trifle with because I came from a power structure equal to his own. But Ranya – she could be a challenge if he wanted to make her into one…

My phone rang out so loudly, I nearly dropped it. It was Abba.

"Are you free for lunch?" he asked. "I'm in the neighbourhood."

"I don't know, Abba," I said, in a voice that I knew he would detect as one I often used when I made excuses to get out of something. Truth was I didn't want to see him. Arjumand's tart words from the morning still poisoned my mood. "I have work."

"Maya…" he sighed. "You cannot be angry with me about what happened at Kesar. I could hardly help any of that."

"It's not that. You promised Arju you'd never visit Kesar again. You already only go there once a year."

He sighed again. "I don't think you should concern yourself with that. You should've told me about Ranya and Jazib. I never would've let her go with you then."

"Yes, very unfortunate. Still no reason why you shouldn't visit Kesar."

"Maya, I really don't need a lecture from my own daughter over this." He sounded bored. "I didn't call you to discuss my married life."

"Why did you call, then?"

"I called to ask about you. How are you feeling, zindagi?"

Oh…

Nobody had bothered to ask me that, and now that he had, I realised I was exhausted. I was exhausted of Jazib going nuts. Of Ranya quitting. Of Arjumand making this all about her and her feud with Ammi. Of knowing that even after all that drama, I was probably still engaged to Jazib. And of course, there was the office with its million issues. Abba's kind concern had me choking on my words for a moment before I composed myself.

"I'm okay," I said. "Just tired from the trip but I'll be fine."

"I know my girl is tough." It felt as though he was smiling. "How's Jazib? You talked to him lately?"

"Just before you called. He's a mess."

"He could use a friend right now. I think you should stay in touch with him."

"I honestly don't want to. He's a grown man who should be able to take care of himself."

"He's not strong as you are," Abba reasoned. "He's just a pampered boy who probably couldn't handle all the stress. You should call him, keep in touch."

"Why are you so suddenly concerned with Jazib's wellbeing? Where is this coming from?"

"From your mother," he said. "She asked me to ask you."

Wait.

So…Abba hadn't called to really ask how I was doing. He'd called to tell me to ask Jazib how he was doing, because Ammi was more worried about him than she was about me…?

"Abba, I have to go." What was next, Ammi calling me for more of the same? I powered off my phone and decided to go out get some air.

I parked in the familiar parking lot of a square, silver building reflecting intense sunlight. Despite my sunglasses, I shielded my eyes against the glare of one-way glass panels and walked in, past the marble mezzanine lobby, up the elevator to an enormous receptionist desk. She wasn't there and I thanked my stars for not having to explain to her why I was there without an appointment. Again.

I went straight to Arhaan's office and pushed open the heavy wooden door. He was in, clad in a steel-grey suit, no tie, standing at his desk, bent over some papers sprawled all over the tabletop in front of him. He instantly looked up as he saw me barge in.

"If I killed someone, would you defend me?" I asked.

"Well." He smiled. "I'm not a lawyer but I'll get you one."

"Good! Because I have a bunch of people I just—" I was suddenly aware that we weren't the only people in the room. I turned around slowly and saw three elderly men in business suits sitting on heavy chairs, staring at me, their laptops, notepads, files, and binders all stashed on tables in front of them. "Oh… you're in a meeting."

"Apparently not anymore," Arhaan said. "Gentlemen, let's do this tomorrow."

"We need to work the numbers out by tomorrow night," the least formidable of the three men spoke gruffly, casting a passing glance at me. I believed there was a hint of a frown there.

"We'll do it tomorrow," Arhaan said, with a polite finality to his tone. "Thank you."

The three men silently collected their things and left.

"I'm so sorry." I clasped my hands together. "I didn't mean to interrupt. Your assistant wasn't outside, so I just…I shouldn't have. I should've called first. But my phone, I switched it off because…this day has…it's just been…" I stopped and pursed my lips, I'd run out of words and steam.

"Maya?"

"Yes?"

"I'm going out to eat," he said grabbing his keys and wallet. "Want to come?"

We sat at our favourite spot at our favourite seaside burger joint, devouring beef patties, enjoying a healthful sea breeze and sparkling sun. It was an hour too late for students and officegoers to crowd the place and too early for diners to pour in for a bite. A few people sat indoors, but the deck where we were was vacant. Arhaan was giving me a rundown of his day, divulging in heavy details of his new project that strangely interested me. It made me forget about my day, the weekend at the haveli, and all that went with it. He'd asked me if I wanted to talk about whatever I wanted to talk about when I'd burst into his office, but I refused.

"I don't even want to think about it," I told him. "Tell me more about your day."

"I'm completely against high-rise plazas," he went on. "It takes away from the sky."

"But it builds the skyline."

"Not a fan of skylines much. I like fresh, open spaces where you can see the horizon uninterrupted for miles on end."

"You'd love the haveli then," I said inadvertently and stopped just as the words came out of my mouth. The food in my mouth suddenly turned to sawdust. I washed it down with soda till my cup was empty. Then I slumped back in my chair. Arhaan said nothing, but I could feel his gaze on me, and I didn't dare to look up lest I exposed my thoughts to him.

I'd never felt this way around him before, and that annoyed me. I could always tell him everything and he had the best advice, always. That's exactly why I'd gone to him earlier, but something changed from the moment I entered his office and saw him standing by his desk. He looked so perfect, so ethereal. The sun behind him made him shine with a halo and he looked like an image I didn't want to mar. I decided I wanted to have only happy moments with him. But now, my own mind had turned against me and he was seeing me gradually lose it. I felt hot, like the air around me was being sucked out. My stomach began to churn, and I felt a chunk of something push against my insides and up my throat.

"I think I'm going to be sick!" I placed a quick hand over my mouth and rushed to a nearby trashcan, just in time for my stomach to hurl all its contents back into my mouth and out. While I puked, Arhaan held back my hair and hollered for an attendant to fetch some water. I rinsed my mouth, drank a few sips, and washed my hands, wiping myself dry with napkins that he gave me. I looked up to thank him and that's when I just couldn't hold back my tears.

"Maya, it's okay," he said. "Whatever it is, it'll be fine."

I wanted to say something, or at least stop crying, but his presence made me want to collapse even more. So I gave up. I buried my face in his chest and sobbed. He held me close. Tightly. Securely against him, resting his cheek on my head, hiding me in his complete embrace. I felt safe, exhausted, and light after all my tears were shed. My head still rested on his chest and the rhythm of his heartbeat made it easier for me to breathe again. I listened to it, counting the beats, feeling the gentle rise and fall as he breathed.

I wanted to stand like that forever...

"I ruined your shirt." I noticed a wet smudge on his white shirt. "Sorry."

"I have a closetful of white shirts," he said. "Don't worry about it."

I wanted to respond but my mind went blank. All I could think of was how close his face was to mine and that his arms still encircled me. He hadn't let go. If we were in a movie, this would be the part where he kissed me.

Kiss...we almost did in his car...

My heart suddenly raced, thumping in my ears and my cheeks started to burn.

"Maya," he said, "there's something I need to tell you."

My heart skipped a beat. *Could it be...?*

His eyes sparkled like honey in the sunlight, with amber

threads. He casually brushed a wanton strand of my hair behind my ear and then slowly peeled himself away from me. "Nothing," he said, shrugging dismissively. "You should go home now. You look tired."

But!

"I can stay if—"

"No, I just realised I have, um, a few calls to make," he said. "We'll talk some other time."

"Oh." I stiffened a little.

"You take care, okay?" he said, his tone was still warm and concerned, but with a trace of the finality that I knew so well.

"I will," I replied. "Thank you."

This was an even worse end to my day than if I'd kept talking to Jazib!

14

INITIALLY, I THOUGHT I was dreaming of my phone ringing out of its skin. It took about three bells for me to wake up and look for the device on my nightstand, nearly knocking off a lamp to find it. My clock ticked three in the morning.

"Maya?" a familiar, very stoned voice floated off into my ear from the other end. "I'm calling from the, uh, what?" He listened to someone shouting some words in the background, "...from the, uh..." he sniffed, "...Khaki...something...Chowk police station. It's like, I don't know, close? Can you get me?"

"Khaki Chowk? Jazib? You're at a thana?" I wasn't sleepy anymore.

"Yeah, you have to bail me out."

"Why are you at a police station? When did you come to Karachi? What did you do?"

"Can you get here, please?" He sounded annoyed.

"Yeah, okay, I'll be there!"

I hollered for Aya-Ji to wake up as I rushed to dress, grabbed my bag, and dashed outside to the car. Aya-Ji clambered down the steps behind me, stuffing herself into the passenger seat, running her own list of queries that I barely had apt responses to.

Khaki Chowk police station was a small precinct, just two roundabouts down. Not that I'd ever been there before, but all hail GPS. I braked in its parking lot with a loud screech and jumped out. Aya-Ji followed me at her own pace. When she reached the front doors, I was already at the station house officer's desk.

Apparently Jazib had been in a fight and there was a scratch above his left brow to prove it.

"We don't usually let people leave like this, I mean, without proper paperwork," the SHO told me, popping a cigarette in his mouth. "You mind?" he asked, before lighting it up with a matchstick. He looked at Jazib and frowned. "He's high. I had to bring him in."

"I'm so sorry, I'll fill out all the necessary paperwork. I don't mind. Is there any payment? I don't have any cash on me. Will a cheque do? Or credit card?" I said, feeling a little nervous. I'd never seen the inside of a police station in real life before. I'd never imagined one to be this neat and organised somehow. There were no beat-up furniture pieces, dirty floors or a ghastly lock-up smelling of unwashed bodies in sight.

The officer looked at me with sympathy and sighed. He was a young man and his livery of a dark-grey shirt and tan trousers accentuated his toned body. He had a hardened, no-nonsense look about him that was peculiar to men in his line of work. His tone of voice was firm but not rude, though it didn't fail to remind the listener of how quickly it could turn threatening when needed. "Bibi, you're from a good family," he said. "He had identification, so I know. Saeen Farid is a big name. I'm willing to let him off with a warning, especially because the other party didn't file a complaint."

"You mean the boy he punched?"

"Or tried to. He was served more than he dished out."

"Why didn't you arrest that other boy too then?" I asked, sounding a bit sharp.

"I didn't arrest anyone," he said, blowing another smoke

ring. "And your cousin there was harassing that boy's fiancée. His reaction was normal in that case."

"She's not *his* fiancée!" Jazib shouted. "She's mine!"

Oh…no…!

I felt a pit in my stomach. "Is this about Ranya?" I asked Jazib, but he simply scowled and looked away. I pursed my lips and turned to the officer. "You know what? I don't think I want to take him home. You can keep him."

"Maya!" Aya-Ji's horrified voice added to the drama. She requested the officer to ignore me and tell her what should be done to bail Jazib out. He shook his head, repeated that Jazib wasn't under arrest, and we could take him home. Then he asked one of his subordinates to help Jazib up.

"I can walk." Jazib refused to take the sub-inspector's arm and stood up on his own. Aya-Ji was by his side instantly and offered him her arm. He didn't refuse her.

I thanked the SHO, and still wondering if he wanted something in return for this huge courtesy of letting Jazib off the hook without a record – as was the stereotype attached to our police force that they were corrupt, forever looking for illegal means to make money – I asked him if there was anything else I could do for him, er, *monetarily*. He stared at me for a moment. I couldn't decide if he was offended or just plain disappointed in how little I thought of him and his department and the police force in general.

"Don't do drugs," he said briskly, "and stay indoors at such ungodly hours for fuck's sake!" He stubbed out his cigarette and walked up to Jazib and gave him a stern onceover. Jazib too seemed to stand attentively on an instinct, recongising authority. "Saeen Jazib," he said. "If we ever meet again, I hope it's under better circumstances."

Minutes later, I was driving back home with Jazib sprawled in the backseat and Aya-Ji sitting in front beside me, reciting Quranic verses for our safety.

"It's just a scratch, could you be any less of a drama queen?" I scowled at Jazib.

"It burns," he hissed between gritted teeth and let out a whistling howl as Aya-Ji tried to clean his dried scratch with an alcohol wipe.

"I don't understand," she said, "how could Ranya be engaged again so quickly?"

"She probably said that to stop things from escalating, Aya-Ji," I said. "Pretty sure she's not engaged to anybody." The idea of being the centre of a boy fight with police officers busting you, while you're totally unrelated to any of the men you're out with late at night was scandalous and a sure shot case for inappropriate public behaviour and everything in that realm for the police to have a field day with. If I were her, I'd have engaged myself to anyone on the spot too.

"Well, that's not very ethical," Aya-Ji said.

"The only one unethical here is that sorry excuse of a man stalking and harassing her." I glared at Jazib. "All the way from Gurhkot."

"What's it to you?" he barked at me in his slurred speech.

"Do you know what time it is? I've never been to a police station before, but I had to today. Because of you! And that alone is very unethical compared to anything at all," I said the last part sharply to Aya-Ji, simply because I didn't appreciate her 'We're holier than that Ranya' attitude one bit, and because no matter how high he was, even Jazib could understand the cultural shame and dishonour of dragging the women of your family to a police station.

"Maya, go warm some milk with turmeric for him," Aya-Ji said.

"It's a tiny scratch for heaven's sake, he isn't dying. He can warm it himself." I frowned.

She pursed her lips, handed me a wipe, and looked at me

sternly. "Wipe the wound clean, then put on a bandage. I'll warm the milk."

"The wound?" I plopped beside Jazib and laughed. It was literally nothing more than an inch-long red line. My tuxedo feline gave me worse scratches with his claws whenever I forgot to trim them. "What did he hit you with? Marshmallows?"

"Could you go easy?" He fiercely gripped my hand that was still a centimetre away from his skin.

"Let go," I said.

"No."

I took the wipe in my other hand and jabbed that stingy little square on his tender skin. Of course, he jumped up screaming bloody murder. Aya-Ji came rushing out of the kitchen with both hands over her heart and her face distorted in plain horror in anticipation of what she might see. And I just lay rolling on the couch with laughter.

"You're such a wuss!" I sat back up, wiping tears off my cheeks. "Honestly, if you couldn't take a beating, why'd you get into a fight?"

"I didn't get into a fight!" He frowned, caressing his brow. "I just wanted to talk to her, but she wouldn't take my calls, so I went over to her place…your dad's I mean…thinking I'll go in and, you know, talk. I was there in my car and…" he paused. "I saw her come out with some guys, get into a car, and drive off, so I followed them."

"You *followed* them?"

"I had to make sure she was okay," he said angrily. "I mean she shouldn't even be behaving this way with me, I mean, it's *me*."

"What happened then?" I asked.

He followed them – a group of two boys and three girls – to a private party, and Jazib, being as high as he was, sprung out of his car and was at them in the driveway. His fierce attempt to talk to Ranya and her stubborn refusal quickly turned into a heated argument between him and the boys she was with. Jazib took a swing at one of them and missed before he punched Jazib in the face, pushing him to the floor. Someone in the group called security and hours later my bedtime was ruined.

"Was Arhaan one of them?" I hadn't meant to ask but it just slipped. I mean, I had seen Arjumand visibly ogle him for Ranya. Besides, his behaviour at the beach was puzzling. *What exactly did he want to tell me…?*

"What? No! And why would Ranya go for *that* guy?" Jazib said crossly. "What's so grand about Arhaan?"

"Arhaan is a dream," I said. "He is handsome, educated, and talented, with an actual career and a future. And you, Jazib Sultan, are a brat who's high on drugs and daddy's money."

Jazib didn't reply. He just stood there for a second, then shaking his head, fell into the bigger couch by the window and covered his eyes as if to shade them against lamplights. I felt sour. I couldn't feel sorry for him. I threw the used wipes in the trashcan and marched off to my bedroom to get some shut eye for whatever hours of the night remained.

When I came downstairs for breakfast, Jazib was sitting quietly at the table, staring at his dry toast. Aya-Ji was standing at the sink, rinsing some apples. I asked her for tea and grabbed a plate from the dish rack, took out a jar of cheese spread from the fridge and settled in a chair opposite him. He didn't look up, and I didn't engage him. I quietly layered my toast and bit into it. The crunch echoed in the quiet of the house, breaking Jazib's concentration.

"Morning," I said. "You look fine."

"Yeah." He touched his bandage. "I'm going back."

"Good." I took another bite. Aya-Ji set my tea on the table. I slid it closer and added sugar, stirring with all the interest in the world.

"I meant I'm not sure when I'll be back again," he said. "Maybe never. I'm going for good."

"Good." This time I looked him in the eye. "And while you're there, get to actually know the land you so proudly declare as yours. Till it and sow it and plough it sometime like a real farmer."

"Real farmer." He chuckled softly as if in a dream. "Ranya wanted that."

"What?"

He shook his head. "I'm just going back. It's over. I know that now."

I couldn't think of anything gentle to say to him, no tender farewell, no asking him when I would see him again. I didn't feel anything in the vicinity of those emotions either to word them.

"Good," I said after a while, and stood up to head off to work.

15

BACK AT THE OFFICE, it was a war zone.

That Facebook post we'd been ranting over, and thought would disappear in no time, had really gone viral in the form of a tweet. And now everyone at Edit₂ & More was scared.

"If my brother finds out – and he will because it's *everywhere* – he won't let me work here anymore," a girl said nervously. "And I really love my job. I don't want to quit!"

"Me neither!" Another was in tears too.

"Would you all stop?" I glared at them. "It's just a stupid tweet!"

"People are making actual threats, Maya," Meera said, her voice shaking a little.

"Both are Twitter eggs with zero followers," Kareena said, rolling her eyes. "I checked their profiles."

"See?" I looked at Meera and the other girls.

"Are we discussing *the* tweet?" Zarish, another editor, and a Christian at that, joined the conversation that was quickly turning into a panic-room meeting. "Why is everyone so scared? It's just a silly tweet."

I quickly shot everyone a reassuring smile, hoping they'll take heart from her.

"It all spiralled out of control because Asim Roy tweeted about it," someone said. "And now it has a life of its own. Now, they're saying we're unprofessional."

Apparently, Kareena and her gang had managed to get Fazal's bigoted Facebook post deleted, but not before screenshots were captured and shared across social media. Asim Roy tweeted out such a screenshot, tagged a few friends, and started spewing crap about Editz & More: *Hashtag Feminazi. Hashtag Toxic Matriarchy. Hashtag Unfollow West*

What none of us understood was why Roy would do that. His boss was a huge client of ours and on very good terms with Kulsom. Had Roy gone rogue? Was he fired? Fired because he didn't get along with our staff? And now he wanted revenge?

"I have a mind of putting Roy in his place," Kareena said. "We got enough stories about him being sleazy. A total Me-Too."

"That's risky. He'll come after you with whatever and some people will believe him," I said.

"I won't use my personal profile. I have several. He won't know it's me."

"Okay," I said, hugely impressed. "You do that."

"I will too," Zarish said.

"Ask others too if they can do the same, but please, be very careful." I warned them. "We don't want issues of breached privacy on top of everything else."

The girls had barely left my room when Kulsom called me to hers. She asked me to take a seat, downed a full glass of water, and set it down with a slight thud. Then she slumped back in her chair and looked at me.

"Bad day?" I asked.

"You heard about the social media fray?" She groaned. "I should've known."

"Meaning?"

She sat up straight. There were deep frown lines crowning her forehead and her eyes kept darting from my face to her hands to my face to any other random object. She finally managed to focus on my face before speaking. "For a couple of months now, I seem to have been spending a lot of time with Akbar Gill. You know, Asim's boss? Yeah, so…every social gathering that I'd go to, he'll just be there, and I kept running into him and we became friends. He was very appreciative of Edits & More, of our work and its quality. And I mean, we *do* have great quality. Everyone knows that. We get more orders than we can fill. I have to say no to so many." She paused. "So, he offered to finance some of the business."

"You mean like a partnership?"

"Yes," she said. "He offered me a good deal. He only wanted twenty percent share in profits while he was willing to finance up to fifty percent of everything, simply because he saw Edits & More as an enterprise that empowered women. And with the overheads rising and lack of space…Jazib's stuff is strewn all over your room because of it…Gill's money could solve all these problems," she explained defensively.

"Of course," I said reassuringly, "it only made sense you'd take the deal."

"Last night, I went over to his office to finalise everything and…he made me another offer. He proposed."

"What?" I blinked. "Isn't he already married?"

"Yes. I told him I couldn't. I quite like my life the way it is. I'm single and I'm fine. He laughed, said it's okay, we don't have to get married. We can just live in sin. Those were his exact words, 'Let's live in sin.' Because, that's how single women sustain themselves, right?" Her face reddened. "I thanked him for his offer, for *both* his offers, and walked out. No deal."

Scumbag!

So much was clear suddenly. The twitter spat was how Gill had chosen to react to Kulsom's rejection.

"The girls have a plan to deal with the social media spat. They're just as passionate about this firm as you are." I put my hand over Kulsom's. "None of them would let a sleazy old jackass get away with this."

She smiled faintly, giving my hand a gentle squeeze. "I know."

I wished I could do more for her. Like, egg his car or run it over with a tank. I knew I'd find a way to rent one if I had to. Or I could call and cuss him out in legit Shakespearean. She laughed, shaking her head. We joked for a few more minutes until she looked better. Then I got up and went back to my work.

16

LIFE WAS PRETTY MUCH on track for a few weeks.

The Twitter feud had ballooned, then plateaued, taking the fight from Editz & More's character and talent debate to an all-claws-out sassfest between misogynist men and feisty women. Meanwhile, Meera had hired three interns, all college undergraduates with excellent credentials in business writing. As per Kulsom's hiring policy, the interns too were women.

"It's not that I have something against hiring men," she'd said to me when I was hired, "it's just that I want to be the employer that gives a hundred percent opportunity to skilled women."

"Won't that get you accused of being biased?"

She'd shrugged and laughed. "It's not illegal."

True. And she wasn't the only one to hire only women for her business. Beauty salons and garment and spice factories, for instance, did that increasingly. Kulsom was just the only one to do it in a field that men wouldn't otherwise feel ashamed or awkward or bored to work in. She was also working on a unique women's empowerment project that was her brainchild. She'd picked me to assist her team of photographers.

"It'll showcase the contributions of a housewife to the economy via pictures," she explained. "It'll be brilliant!"

"You're talking about the unpaid work category of the GDP that nobody cares about?" I asked.

"But they must care about it," she said passionately. "Being a housewife is synonymous to being good at nothing when it's simply not true. A housewife is a great poster child for a multitasking unpaid worker."

"But she isn't employed by the household. She's married into it."

"She's pushed into that system, brainwashed and indoctrinated to accept it since childhood. It's not as though she has a choice. You can quit a job. You can't quit a marriage or housework. Not here."

"So, it'll be a public service message?"

"At best!" She was obviously very hopeful and pumped up.

There wasn't much research about unpaid worker contributions to the GDP in Pakistan to begin with, but whatever little outdated reporting we did have revealed that unpaid work was about a quarter of the entire GDP for the year the surveys were conducted. Amazingly, all contributors of said unpaid work were women – rural and urban. If done right, this could be great information.

But to what end?

"Just to throw out figures at the public?" I said. "Dishes your wife washes cost six hundred rupees a month, cooking costs twelve hundred, with so many hours on the line?"

Kulsom thought for a moment. "Attaching a monetary value to work is important."

"For husbands to pay their wives?"

"No!" She laughed. "That would be insulting to women and men alike. Women want respect, not payment for their toils. They contribute to making a home, to sustaining a family just as much as the men do, maybe even more. But nobody sees it that way. People understand the value of something better when money is involved. I don't want to make it about *payment*."

Getting paid wouldn't be so bad either, I thought.

I understood what she meant though, it felt like a long shot in terms of getting the message across. It would still come down to the mantra of 'but it's her job as a wife/mom/woman' in the end. There had been plenty articles written on the subject before and yet, there were recent stories of men killing women under their care for the huge offence of not serving dinner on time *because that was her job.*

Perhaps a photo-shoot might be better received than all other media.

By the following week, I was knee-deep in tripods and power cables, drenched in light kits and reflectors, and dictating quick poses to stiff models. "This isn't a fashion shoot." I frowned at my subject. "Don't pout!" I could tell she was about to cry because I was not being nice for the twelfth time in ten minutes. So I called time out and let her prance off to grab a drink, make a call, smoke, or whatever calmed her down.

I went and sat with Yasir, an actual photographer who owned a professional studio. He looked like someone we'd dub as an ageing hippie, and by "we" I meant we in Pakistan. Greying long hair tied back in an unkempt ponytail, stick figure, and a lit cigarette in one hand. A guy who'd gone to the States in his youth and returned a free spirit, wired all wrong, unconventional, and generally annoyed with the universe, a camera forever dangling from his neck. Nobody cared if actual hippies fit that description, but hey, he fit our perception of them, so he was one. His business partner, on the other hand, was a clean-shaven, crisp-shirt-and-pants kind of upwardly mobile nice boy. He was the celebrity in this team of two. He worked with the hot models and hip fashion houses of the country and was mostly out of town on business. Together they ran a studio where they catered to all sorts of photo needs.

Kulsom's project hadn't taken root in a vacuum. Yasir had been looking to do something exactly like it for ages. His partner liked the idea as well, but since his schedule was already booked with national and international fashion shows, he promised to look after campaign promotions when he got back.

I took a sip from my water bottle and sullenly looked at the studio. It was a long white rectangular den with large skylights and a window wall on one side. Yasir and I lounged on a couple of leather chairs that seemed to have been salvaged from a spaceship built for a sci-fi flick.

"These are not the models for this project," I told him. Surely, he could see that too.

"Why?" he asked casually, dragging on his cigarette.

"They're not inspiring. They're not real. They don't look the part."

He took another puff and stared into the distance. "You have suggestions?"

"Real housewives?"

"They're a rare breed in our field of work."

"Because you work with fashion models. This project isn't about fashion. It's to empower real housewives."

He stubbed out his cigarette in the ashtray and lit up another. He'd been nodding at my analysis and staring at our model in the distance. "You're right."

"It shouldn't be hard for you to find appropriate models."

"I have a few in mind." He smiled and I noticed his skin slightly dimpled over the cheekbone on the left side of his face. He ordered everyone to pack up and spent the next hour criticising the few pictures I'd taken that day.

"You need to veer off your AV mode. Manual everything. Except your ISO. Leave that shit alone. Your shutter speed needs attention. See, like here." He continued tutoring me and I listened, drinking up every detail. Amazed at his depth of knowledge. The most important lesson I learned was to take pictures. Lots of them!

I experimented with different combinations of aperture, shutter speeds, and zoom. Outside in sunlight. At sunset. Under a cloud cover and a starry sky. Indoors in lamplight, candlelight, tube light, and more. I shot frame after frame of objects and people. Portraits. Landscapes. Objects in motion and objects that were still.

I preferred a tripod initially, but Yasir eventually took that away. "Experiment with your posture," he said. "Photographers like tripods but we like our hands more."

Being involved in Kulsom's project meant I spent more time at Yasir's studio than I did at the editing firm. After a while, it didn't feel like someone else's project that I was working on. It felt like an on-the-job training to me. I was a photographer, doing meaningful photography under professional guidance from experts.

I requested to assist Yasir on his other shoots that he regularly did for fashion magazines, dress designers, and garment retailers. I was learning to get models to strike the kind of pose required. To manage exposure. To manage lenses. To observe and compose a shot. To pick out the best shot from a series of similar shots and enhance it with the right software.

I'd finally found my dream career.

Definitely better than my current job, isn't it? I smiled, thinking about how Arhaan would react to this new development in my work life. He didn't know about any of this though. We hadn't talked since – since the beach.

Somehow, finding an appropriate model for Kulsom's project took longer than expected. Yasir had decided to go with real-life housewives, fresh and unknown faces, and that was the crux of the problem. Real housewives didn't model. They were too busy keeping house. He drowned Kulsom in pictures and portfolios of models he'd rejected at one time or another, so they weren't exactly known names in fashion. They could still make the project appear legit. We picked out a few of them but to no avail. The project idea failed to interest some, while others really wanted opportunities to flaunt their beauty – like a shampoo ad or skincare or clothes. Nobody seemed to respect the spatula.

"I have one in mind," Kulsom said hopefully. "My neighbour."

Two days later, we were sitting and munching sandwiches with said neighbour at a club café. A dainty figure, in her late twenties, coming from a cookie-cutter "liberal" background, aka conservative values dressed in fashionable clothing. A fine arts graduate, she was married right after her finals. Nearly eighty percent of Pakistani women stood in her shoes. She seemed eager to give voice to this idea of recongising a housewife's worth in economic terms. She'd also modelled before for clothes for a friend's boutique and her family (husband included) had no objections.

"The project isn't against the idea of a housewife," Kulsom explained to her. "We just want to highlight the value of her work."

"I completely get it." She was excited. "I think it's amazing that you're doing this."

With everyone on board, the shoot was set for a week from then, but just a day before, the girl excused herself. She wasn't coming.

"Her husband isn't exactly comfortable with it," Kulsom told us. "Apparently the project is controversial and will get loads of criticism that he can't deal with, and neither can she. They wish us well though."

"How can he say it's controversial?" I frowned. "It doesn't even exist yet."

"Don't be naïve. It will be a pot-stirrer," Yasir said casually. "I want it to be."

"Only we don't have a model yet."

"I can ask my cousin," he said thoughtfully. "She's a housewife but not your average *homey* kind."

"Ask her," Kulsom said. "We're running out of options."

And that's how I met Kishvar Doltana.

Her heels clapped against the studio's white concrete making every head turn: a buxom figure in white clothes and bright red lipstick, her long curls bounced at her waist, and dark kohl-lined eyes sparkled like jewels in a face that was as smooth as glazed chocolate. A thick gold ring glinted in her nose and she held a glittery cellphone in one hand and a lit cigarette in the other. Her dazzling smile was unpretentious and warm.

"I didn't know what you'd have me wear," she said to Yasir in a raspy smoker's voice, stubbing her cigarette in an ashtray. "Kishvar," she said to me, clutching my hand in a strong grip. "You must be Maya."

I was mesmerised. I'd never seen anyone quite so exotically beautiful.

"You're fine," Yasir said to her, holding his camera in one hand as if he was weighing it. "Today, I just want a few shots of your face."

Minutes later, when Yasir put her in front of the camera and lights, it was obvious she was born to be there. The camera loved her. And she loved it back. She could command her expression to go from completely jubilant to absolutely mournful in a matter of seconds. Yasir and I sat in the studio that day, praising her pictures long after she'd gone home, already confident that our project was a hit.

Kishvar could've been a model if she wanted to. But, as Yasir told me, she already was everything she ever wanted to be – a housewife. Yes, she was that rare gem. She had a degree in finance, had interned at a multinational bank, and then worked at a brokerage firm for two years before marrying her businessman boyfriend. She could cuss like a sailor, reaffirming my belief that every swear word sounded more insulting in Urdu than it could ever hope to in English. I usually auto bleeped out her conversation in my mind as I heard it: "*Kulsom, this project will have all the haram***** coming after you to preserve the honour of their behn**** status quo!*"

"I'm cutting down on my cussing and smoking," she told me one time, puffing on her unlit cig during a break. She was dressed in a very run-of-the-mill Sunday bazaar lawn print, standing over a stove in a mock kitchen set with a spatula in her hand. The idea was to have her play the dutiful housewife in the kitchen, then take another shot in the same setting with her dressed as a professional chef and insert the economic value caption to highlight the difference. The same idea was to be repeated with her doing laundry, dishes, making beds, ironing, and babysitting. Kulsom wanted to add 'driving' to the list but wasn't sure as many housewives didn't drive.

"Do you cook?" a makeup artist joked with Kishvar as she touched up her lipstick.

"The question you should be asking is, 'Is there anything that Kishvar doesn't cook?'" Yasir replied instead.

The makeup artist raised her eyebrows and looked at Kishvar for a confirmation.

"I couldn't even boil an egg when I got married." She laughed. "A decade and four kids later, there isn't a dish I can't make."

"And it is all finger-lickin' tasty," Yasir said. "I never lie about food."

One day, Kishvar baked us some fudge brownies from scratch and brought over the entire batch at the studio as proof of her mad culinary skills. After that, it became a sort of ritual for her to bring some snack over every other day.

"If my ex-fiancé saw me cooking now, he'd die." Kishvar told me.

"You were engaged to someone else?"

"Oh yeah!" She laughed. "My parents chose that one. He was planning my whole life for me. Where to work. How many hours and what salary, his expectations of me as a member of his clan. I was like, dude, fuck off!"

She was just so full of interesting stories; I could listen to her all day.

17

IT WAS A LAZY afternoon. We were lounging in Yasir's tiny apartment as he and Kulsom finalised the Housewife Project with regards to its release, skyping with Yasir's partner, updating and discussing with him about the promotion.

"It would be good if we got a TV spot," Yasir was saying, sprawled across the length of his living room floor. Kulsom sat next to him on a floor cushion, shaking her head and saying she didn't have the budget. I occupied the only couch, changing channels on a mammoth flat screen that nobody was interested in watching.

Yasir was a minimalist, which suited his tiny place perfectly. You basically walked into his kitchen from an entryway that wasn't more than two feet long and you could hear the dull din of traffic outside his living room window. I had almost dozed off when the apartment door swung open and Kishvar made her loud entrance. Shouting hellos all around and balancing a paper bag and two plastic containers in her arms, she headed straight for the dining nook.

"I made some biryani today," she said, taking paper plates and plastic cutlery out of the bag. "And oh, there's chaat for you, Maya."

"Awesome!" I loved chickpea salad. I could even forgo biryani for all the savoury scents and flavours of fresh tomatoes, onions and coriander seasoned with chilli powder and lemon juice. I pulled out a chair and the others joined me with their own platefuls.

"So, I was looking at that post about your firm, Kulsom," Kishvar said, taking a forkful of rice. She'd recently found out about the Asim Roy story and quite enjoyed the end of it. "Your girls handled it so well. I'm sure you'll get more of the same after the Housewife Project, and I'll be there to troll any kam**** who might need it." She was regularly active and vocal on social media, with a great following. Every post of hers was nothing short of an articulate opinion piece. Kareena would've been jealous as well as a fan.

"Chai anyone?" Yasir asked as we finished eating.

"I'll help," Kulsom said, and went for the kettle and tea-leaves while we cleared the table.

"I only make doodh-patti," Yasir declared, turning on the gas stove.

I still had to meet a person who didn't like this version of tea, brewed in boiling milk and sugar until creamy with froth and served hot. I complimented him after emptying my cup, leaning against the couch, and feeling lazier than a stuffed cat.

"Let's take a selfie to remember our afternoon, guys!" Kishvar rallied us behind her and positioned her smartphone to catch us all in the frame. "Ready?" Yasir raised his mug as if to toast the selfie. I bared my teeth in a grin like I always did, secretly wishing I could gracefully curl my lips like Kulsom did in her quiet smile without looking stiff. Kishvar made her pouty duckface and clicked. "Let me upload. I'll tag you all. Maya, you're on my Facebook, right?"

"You're a celebrity there," I remarked.

She giggled and told me to check the picture on my timeline. I looked good. Fresh and natural and so oddly at ease. I pressed the love reaction and watched as the picture gathered more likes and comments, mostly directed at Kishvar, telling her how gorgeous she looked. And then, there was one comment that made me gasp. Somebody, one of Kishvar's contacts, posted another picture with "Just like these times from eons ago" as a caption. The picture was of a much younger Kishvar with that girl who commented and a man I would recongise even if he stood as a silhouette against the horizon.

"How do you know Arhaan?" I turned to Kishvar.

Yasir peered into my phone and pointed to Arhaan's picture. "I know him because of Kishvar. I don't know the girl. She's cute." Then, without waiting for a response, he collected the empty teacups and mugs and went into the kitchen. Kulsom was standing in a corner talking into her phone, too busy to notice us.

"Oh, we grew up together," Kishvar told me. "Family friends. He's five years younger and his mother was so strict, she made him call me Baji and I hated that! I mean, I'm nobody's older sister, and two, hello, I have a name that I like. So one day I cornered him and told him if he didn't stop, I'd French kiss him in front of everyone and tell them he was my boyfriend." She clapped her hands as she laughed out. "I still remember the look on his face. He was horrified!"

"You're mean." I chuckled. It was hard to picture Arhaan being intimidated, not with that ironclad exterior of his and the confident aura he wore. "And who is she?"

"That's another close friend. She and Arhaan went steady for a while. Then he went off to the great States and ruined his life. And she married someone else." Kishvar rolled her eyes. "But hey, how do you know him?" Suddenly her eyebrows arched all the way up to her forehead as her lips curled in a perfect O shape. "You're Maya!" She gasped. "Oh my God, you're *the* Maya?"

"The Maya?" I asked.

155

"You were his student," she said it like a question.

"Yes, for one semester in business school."

"Girl!" She clasped her hands. "He's totally fond of you, can't you tell?"

"Who is fondling whom?" Yasir was back, puffing on his cigarette and making smoke rings in his casual style.

"*Fond of*." Kishvar slapped his arm. "Not fondling, you perv." She turned to me again. "He thinks you're very talented, thinks the world of you."

Oh.

Fond *of me?*

Not crazy, smitten, totally down, hopelessly in the vicinity of being hopelessly in love, maybe?

Kishvar's piercing gaze rested on my face, pressing me to collect myself. I switched off the phone and faked a bright smile. "Such a small world," I said.

"Very." She smiled back, giving way to one of those awkward pauses in conversations that no one in the world knows what to do with.

18

SUMMER WAS TECHNICALLY OVER, as mornings decided to stay chilly for an hour before sunlight turned on full blast for the rest of the day until the evening breeze pushed the sun over the edge of the horizon, blowing cooler than it had a month earlier. My friends who lived abroad had started sharing pictures and videos of trees burning beautiful with orange and yellow foliage, of raking dead brown leaves in their backyards, piling them into small mountains for their children to dive into.

Here in Karachi, we only pretended it was autumn and enjoyed our swaying palms.

Kulsom's Housewife Project was due for launch in a week. The entire Editz & More personnel were preparing for a huge party and it was really all the buzz everywhere I went. Kishvar had decided to throw us a small dinner at her place a couple of days prior to the grand launch.

Since it wasn't chilly, I opted for a sleeveless cobalt-blue shalwar kamiz in a fabric combination of net and silk, with dark rust sequins. Not to brag, but the dress made me sparkle.

"I'm leaving, Aya-Ji!" I told her goodbye and was barely out of the house when my cellphone rang. "Salam, Ammi, how are you?" She hadn't called for days.

"I'm good, how about you?" she asked and went quiet.

"I'm good too. Little busy these days. With that project I told you about?"

"Hmm, yes, that's nice," she said and there was deafening silence again.

I hated those pauses. I was never for small talk and that too with my own mother. Why couldn't she just get straight to the point? I knew there was always something specific she had to say to me or advise me about. Besides, she knew exactly how I was doing. It was plenty clear she was in touch with Abba more than either of them let on and if I wasn't okay, she'd know.

"I'm driving now," I said. "Everything okay?" Of course, it was always left to me to ask the tough questions.

"Yes...it's nothing. And you're busy," she said and took another long, never-ending pause.

"Ammi, I'm not that busy. I'm just driving. Is everything okay? What is it?"

"Nothing!" She sounded offended now. "Can't I just call you to say hello? It's been so long since we talked last. I just wanted to hear your voice and know what you were doing and how you were. That's all."

"Okay." I sighed, giving in to a smile. "I'm fine. I'm headed to a party. Kulsom's project is due for launch next week so we're celebrating."

"Who'll be at the party? Is Badr invited?"

"No, Ammi, these are just people I know. Abba has nothing to do with them."

"Why do you have to get involved in such controversial projects?"

"It's not even launched yet. How do you know it's controversial?"

"Such things always are, and even if it isn't, you know Bhai-

Jaan doesn't approve of such activities," she said dismissively. "He doesn't approve of you working either."

"Is that why you called? To tell me what your brother thinks?"

"There's no need to get upset. I mentioned him just like that. He isn't well these days."

"What happened?"

"It's Jazib." She sighed. "That boy is so disturbed. Ever since that little adventure of his with that tramp. Aren't you in touch?"

"With the tramp?"

"With Jazib!"

"Nope."

"He hasn't called you since he came back from Lahore?" She sounded surprised.

"He was in Lahore?" I was just as taken aback as her.

"Yes! He was there for his bar exam. And now he's back and growing corn and sugarcane and thinking of cotton and mingling with every colour and kind of peasant out there, asking their advice on what soil and how to till and—" Ammi was talking but I was stuck at her first comment.

"Jazib went *back* to law school?" I asked.

"Yes!"

That gave me a moment's pause. I recalled the conversation I had with him the last time he was here. *Could it be?* Was it possible that Jazib could take his life seriously? Take my advice seriously? He'd said something about Ranya being interested in farming. Was he doing this all to win her back?

"Maya? You there?" Ammi's voice killed my reverie.

I was already at Kishvar's house and her chowkidar was ushering my car in, telling me where to park in a winding driveway. "Ammi, I have to go," I said, not really wanting to cut our conversation short. I wanted to ask more about Jazib.

Kishvar's house was a two-storey, Spanish-style construction, and a lot bigger than mine but a lot smaller than Abba's. Her front yard looped around her house and spilled into the backyard that was alive with voices and soft music. I could smell fresh barbeque on the air.

"Maya!" Clad in an ivory-and-gold chiffon sari over a low-back blouse, Kishvar looked like a silver-screen beauty. "I'm so glad you came. Come, meet Farris."

Farris, a thickset man dressed in a casual suit, was exactly the kind of man who should've been Kishvar's husband to put the yang in her yin. He spoke softly, didn't smoke, didn't cuss, and just was so proper. Yet you could tell by the way he looked at her that he completely doted on her. The couple could restore one's faith in Happily Ever After.

"I didn't cook anything today," she confessed, serving me a plateful. "It's all catered, but I can swear by this chef. He makes the best kebabs."

I noticed him in his white apron, and his staff, working the grills in Kishvar's outdoor kitchen, filling up the dishes at the buffet table as they emptied, keeping everything fresh and made to order.

Kishvar handed me my plate and excused herself to greet her other guests who were just arriving. I took my food and drink and went to a corner where I'd spotted Yasir and Kulsom with some other people I knew. We were deep in conversation when Kishvar called my name, asking me to come over.

My heart flipped.

I hadn't seen or talked to him since our awkward goodbye by the beach despite having a truckload of things to tell him about my new project. I'd kept telling myself that I was too busy, had so many new things to learn that I totally had no time to call him but the truth was…I was afraid and a little bit cross with him. I was afraid of whatever it might be he'd wanted to say to me that day but hadn't…something I didn't want to hear maybe? And I was upset that he'd never called. Didn't *he* feel we needed to finish that conversation? Or was it just me stuck in that moment while he'd just dismissed the thought and moved on?

What exactly did he want to tell me?

"I knew you'd be surprised." Kishvar was smiling at me, placing three manicured fingers on Arhaan's arm. "I told you I was having all my favourite people in one spot. Oh, and where's your plus one you said you'd bring?" The question was for him, but it made my ears prick.

He was there with someone?

"Just a friend," he replied. "Maya knows her."

I looked at him questioningly as Ranya, wrapped in all her innocent glory, joined us by taking her place nicely by Arhaan's side. She was his *plus one*? I didn't know how to react. I just stared. I could tell by Ranya's face that she hadn't expected to see me either.

"So, you two have met?" It was Kishvar who broke the awkward silence.

"Yes," I said. "We know each other. She interned at Edits & More for a while." *Also, she's my stepmom's sister and my cousin's ex-fiancée and the reason my stepmom has one more reason to hate my mom, and now, she's here with the man I'm sure I'm in love with…*I said none of that. Maybe I should have.

Kishvar indulged in small talk with Ranya, then excused herself to attend to someone else, leaving the three of us standing and staring at each other.

They both wore black. Like a couple. Did they colour coordinate?

"So? How are you?" I looked at Ranya. "Called you a few times but you wouldn't pick up."

"I know. It was rude of me." She flinched. "But let's not dwell on the past. How are you? How is Jazib? I hope he's doing well."

"I'm surprised you even asked. You shouldn't. Tell me more about what's happening now? How come you two are together? When did *this* happen?"

"When did what happen?" Her confused smile annoyed me even more.

"You and Arhaan, of course. Arju must be ecstatic! She was planning for this day the moment she first saw him that night."

"What nonsense, Maya." Arhaan knotted his brows.

"Seriously?" I scoffed. "She didn't tell you how Arju wouldn't shut up about you being *such* a lovely catch? Why do you think she invited you to dinner? It's not like she invites random people over all the time or cooks for them or hints at how they should come over *again*! Did you really think it was a coincidence that you got to sit next to Ranya at the dinner table? Or the fact that you're even standing here with her? And the constant…" It was a jealous, mean word vomit that wouldn't stop.

"That's enough!" He glared at me, then asked Ranya to "please" excuse us. He waited until she was out of earshot before turning to me. "What the hell was that Maya?"

"Are you kidding me?" I wanted to scream. "You can't tell?"

"Whatever you're thinking isn't happening." His eyes became sterner. "I'm not dating her. But even if I were, wouldn't it be part of *your* plan?"

"Excuse me?" It helped that we stood in a secluded corner or else we might've attracted attention. "How is this any of my doing?"

He quietly reached for his cellphone and scrolled down a message just to shove the screen in my face seconds later. My jaw dropped. There were screenshots of a text conversation between Ranya and me from centuries ago, when I'd sent her pictures of Arhaan with suggestive captions, essentially pimping him out to her.

> Forearms, baby…imagine the rest…
> Too hot? Are you melting yet?
> Stubbles…Mm'mm!
> I could smell the aftershave through the lens!

My messages with his pictures. Pictures I'd taken of him during my college days when he was my teacher. Pictures he wasn't ever supposed to know even existed!

He switched off the infernal screen and looked at me.

I wanted to *die*.

"Ranya sent me these as a joke," he said. "She thought I might already know about them since you and I are such good friends. And you told her it was okay for her to go for me."

"I didn't think you'd reciprocate." I felt I might be turning blue for lack of air. "She's not your type. And you wouldn't be standing there mocking me if you knew exactly how I felt about you!"

"I'm not blind, Maya. Of course I knew!" He let his confession hang heavily between us for a second. "But Ranya didn't. Nobody does. And there's so much more about me that even you don't know."

"You knew?" I expected to feel warmth but there was a coldness about him. "What are you saying? What don't I know?"

"I'm divorced," he said. "I was in love. I proposed and she accepted. After three months of marriage, she filed for divorce because she decided the love was gone. I didn't see it leave. But she did, and she left with it. So, anyway, I wish her well but…I can't experiment again. Not with Ranya. Not with anyone."

So many words…a thick fog seemed to settle around me as all those words seeped into my brain to make sense.

Divorced.

It was an unexpected, heartbreaking detail. Surely. But it was *divorced*.

Past tense.

What did it have anything to do with us now? What did he mean he didn't want to experiment with anyone? I wasn't just *anyone*. There was an unmistakable hot vibe between us. He must have felt it too. He probably already loved me but just needed time to recongise it. He needed to give himself time. To give *us* time.

"How long ago was this?" I asked.

"Seven years."

Seven years?

That was nearly a decade ago!

I wanted to laugh. But if he still needed time, we could do that. I could wait. "It's time to move on. Please, don't reject the idea of…whatever we have."

"Maya—"

"You just need more time to think about this." I stepped closer to him and gently put my hand on his cheek. I just wanted to touch him to emphasise my presence. Maybe, if he felt me near, saw me up close, he'd realise the reality of what we had, what we *could* have. "Please, Arhaan, think about us."

"I have." He held my hands in a tight grip. "I've thought about you for so long."

"Then you know we're right for each other. Maybe she wasn't but I am. I know I am!" I felt a surge of warmth wash all over me as passion gripped my tongue and I felt fearless to say all that was on my mind. "I don't care what happened before. About your marriage and divorce. I don't care. I love you, Arhaan! I've loved you for so long, I can't even say since when." I laughed, feeling dizzy with joy. This was so easy! Why hadn't I said it all before? "I choose you. I really do! That's all that matters to me. None of the other stuff matters."

"But it matters to me. And it will matter to your family."

"Do you still love her?" It burned me to ask but I had to know.

He looked surprised, but not entirely in an exposed kind of way. He seemed to consider the question for a bit, as if evaluating his own emotions for the first time in a long while, and then he calmly shook his head. "No," he said easily. "I don't."

"Then, what? What is it? What is it that's stopping you?"

"I just can't."

"That's not good enough. I need answers!"

"Sometimes there are none!" he snapped back. "You need answers and your family will have a million questions of their own about my past and they'll need answers too. I won't put myself or you through this." He paused. "Don't do this. You are young. You'll find someone who—"

"Oh, stop it!" My eyes stung. "Don't pretend to care about me. You're too afraid to take a chance on yourself and that's what's stopping you."

"Yes," he replied flatly. His honey-warm eyes were bloodshot. "This ends here, Maya."

He was so cold, like stone. I edged away from him, trying to believe that I'd walked into a bad dream where a heartless man who resembled Arhaan had been exceptionally cruel to me. I needed to walk out of this nightmare. I turned away from him and ran. There was a garden, a pathway, brick floor, and then, my car.

I don't remember the drive home. I remember Aya-Ji was there, and my bedroom. Did I cry myself to sleep? My cellphone rang out. I splintered it against a wall. My eyes hurt. My head hurt. My heart hurt. And I lay back in bed for who knows how many hours, maybe days? Counting the rotations of my lazy ceiling fan.

After a while, there was no pain.

19

"FIRST YOU BROKE YOUR phone. Why?" Aya-Ji grilled me while I quietly sipped my tea. "Then, Sahib came over to see you, but you refused to meet him. Why?"

"Because Sahib can go to hell!" I slapped my cup on the table and stood up. The hurt in my heart was back. I didn't feel numb anymore and that made me furious. I wanted to be numb. I wanted to not feel anything ever again!

I looked outside the big living room window, watched as a few cars rolled by. Kids played cricket in the street, enjoying their after-school evening. I tried to remember what day was Kishvar's party. I think I'd been locked up in my room mostly. Lying in bed. Maybe had run a mild fever that had Aya-Ji fussing over me like the world was about to end. And maybe, in her anxiety, she'd called Arhaan to come by because Abba couldn't be reached.

I didn't care to find out much else.

"Maya," Aya-Ji said softly, caressing my shoulder. The concern in her voice was motherly. "Did something bad happen? Did Sahib do something? Did he say something wrong?"

"No, Aya-Ji." I sighed. "I think I said something wrong. I think it scared him."

"Then, just clarify it. He even came to see you. Why won't you talk to him?"

I remembered the moment I'd flung my phone at the wall. The screen had blinked Arhaan's name, and I didn't want to see it then. "I'm ashamed to face him," I said. "That's all."

"Don't be ashamed to admit your mistakes, Maya. You were taught that." She patted me on the head and walked away to get back to her chores. "Jazib also called. He was worried too that you weren't answering."

"What does he want now?" I frowned. "Was he arrested again?"

Aya-Ji stopped chopping her onions and stared at me. "It wouldn't kill you to be nice to people. You should've been in touch with him yourself after the way he left here last time."

"That was his own doing. I don't know why you say it like it was my fault."

"It's not about blame. It's about courtesy and caring for family. Be a good cousin and call him, okay?"

"Fine." I marched towards the handset and picked it up as if I were choosing a weapon for a fight. I called him and as soon as he said hello, I grilled him about why he'd called.

"It's been a while," he said, sounding quite relaxed. "I thought we should talk. I went to Lahore."

"I heard. How soon do you plan on dropping out this time?"

Aya-Ji gave me a reprimanding look, which I stubbornly ignored and carried on the conversation.

Jazib was laughing at my jab. "I completed it, darling! You want to see the degree on the sacred plaque hanging in my room? I mean, it hasn't arrived yet, but when it does."

"You're kidding."

"Not at all."

"So, you'll work now? In a law firm?"

"Nope."

"Excuse me?"

"I'm growing sugarcane now."

"With a law degree?"

"No." He chuckled. "The law degree was part of my new plan where I complete all my unfinished projects. It's going pretty well so far."

"Oh, wow. So, law degree was a project. And the next one is farming. What after that? Scaling the Nanga Parbat?"

"I'm serious, Maya, I think I found my calling," he said. "You were right. What good is a zamindar if he won't get to know his zameen? I should have connected with the land a long time ago. I might've found peace a long time ago too."

There was something about the way he uttered the word "peace" that pierced through my heart. I had given Jazib all the crap for his fall-out with Ranya, but in doing so, I'd forgotten that he had loved her. I didn't make much of it because I didn't believe his sentiment. But what if it was true? He might've lost the only girl he'd ever loved, and here I was, giving him grief about it.

"Why are you doing this, Jazib?" My tone was kind this time.

"Because I think I'm good at it." He sounded honest. "I'm learning from the farmers who've worked our land for generations and they're just…they're such nice folk, Maya. I wonder why I never got to know them before."

"What will you do with your law degree?"

"I'll help the farmers with any legal problems they might have. For free. It's called pro bono." I smiled at that. I could almost see his face beaming like the sun, him winking as he said it. I couldn't deny I felt so much better than I did before I'd called him up. "Maya," he was saying, "Come down here. Even if just for a day. We can go for a ride across the acres like we used to. I could show you what I've done."

The suggestion sounded soothing, but I quickly recalled what had happened the last time I was there. Was I ready to meet Ammi and Mamu-Jaan so soon? Besides, there was that launch party, and everyone would be there. *Everyone...*a stinging sensation shot through my entire body at that thought. I lived in a ridiculously small world and "everyone" in that world included Arhaan. I'd rather kill myself than see him again.

"How about a few days instead of just one?" I asked, calculating the exact number I'd need to stay in the countryside to avoid the launch party.

"It's home, Maya. You can stay forever," he said.

"I bet that'll solve so many issues for the both of us, wouldn't it?" We both laughed at that and I realised that there was no one else in the world besides Jazib who knew my life and shared his with me exactly the way it was. We could've been twins.

"I can send Haji tomorrow to pick you up," he said, referring to his trusted driver. "He can be there in the morning."

"Okay, I'll be ready," I said.

When I turned around after hanging up, Aya-Ji was standing with her elbows resting on the island, wearing a meaningful smile. I rolled my eyes and started walking up the stairs to my bedroom.

"You two are meant to be!" she called after me. "You should write that down and stick it to your forehead."

"I'm going over to Abba's," I informed her, rummaging through my closet for something cheerful to wear.

Abba sat in his library at his ginormous desk, typing away at his laptop in his pyjamas. There was a large window behind him that looked over a deep swimming pool. The wall-to-wall bookshelves and leather couches, the entire décor of the space reeked of timeless elegance.

"Just a minute, zindagi," he said, raising a finger. "I'm in the middle of an email here."

I dropped my bag on the floor, picked up a random magazine, and plopped in one of the chairs in front of him.

For five minutes, all I heard was his typing and the tick-tock of a desk clock. I put the magazine away and sat staring at him, tapping my fingers on the naked wood.

"Done!" he said, punching the last key, then he reached inside a drawer and pulled out a box. "I hear it's the latest model. You like it? Want another brand? Or model?"

"I don't care, Abba. I just need a phone," I said, examining the brand-new smartphone, scrolling through my contacts, then dropped it in my bag. "I don't know why you insist on keeping me on your phone plan. I can afford to have my own."

"Because you're still my baby girl."

"Joy."

"May I ask why you smashed it against a wall?"

"Nope."

"Okay," he said, eyeing me curiously. "Will you stay for dinner?"

"No, I'm going to Gurhkot tomorrow morning. I have to pack."

"Really? How come?"

"Well, Jazib is a farmer now and he'd like me to see that."

"Impressive. Say hello to Gohar for me."

"I'm not your messenger girl, Abba. And FYI, Jazib is also a lawyer now, so if you and Ammi finally decide to divorce, he might help you there. Free of charge. It's called pro bono."

"Don't be rude, Maya." He frowned. "And now that you're going there to visit, don't say anything untoward to your mother. Mind your temper."

"Fine, I'll be nice. See you when I get back." I'd hardly said my goodbye when someone softly knocked at the door and opened it a crack, lingering in the doorway. It was Ranya.

"I'm sorry, I heard Maya was here," she said.

"Oh, come, come," Abba said graciously. "Excuse me, Maya, I have to take this. Have a safe trip, sweetheart." He grabbed his phone, gave me a quick peck on the cheek, and left, slamming the heavy oak door behind him. Now, it was just me and the girl I didn't want to see anytime soon. She looked paler than I remembered and her faded peach shalwar kamiz didn't help her much either. Her luscious hair that would otherwise be cascading down her frame was neatly braided.

"Are you ill?" I asked.

"I'm fine." She smiled and that made her look alive for a moment. "I'm so glad I could catch you before you left. Just wanted to say hello."

"Oh. Hello."

"Do you have a minute?"

"It's getting late." I tried to wiggle out as politely as I could. "I have to pack. I'm leaving for Gurhkot in the morning."

"Isn't that Jazib's town?" She took an eager step forward, then restrained herself, clasping her hands together in a calm gesture. "He told me that it was. How is he?" She seemed so different from the girl I'd seen with Jazib or the girl I'd seen with Arhaan that night. What game was she playing?

"Yes, it is." I felt edgy. "And he's fine."

"Will you tell him hi for me?"

I wanted to scoff, roll my eyes, *and* sympathise with the pitiable expression on her face all at once. Instead, I just muttered a confused 'okay' and smiled. She really looked unwell. "Shouldn't you maybe sit down?"

"Oh, I'm fine!" she spoke brightly, then paused. "Maya, I just wanted you to know there's nothing between Arhaan and me. I just asked him if he knew of any jobs or internships I could do, and he helped me connect with a few people. That's all."

"You don't have to explain yourself to me or to anyone else," I said. "I'm sorry for acting badly."

She quietly nodded and I took that as a sign of us being in the clear, as well as permission for me to finally leave. And I couldn't have been happier to do just that!

20

THE SUGARCANE FIELDS LOOKED like expansive dirt pools where heavy machines and bulls ploughed through, tossing, and turning, and mixing the soil, combing through to make straight rows for seeds to be planted in. Jazib in his muddy trousers, rubber long boots, and a wide straw hat, when all the other men around him wore shalwar kamiz and head wraps, stuck out as a green tomato in a field of red ones.

I hadn't brought any farm boots, but my sneakers felt like a better choice compared to the flip-flops everyone else was wearing. I'd long stopped fidgeting with my billowing chador to keep my head covered. It was enough that my hair was all tied up in a bun and not getting in my face. It usually didn't get this windy over the fields, but maybe they'd just rolled by to see me. I readied my camera again as Jazib walked me through the entire process of planting sugarcane.

"You see these stalks?" He pointed to a pile of what looked like pale sticks that three men were fishing out of a large drum of water. "These are sections of sugarcane kept as seeds to grow the next crop. First, you soak them in warm water, then lay them in the burrows, and cover with dirt. Did you know one acre uses about forty bags of these setts? I didn't know that!" He was totally energised, educating me on what nodes were and how to properly harvest the crop. "It's just so fascinating how much science goes into getting a ganderi out of the ground."

Farm machinery was expensive, mostly imported, and since our landlords had enough manpower, most of the farming was done by field hands. It provided work for the locals and saved money for the landlord.

"People have been doing this for generations, and if we don't use them, what else would they do?" Jazib explained.

"Go to school? Find a better job?" I suggested. It must have sounded funny because a young farmer who heard me talking laughed out loud. Then instantly apologised for fear of being disrespectful. I encouraged him to speak his mind. He had nothing to fear from me and I wanted him to know that.

"You said school, Bibi," he said. "I went to school. It's only elementary. And we don't have money for me to go to the city for higher education."

Wow, that was quite a slap to my ignorant self!

"So, we need a school here." I turned to Jazib as if it were his fault there wasn't any to begin with. In a way, it was. He was twenty-seven years old and hadn't done a thing about it yet. *Did we have schools in Kesar though?* I didn't know. I was twenty-four and I hadn't ever taken an interest in anything but my mandatory visits to the haveli in that rural town.

"But Bibi, I'd still want to be a farmer," the young man said.

"Really?" I was surprised.

"Yes," he said passionately. "Somebody has to grow plants too. I helped my father in the maize fields last season. I like this, growing and gardening, and then, when you eat that fruit that you've grown yourself? It tastes better than anything in the world! I have a small vegetable patch at our house. I grow tomatoes and chillies."

"So maybe you need education that'll help you be a better farmer."

"There is that kind?" His eyes became round as saucers, making his sun-kissed face more curious than before.

"Bibi, we're all farmers!" His father joined the conversation from a distance. "Our ancestors were farmers. We'll die farming!"

"He seems resolute," I said to Jazib.

"Or afraid to really speak his mind," he said.

"What do you mean?"

He took my arm and walked away from the farmers, towards the edge of the field where his cruiser was parked on a dusty lane. "My father owns these people," he said. "They're not termed slaves because there are no markets where we buy and sell them, but once you get hold of their land, you get hold of their livelihood, and they're doomed to be here for life. Imprisoned on these open fields. There are no schools because if there were, the new generation of these farmers would find different careers and leave, rendering the mighty landlord peasant-less and at a huge loss."

I'd heard stories of how small farmers had to mortgage their land to the bigger landlord to fulfill one financial need or another. They would never come into enough money to buy back that land or pay off that loan or even its interest. No bank entertained them, and trapped in this vicious cycle, they ended up letting the landlord legally usurp all they had. The small farmer, being a powerless pawn in this unjust setup, would sell his dreams, his children's dreams, and dreams of all generations to come.

Abba was the only man I knew who'd given away all his land to his farmers.

"These lands have been in the family forever," Jazib said, "meaning whatever land was snatched happened a long time ago. But I found two families down where we grow cotton who used to own some acres. They still have the old mortgage papers."

"Are you serious? You've seen those?"

He nodded. "This man, his great-great-great grandfather owned quite a few acres, and over time, lost them all to one of my ancestors, but his family kept the papers. I suppose as an old memory. But they're legit documents."

"So they still own the land?"

"No." He shook his head. "The documents only show them as legit previous owners. But I'll give it back."

"You'll give that land back? For free? Just like that?"

"Yep."

"You can't do that, Mamu-Jaan will kill you!"

"That's not all I'm gonna do," he said impishly. "I have many plans that Baba Saeen wouldn't like."

"Such as?" I was all ears.

"You know these farmers aren't paid, right?" he asked. "They get a small share of the crop they grow for us, just enough to sustain them, and if they need anything else, they have to come begging for it at our doorstep. A luxury like possessing cash, that's out of the question. So my plan is to start paying them. Money. Like a real job."

"Oh!" I gasped. "That would be groundbreaking in these parts."

"I haven't worked out a system to calculate daily wages, or if it would be a monthly salary and how much, but I'm looking into it."

"Gosh, Jazib," I said with a hint of admiration in my voice. "You've matured. So noble too."

He laughed. "Do you think they'll build a monument in my name or something?"

I smiled. It was good to hear what he was saying and great to see him using his time so productively. Maybe agriculture was his calling after all. The land had finally owned the lord back.

Gurhkot and Karachi seemed to exist in two different time dimensions: one frozen in time and the other vibrant with life.

Kulsom's Housewife Project launch had happened. Yasir and Kishvar had called me frantically, demanding to know when I was coming back. And I wondered, what if I never did? I could hide away here from Arhaan forever. They'd miss me for a few days, but then get drowned in life as it brought in new waves of stress and hectic routines with the daily sun.

As if I didn't have crazy thoughts of my own, Ammi had hers to add too.

I was back at Kesar to see her after two days of roaming all over Jazib's farmlands. We were sitting out on the roof garden, enjoying the benign autumn sun while Ammi ardently lectured me on the dwindling marital prospects of a tan complexion, which naturally fed into her next topic: *Jazib*.

"Give me one reason why he isn't right for you," she said.

"Because…" I got ready to list all my previous excuses: *he isn't educated, doesn't have a job, is immature, we aren't compatible…* but I realised none of those reasons worked anymore. Except maybe just one: I didn't love him, and he didn't love me.

"Rubbish," Ammi said dismissively. "You need money. Stability that brings honour and respect. Love is fickle and feeds no one."

"Goodness, Ammi, do you want me trapped in a loveless marriage too?"

"Jazib is not like your father. You two get along so well."

"And yet, he wanted to marry Ranya." I could have told her about Arhaan too, but what would be the point of that?

"Maya, try to understand," she said, "if I died today, your father would forget you in a heartbeat because of that tramp he's with. Thinking about it kills me."

"What are you even talking about, Ammi?"

"She talked him into never coming to Kesar because her sister had a few bad hours. I'm still his wife! If I died, how long do you think it'll take her to talk him into disowning you as well?" She paused and continued in a softer tone, "Knowing that you're taken care of, that you're married into a family I can trust, will give me peace."

Peace.

It was a rare commodity and nearly an impossible one to come by for parents of an unmarried girl. They spent sleepless nights worrying about her destiny that depended on her landing a good match. If she didn't, it was seen as their failure. If she did, they were hailed as responsible parents with a success story. It was a matter of honour and prestige. So, yes, I understood Ammi's concern. I just didn't care for it.

"Maya," she said, sinking back into her swing tiredly. "We all want love. I fell in love with your father. I still love him after everything. But we were never friends. We never really understood each other."

She'd never shared anything so cutting about her life with me before. For an instant, I saw myself in her – loving Arhaan, finding him, and yet craving him from a great distance, never really knowing him…

It wasn't a pleasing image.

It was the last day of my trip. Jazib had come by Ammi's to say goodbye, and we lazily lounged in our old shack, just for a couple of hours before I was set to leave for Karachi.

"This was a good trip, wasn't it?" he said. "Glad I talked you into it."

"Me too." I smiled back at him, studying his face for a second, and then, out of nowhere I blurted out what Ammi had said to me about our match. His sunny expression darkened a bit as he averted his gaze from my face. I knew I'd made him uncomfortable, so I tried laughing away the awkwardness. I shouldn't have told him. He'd only told me a million times before how the very idea grossed him out.

But…something about his prolonged silence didn't sound right either.

"I did tell them I'm okay with it," he said slowly. "With us."

"Jazib…" I was stunned. "But…why? And Ranya?"

"She's gone."

"So you don't love her anymore? Just like that?"

"She's gone," he repeated. "I can't run around anymore. I need to settle down, start a real life. I never asked for you or had you in mind, but when they brought you up, I couldn't refuse. Maya…I'm not asking you to marry me. I'm just telling you that I'm here."

Those were sincere words. I could value those words after the sordid rejection both of us had faced at the hands of what we had thought of as true love. Perhaps that was the string that could bind us.

We made a good team. I thought of all the times we'd shared since we'd spoken our first words to each other as kids, the times we'd bailed each other out of trouble without letting the world know. What if this marriage was a time like that? An idea to give stability to both of our roaming minds.

An anchor.

A harness.

"Are you sure?" I asked him. "About us?"

"I'm sure about the kind of life we'll have. I can predict it," he said. "But predictability doesn't scare me anymore."

"It's peaceful," I said, understanding for the first time that maybe this was what had gone through Ammi's mind when she decided to stay with Abba after he married Arjumand. She could foresee a peaceful life that still promised her everything that made her honourable in the eyes of her society – lady of the haveli, faithful wife, mother to her husband's child, strong roots, and not a gold-digging tramp like Arjumand. Yes, she wouldn't have love. But then, love wasn't peaceful. Love was harsh. It was painful. And now that she was a mother, her peace was tied to mine. For her to find peace again, I had to find peace too.

"If we're together, I promise never to mention Ranya," Jazib said earnestly. "I promise to never give you grief that way." It was sweet and innocent.

I hugged him.

He held me close, but there was nothing sexual about it, and in that moment, I knew this was how our marriage would be. There wouldn't be wild passion. There wouldn't be mad romance. But there would be companionship. That was more than what I'd seen my mother live with all her life. I peeled away from him, looking him straight in the eye, shutting down all voices of doubt and heartache. My mind was made up and I was going to do it.

"Okay, Jazib Sultan," I said. "I will marry you."

21

THE DAY I SAID yes to marrying Jazib, Ammi seemed to wake up from a deep, lifeless sleep. Her eyes began to sparkle with a long-lost energy that once fuelled her when she lived in the city with Abba.

It was going to be a winter wedding.

Ammi had moved into my tiny house to help me shop for dowry: a truckload of expensive gowns, shoes, clutches, and boxes full of jewels for every occasion. There was the traditional talk of how many furniture pieces, dinner sets and cash I was to bring, to which, as I heard, Mamu-Jaan greatly objected because what would Jazib or I do with all that anyhow? His wing of the haveli where we were to live was already furnished. If I wanted to redecorate, I could do that with his money. And dinner sets and stemware and such? Really? The haveli had those things too. Hence it was settled that I would bring whatever I liked for my personal use, which included gifts from my parents, a hefty bank account and investment portfolios.

"A woman must always have her own money," Ammi explained to me the need for all that as I slipped on a pair of sling-backs and got ready to go to work. "Why are you still working? Resign already!"

"Earning my own money," I said and dashed out.

Back at the office, the girls were thrilled that I was getting married, but bewildered about why I wasn't taking days off to prepare for the big day.

"I won't be working again," I tried explaining to them. "This is my last job before I turn into a full-on Bibi Saeen and am sentenced to being cooped up inside a haveli for life."

"Oh, but such a lavish and gorgeous haveli though!" Kareena swooned as if she'd seen it with her own eyes. "I googled it. There were a few pictures from days when your father-in-law was a minister. They're so high profile. I had no idea you came from *that* family."

"I don't." I smiled at her. "My mom does."

"But you have to request leave, Maya," Nina reiterated. "You only have a few weeks left."

Kulsom took it a step further and put me on mandatory leave. "I'm not firing you," she said. "You'll always have a place with us. Although I think Yasir would snatch you before I ever got you back. Our Housewife Project is trending everywhere! You will work after marriage, won't you?"

I wasn't sure. I would be a vadera's vaderani, adding value to his haveli as his obedient wife and the mother of his future children – the heirs to his acres. It was so strange for me to hear myself chalk out my life the way I'd always wanted to never have. I had big dreams. I wanted a career. I was going to be somebody in my own name, not live under someone else's shadow. I was going to marry for love, not settle for a compromise.

What changed then?

As the wedding drew nearer, my house became messier. It lay strewn with glittery things from ceiling to the floor. Brocade, moonlight, silk, gauze, georgette, cotton, chenille – there wasn't a fabric that hadn't found its way into my dowry closet, and there wasn't a glitzy stitch that hadn't found its way on those fabrics. There were purses for every occasion, from a formal dinner clutch to a beach tote; shoes, from flats to stilettos to boots; jewellery pieces for every visible part of the female body, from pure gold to studded with gems to only gems.

I picked up a thick choker of uncut diamonds, tourmalines and kundan, and watched it sparkle in the sunlight. The weight of that piece spoke volumes of its value and did justice to its grandeur. It was part of the heritage jewellery that was passed on to Ammi by her mother, and now I was to become its rightful owner.

"That's not for your wedding day," Ammi said, as she rummaged through a dozen black velveteen boxes. "This one. This is for your barat. Try it."

It was an intricate gold mesh of beads and chunky medallions studded with emeralds that covered my décolletage. I had no doubt it would glitter from miles away and look absolutely stunning against the dusty pink of my wedding gown. I'd refused to wear the traditional red. Red was such a bridal colour and I didn't feel like I was that bride who would wear that red. I was more of a dusty-pink bride. Since modern brides wore all sorts of colours anyway, my forgoing red wasn't even noticed. But in my mind, it was a statement against something. I just wasn't sure what, yet.

"Arjumand called," Ammi said, cutting my thoughts short. "She wants to host a dholki for you."

My friends had been pressing me for my pre-wedding dance and musical nights since forever. "We won't be able to come all the way to Kesar to see you take your wedding vows!" They had mused over it a million times, so obviously they'd welcome a dholki party.

Except…

"I don't think we should hold it at Abba's house," I said to Ammi. "It might make Ranya uncomfortable."

"Ranya?" She frowned. "It's *your* house, not hers. What does it matter what she feels about this? Besides, Badr told me she has moved out."

"What? Where?"

"To some cousin's house in the city."

"When?"

She left the box she was handling and stared at me. "I didn't ask, nor do I care, and neither should you. The only thing that matters is that you're marrying Jazib, as it was always meant to be. Everything else is insignificant."

I just quietly looked at her and peeled off the heavy necklace. It felt like I freed my neck from a chokehold, and I could breathe again.

The wedding invitations arrived soon after. I'd placed the order myself, so they were every bit what I wanted. Gloss and glitter free. Hand-calligraphy by a local artist. They looked like specimens from a tasteful arts and crafts exhibition. Ammi handed me the guest list to write out the envelopes. Some five hundred people.

I gasped.

She peered at the paper she'd handed me, then, making a clucking sound with her tongue, took it back and handed me another sheet. "This is yours. I only wrote down as many as Aya-Ji could remember. You can add the rest," she said. "This other list is already sent."

"Wait, you have two lists? You had different cards made?" I blinked quickly, trying to make sense of what I was hearing. "Because these invitations came today. How could you have already sent them to five hundred people? You had me order these cards just for fun?"

"Of course not. But what you chose is so plain. No tassels. No gold. Doesn't look like a wedding invitation at all."

"So you went behind my back and ordered different ones for your people? This is my wedding, Ammi! I can't pick out what invitations I want to send?"

"Maya," she said in her best patronising tone. "There are three hundred cards in this box. Invite whoever you want. There are certain societal norms and expectations. Your father has a status that must be maintained. The card you chose is young and hip. People our age, our friends and relatives, are old-school. We expect something traditional."

"Where's the one you sent out?"

She asked Aya-Ji to bring a certain box. Five minutes later, I was gawking at a bejewelled scroll that matched the intricacies of my wedding gown. I remembered seeing and *rejecting* a similar style at a high-end shop Ammi had dragged me to. I saw no sense in spending an exorbitant amount of money on a gaudy invitation that would eventually visit the trashcan. However Ammi had refined the original design and made it into a million-rupee masterpiece. "It's our only daughter's wedding." She smiled proudly. "It has to be memorable."

Fine.

I got down to addressing my own set. Three hundred? I only had about ten people who I really wished to see at my wedding. I crossed names off the list as I labelled their invitations to keep a record.

~~Nina~~
~~Kulsom~~
Arhaan

I stopped.

Would it be odd to invite him now? Would he even come? My instincts told me he wouldn't. So then there was really no harm in inviting him. And if he did come, seeing him there among guests while I sat all dressed up next to my groom on the bridal stage might just validate my emotions that I didn't care for him anymore. Also it wasn't as though he would be heartbroken over it or anything…

~~Arhaan~~

I was going to hand him the invitation card myself.

22

I'D BEEN PARKED OUTSIDE Arhaan's office in a large, uncovered lot that seemed more desolate as winter clocks ticked the sun into the horizon. There were very few cars there besides mine. One was his. I glanced back at the glinting marble multi-storey structure and wondered why I'd never appreciated its grandeur before.

I had come to that place a dozen times, always bursting into his room while he'd be neck-deep in work. He never objected. I wasn't sure what his job was. How much did being a top market researcher really entail? Did he own the building he worked in? I knew he was somebody important, but I never bothered beyond that. To me, he was just Arhaan. A man I'd secretly worshipped for years.

I looked at the invitation card in my lap and sighed, gathering every bit of strength for the moment when I'd hand it to him. He wouldn't feel a thing, I knew. But I didn't want to splinter right there like glass upon seeing him after that awful night…

I rested my head against the steering wheel and listened to the silence. Suddenly there were voices. I looked up and saw him. He was shaking hands with two other suited men who walked back inside the building. Then, with his phone glued to his ear, he came towards his car, parked right in front of mine. He stopped.

"Maya?" he said, his phone still blinking in his hand.

I bit my lip, then, squaring my shoulders, stepped out. "Hey." I held out the invitation for him. "I'm getting married. You might have heard. There's also a dholki tomorrow at Abba's. If you want to attend." Not the warmest of invites but...I didn't collapse.

He read the card, taking a long time to do it too. Then he looked up at me and frowned. "Why are you doing this?"

"It's called marriage. People do it every day."

"I'm not concerned with people. Why are *you* doing this?"

I took a hard look at his expression. Was I missing something? Any hints of suppressed feelings and such? Why was he being obsessive? I saw nothing, but I was willing to take my chances and assume.

"Are you jealous?" I asked.

"I'm disappointed," he replied flatly. His expression was so deeply sour. I didn't understand it. "You have such potential. You're one of the few women I know who not only has the talent but the opportunity to do something meaningful with her life. To be somebody. Why would you throw all that away?"

"I *am* going to be somebody."

"A feudal lord's housewife?"

"A housewife is somebody." I frowned. "Maybe you should've attended Kulsom's Housewife Project showcase."

"That's cute, Maya."

"Don't patronise me!"

"That project wasn't about you. You don't want all that," he said sternly. "You are not those women!"

"What if I am? What if that's what I want?"

"You *want* to marry Jazib and be his wife? Is that what you want?"

"Kishvar is a housewife too, in case you're forgetting." I secretly cringed at my childish comeback. "She could do it, so why can't I?"

"Kishvar is a unicorn." He rolled his eyes.

"A unicorn because she married for love?"

"Are you marrying for love? Is Jazib? Since when?"

I felt as if I'd burn under his gaze.

These weren't questions. He already knew the answers to each one and we both knew how pointless the entire argument was.

"You know what? Don't come to my wedding." I snatched the card back from him. "I'm uninviting you. You're not invited. I don't want to see you there!"

"Maya…is this what you really want?"

I searched his eyes one last time for that beacon of hope that might make me want to stay. I saw concern in those eyes. I saw sincerity. I even saw empathy and a semblance of fondness. But there was no love. I pursed my lips and got into my car without another word.

He was still standing there when I drove away, watching me leave.

Arjumand was determined to make my dholki a hit. She was treating this one event as if it was my wedding day. She couldn't, of course, plan my wedding because that was Ammi's forte. Ammi had already left for Kesar to take charge of wedding preparations there. She wasn't going to attend the dholki in Arjumand's presence. And Arjumand wouldn't attend my wedding at Kesar. It was an unspoken deal.

I got ready in my old bedroom with Arjumand's trusted stylist fussing over me – making my eyes smokey, helping me slip on two-dozen blue-green and gold glass bangles that complemented my feroza chandelier earrings and my gold beadwork ghagra skirt with a delicate turquoise chiffon kurti. I gave myself a critical look in the mirror.

You're choosing this, I said to the girl in the mirror. *You agreed to marry Jazib. And it'll be grand. You'll live a happy, useful life. You will do it!*

The girl in the mirror looked back with eyes that were reddening at the rims. She curled her lips in a smile that never made it to those eyes.

I looked away.

"Are you ready?" Arjumand popped in her head and asked. She saw me standing by the mirror and walked in to stand beside me. "Lovely! You look so glamorous. Like a movie star."

"Arju…where's Ranya?"

"Oh, she's with relatives," she replied casually, straightening the fall of my lacy net dupatta.

"Where?" I pressed on.

"Our first cousin. Lives in one of those oceanfront apartments by the old fairground."

I knew by her tone that Ranya wouldn't be attending. I'd hoped she would though. I'd had days to ponder over things and people and decided that Ranya was alright. I wasn't sure if we could be friends after what had happened, but I had hoped to say a polite farewell to whatever we had once.

Arjumand walked me out into the hallway that opened into a large den. I could hear women clapping and singing wedding songs to the beat of a dholak drum. It was a cherished tradition. A long line of girls waited to greet me by showering rose petals. I saw Nina. She came running to me, fawning all over, taking the train of my dupatta as Arjumand led me towards a bridal stage set up in one decorated corner.

This hall had seen all sorts of gatherings and décor when Ammi lived here. Tonight, it was bathed in shades of turquoise and glitter, creating a dreamlike sequence in an enchanted

garden. One section of the floor was covered in silk sheets
and oblong pillows, and on this sat a large group of girls with
a small horizontal cylindrical drum that was beat up by hands
on either side. They waited for me to take my seat on the divan
before resuming their singing, and the other guests settled into
socialising again. Everyone I knew was there. Some were friends
of the family, some mere acquaintances, but seeing everyone
from Edita & More, and even Yasir and Kishvar, made my heart
fill with warmth.

Arjumand had done well.

Dinner was announced after a while and sounds of clanking
cutlery and chatter filled the air. Arjumand offered to bring me
food but I refused. I wasn't hungry.

"Mind if I sit here?" Kishvar came up to me, handling her
plateful of rice and chicken curry. Kulsom and some other girls
from Edita & More joined us too and then I saw Yasir. He came
and gave me a kiss on my forehead.

"Where's your camera, Yasir? How could you not bring it
tonight?"

"I have a phone." He switched it on and started arranging
the people on stage for a picture. He clicked several frames and
selfies. Although Arjumand had arranged for a professional
photographer, Yasir's pictures held an emotional value for me.

After dinner the singing commenced, but after a few more
songs, they wrapped up the dholak and stood up to dance to
loud music by virtue of an exemplary sound system.

"Maya, come on!" a girl I knew because our families moved
in the same social circle called me to the dance floor.

"I don't think your feudal lord would mind!" a boy I'd known
similarly yelled above the noise. "He's not here to object anyway!"

I smiled with the expected decorum of a polite bride, even
though I didn't think his joke was funny. He'd never met Jazib
but felt confident in stereotyping him.

The room became louder with another rowdy number. My ears felt boxed, my head was heavy, and my feet hurt in the new heels. I was parched. And I had to pee. With everyone else on the dance floor, I told a maid I was going to the restroom so she might inform anyone who asked. The bride couldn't just up and leave, you know.

I stared at myself in the bathroom mirror. I didn't look half as fatigued as I felt inside. In fact, I looked fresh. Whoever invented makeup must've been a big fan of sweeping your feelings under all that foundation. I touched my hair just to feel how nicely it was tucked up, took a selfie, and texted it to Jazib:

Dholki Mubarak! You still in your farm boots?

He instantly called. "Sexy!" He whistled. "And I'm in my pyjamas. Sans my shirt. You wanna see?"

"Ew. No."

He laughed as if he expected it, but I realised the oddity of my response. He was my fiancé. We were to be married in less than a month. And I didn't want to see his hot bod…? I shivered and went back to sparring with him over the phone. He wanted to know why I was in the bathroom and not dancing my night away instead.

"I have such a headache from all that noise."

"Noise? It's your own dholki. Go, enjoy it."

"I will." I felt tired. Then for no reason, I told him about Ranya.

"It's only right." He didn't sound too heartbroken. "Who are these cousins? You know them?"

"Nope. They live in those oceanfront apartments by the old barbeque place. If I knew, I would've invited them tonight."

"Just let it go, Maya," he said. "We need to move on." There was a momentary silence and then he was back to his sunny mode. "And you need to go back to that ballroom and claim it like the belle you are!"

I smiled. "I wish you were here."

"You'll be here with me in no time," he said. "Can't believe it's happening."

"Yeah, me neither."

An awkward silence fell between us again. I wondered why it ever existed. Where were the happy notes that melted away doubt on such occasions, the kind I'd always read about?

"I'll go back to bed now," he said finally.

I said goodbye, wondering if he was noticing and thinking the same things I was.

23

"I THOUGHT I'D NEVER change out of these mayun clothes." I hungrily eyed a silken yellow three-piece outfit Tani laid out on my bed.

I was finally back in Kesar for the wedding and getting treated with beauty naps, massages of essential oils, and yellow ubtan mask made from gram flour, turmeric, and sandalwood. That also meant bad smells and zero socialising. Mayun, our most ancient wedding ritual spanning days and sometimes weeks, was restful as well as stifling.

"My sister wore hers for two weeks and changed straight into her wedding dress," Tani said.

"I don't know why brides have to go through this." I sniffed my sleeve. The dense odour of ubtan and a dozen other things, mustard oil among them, shot through my nostrils. "A million showers won't wash this stench away." And I'd showered every day, despite Aya-Ji's protests, only to wear the same outfit again. "Why is it forbidden to wash the mayun outfit?"

Tani giggled. "It's just tradition."

"Men are lucky they don't have to do this."

"Because nobody looks at the groom. Bride is the centre of attention."

That was true.

Kesar was used to having morning or afternoon wedding festivities as opposed to the all-nighters seen in the big cities. The prime reason, as I'd come to understand, was because rural folk went to bed early. I could hear dholak and songs filling the air of our haveli as girls and women gathered downstairs in the inner courtyard. It was a sunny day outside with winter temperatures.

Tani helped me into my brocade and gota applique lehnga. The velvet lemon of the dress contrasted brilliantly against the rich reddish-brown henna decorating my hands, arms, and feet. I wasn't a fan of its strong scent, but it was a beautiful tradition, essential for a bride.

I looked at myself in the mirror while Tani struggled with my sheer dupatta to cover my head after fixing florets in my ears and braid. I looked like one of those glittery cloth dolls they sold at the handicraft stores.

"Is she ready?" Aya-Ji came in and let out a happy gasp. She extended both her hands at my face, made a scooping gesture, and touched her temples in a sign of cleansing my aura of any evil spirits. "Bless you, my love! May Allah protect you from all evil eyes, all harm, from all bad things. May He bless you with happiness forever!" She kissed me delicately on the forehead.

"I did a good job, didn't I, Aya-Ji?" Tani trilled. "Peel away my evil shadows too."

"Bless you too, girl!" Aya-Ji laughed.

"Aya-Ji, Bano Bibi says..." Zaytun hurriedly burst in to deliver some message, but she too stopped when she saw me. "Mashallah, Maya Bibi, you're a vision!" She made the same warding-off-evil gesture that Aya-Ji had, then said, "Aya-Ji, all the elderly women have gathered downstairs. They're waiting for the bride."

"Has Jazib arrived?" Aya-Ji asked casually, trifling with my jasmine earrings.

"Jazib will be here?" I asked. Traditionally grooms weren't part of mayun festivities.

"Yes," Aya-Ji replied. "Look how pretty your henna is. Darker the stain, deeper the love of your husband." She voiced an ancient superstition. Obviously whoever came up with that never took body temperature into account and how cosmetics reacted to it.

"And her hair and skin are so soft," Tani said. "Saeen would completely love it!"

"Excuse me?" I was a little taken aback by her statement, not that it was too bold for her to say, but simply because...*ew*...why would Jazib love *my* hair or skin or anything?

"Saeen will madly fall in love with you, Bibi." Tani giggled again. "You're so pretty! If I were him, I'd take you away today."

It took a minute for her meaning to sink in: *Saeen would love your...* and I saw him doing just that. My hair. My skin. My –

I thought I'd die hurling all over the place. I'd never thought about this aspect of what I was about to do. Intimacy. *Sex.* That's what marriage was built around – most of it, if not all of it; or at least some of it, if not most of it. But I couldn't be intimate with him even a bit. Not ever!

"Tani, make yourself useful elsewhere," Zaytun rebuked her sharply and she instantly obeyed, her smile still plastered on her lips as she left. "Silly girls, they forget their place," she muttered irritably, then reminding Aya-Ji to hurry up, she followed Tani out as well.

Aya-Ji gave me a critical onceover and was about to usher me out when I held her back with urgency. "Aya-Ji," I was breathless. "I can't marry Jazib."

"What?"

"I'll go tell Ammi to call it off!"

"Maya!" She pulled me back sternly as I readily marched toward the door. "Breathe!" she said. "Breathe, darling. I know what you're going through."

"No, you don't!"

"It's just cold feet."

"No, it isn't!"

"Breathe!" She took in a deep breath herself, as if demonstrating a how-to on breathing. I complied. "Good," she said approvingly. "Now, listen to me. When you go down there, and you see him, and see how happy everyone is – how excited your mother is – you'll feel better. More confident."

I didn't really have a proper response for her, except to nod and be led to wherever she wanted to take me. Maybe she was right about me feeling better once I saw Jazib. Besides, there was no one formula for a perfect marriage. Jazib and I didn't have to get physically close to make it work. I was sure he wouldn't want to. We could be partners on a very sexless, platonic level and still be happy. He could grow his sugarcane and excel at that and I could take pictures of his crop and be happy like that. And if we wanted children, we'd adopt.

The courtyard was all yellow: yellow marigold garlands and wreaths adorning every pillar and doorway, yellow rugs, hordes of relatives and other acquaintances (mostly women, mostly dressed in yellow), sitting with dholak and clapping, singing their lungs out. On an ornate loveseat decorated with yellow silks, ribbons, and flowers, sat Jazib. One look at him and I began to mildly panic. Somebody helped me take my place beside him. Someone else announced it was time for the *rasam* to begin.

"Can married men join in?" asked an older cousin whom I'd always known for his gentle humour. His query prompted hearty chuckles. Of course, everyone knew that mayun rituals were only performed by married women.

I glanced at Jazib from the corner of my eye. In a white starched kurta shalwar, he sat stiff like a statue. His sun-kissed complexion had paled to a sickly green. "Are you ill?" I whispered to him. "Jazib? Are you okay?" He looked at me as if he was surprised to see me sitting next to him. Before I could reiterate, loud giggles erupted around us and Ammi told me to stop talking. Brides didn't talk!

"You're a good listener, Jazib!" One of his male cousins from his mother's side hollered at us.

"Look how they can't help but stare at each other!" some lady with an extra shrill voice remarked. Everyone joined her for a good teasing laugh and engaged in more jests at our expense.

They all expected us to blush, smile shyly, for me to bury my reddened face in my hennaed hands, because that's how any normal bride would react. But nothing about my mayun felt normal to me. I was having an out-of-body experience, sitting next to a boy who looked like he'd spent a good part of his morning throwing up in his bathroom.

"Chalo, chalo, let's start!" somebody said and someone else grabbed my palm, placed a fresh betel leaf on it, then placed my hand over Jazib's. He immediately recoiled.

"I don't think we're supposed to hold hands traditionally," he protested with a wide nervous grin.

"Traditionally you're not supposed to be here either, but we decided to pamper you," his mother teased him and everyone else burst out laughing again.

"Hold her hand, don't act so polite," said one of Ammi's cousins who reminded me of an overly decorated cupcake.

"In his heart he wants to hold more than just her hand!" Someone else decided it was okay to be crass in public because it was a wedding event, and the public around her endorsed it with more laughs.

Jazib and I exchanged horrified glances with each other, and I knew he felt just as frustrated as I was.

A maid brought a large platter of small bowls of henna, ubtan, and yellow ladoo balls. Jazib's mother was the first one to start. She dipped a finger in henna, wiped it off the betel leaf on my palm, and repeated the same with ubtan. Then she picked up a ladoo and asked me to take a bite. The sweet taste of melting gram flour pearls wasn't my favourite, but ladoo was the life of any festivity. She offered the same ladoo to Jazib, who obediently gobbled it down. Everyone cheered as though he'd scaled K2 or something. Her final act was to take a wad of rupee notes and make circular motions with it over Jazib's head, then mine, and then give it to a group of maids to share amongst themselves. After she stepped aside, ten more women lined up to repeat the same ritual exactly.

Jazib shifted uneasily. His hand was getting clammy, but he couldn't move it lest everything I held in my palm fell. He stared at me in exasperation, inviting loud cheers of oohs and aahs.

"He just can't keep his eyes off her, can he?"

"Can't wait to taste his bride too, haan?"

I couldn't wait to be in my room again!

Finally the ritual was over, food was served, and the guests headed to plunder the buffet.

I was exhausted. "Ammi, can I go now?" I begged her. "I literally can't sit here any longer."

"But this is your mayun," she insisted. "Stay and enjoy. Eat something too."

"I'm stuffed with ladoo and tasteless humour." I frowned. "Killed my appetite for the rest of the century. And I have a headache."

"Drink some water then. You're dehydrated."

"Actually," Jazib spoke up. "I don't feel so good myself. I think I'll go rest."

"Hai, what happened?" Ammi was by his side in a wink with her hand to his forehead. "You're warm. I think you should rest. You must be tired."

My jaw all but dropped to the floor. "Hello," I said, waving at the two of them to get attention. "I'm not feeling well *also*. May I be excused? I need to look pretty for the wedding, me being the bride and all."

"Yes," Jazib said. "You look tired."

"Yes." Ammi could suddenly see it on my face too. "You both should rest."

But of course, Ammi agreed with him and let me leave only after *he* decided I should. That was a fine footprint of my life for the future – trailing behind my worship-worthy husband all the way.

"I'm going to take a nap, so make sure nobody disturbs me. And shut the door on your way out," I told the maids who escorted me to my room. Once they were gone, I slipped the latch in place just so no one would enter even by mistake.

The dholak had resumed downstairs and it beat to the palpitations of my heart. I was panicking again, rubbing the back of my hand where Jazib had held it. I was seriously thinking of running away. If I did, I wouldn't have to ever wrap my head around the possibility of being intimate with him. But there was also a possibility that Mamu-Jaan would hunt me down and either kill me or force me to marry his son.

Nah, I thought. He wasn't that barbaric. I'd never heard of anyone ever doing that to anyone in the family. But then no bride had ever run away before either. I mean, honour killings happened every day. One thousand women died that way every year in this country. I could be next. Or maybe I was overreacting. Maybe I could learn to like him that way in time…

Ew.

No!

"What should I do?" I buried my face in my hands and was sitting on my bed wondering when the cellphone rang. I instantly took the call. "Jazib?"

"Come down to the shack," he said hoarsely. "We need to talk!"

"You're calling off the wedding?" I had the strongest hunch.

"Just come, Maya!"

"But I can't sneak out. I'm the bride!"

He'd already disconnected.

I went into my closet and rummaged for a dark, nondescript chador that was big enough to envelop me. On any normal day, I wouldn't even be looking for a chador just to meet Jazib in my own backyard, but now I was the bride and he was my groom and it wasn't proper to meet each other unless it was in the presence of a million people gathered to tease us ceremoniously.

I peeled away my shimmery dupatta, wrapped around a voluminous black chador and opened the door just a crack. The hallway was clear. I silenced my phone and tip-toed to a rarely used stairway in the back. I crept downstairs; the singing voices grew louder with each step. At the last step, I covered my nose and mouth with the chador and turned a corner to a small hallway that the maids used as a shortcut to the backyard.

Jazib was standing in the shack. He looked at me with an expression of regret and sympathy, with a side of undying fondness. "Maya." He clasped his hands. "Please, don't take this the wrong way. You are, by far, one the most attractive women I know, but...but I can't *touch* you. I don't want to be crass, but I can't have sss...you know...we can't be intimate. We just can't!"

I gasped, and it bounced off the wooden walls of our shack. Next thing I knew, I was hugging him so tightly my fingers hurt. I may also have shed one happy tear or so. "I can't tell you how happy I am, because me neither!"

"Are you serious?" His stiff expression melted into a sunny smile. He threw back his head and sighed heavily. "Oh, Maya! Ohhhhhh, Maya!"

"Are you orgasming? Because it sounds like you are."

"It does feel that good." He chuckled. "What a relief!"

"I know, but now what?"

"I have a plan. Are you ready?"

"What plan?"

"Come on!" He headed out around the back of the shack.

There was a door in the back wall of the garden. Nobody ever used it, but it led out to a dusty path that curved and cut through large clusters of trees and cornfields and eventually led out of Kesar. As children we used that door to sneak in and out of the haveli at odd hours. Jazib pushed the door open and I saw his rugged four-wheeler there with Haji sitting at the wheel, all poised and ready.

"Okay, if we're not marrying, why are we eloping?" I asked him as he helped me get in the backseat. "Salam, Haji Bhai. Do you know what he's planning?"

"Whatever Jazib Saeen wishes," he answered politely to the air in front of his nose.

"Step on it, Haji!" Jazib ordered him as he slid in beside me. "To Karachi."

"Why Karachi?" I asked.

"Because I'm suddenly in the mood to get married." He looked at me and smiled.

24

IT TOOK ME SOME time to figure out we weren't merely going to Karachi. Jazib had an address, and motivation to get there as soon as possible.

"How did you even find this?" I said, reading the screen of his phone before handing it back to him.

"You said it was in the white apartments by the old barbecue place."

"There are like a trillion apartments there, Jazib."

"I know a guy who knows a guy who lives there," he said, with a satisfied smile.

"I sure hope you know what you're doing," I said, shaking my head.

I'd grilled him about it quite a bit. Didn't he remember what had happened the last time he'd tried to be assertive with her? And this time he was planning on going over to her and…but Jazib had promised me he would be calm and respectful and only meant to take his chance one last time. He deserved that much, didn't he? He deserved to say he was sorry and be heard at least once. If he wasn't forgiven, he said he'd accept that too. And he'd accept that as the end of it all.

"I'll be out of her way like I never existed," he promised me. "You know I'm not the obsessive type."

I couldn't be sure. And if he faltered, it would be on my watch. I would have to hold him back if things went awry. No matter what!

"Saeen, I think we're here," Haji said as he slowed down and rolled the car in front of a cluster of five-storey white apartments grouped together inside a rectangular boundary wall.

"Ask the watchman if they live here?" Jazib said and Haji jumped out of the vehicle. It was thirty minutes past midnight and the street where we'd parked was silent as death. There wasn't even an occasional bark of a stray dog to be heard for miles.

"Jazib," I said, "you know that Karachi isn't the safest city in the world, right?"

"Haji has a gun," he replied, shifting in his seat as he stared outside his window at Haji talking to someone in the watchman booth. "What's taking him so long?"

"What if Mamu-Jaan appears here out of nowhere? They must've figured out by now we're missing."

"It's an awfully long drive. They'd still be way behind us."

"He has a private plane." I reminded him. "He doesn't need to drive."

"The airport itself is hours away."

"But—"

"Maya, think nice things!" He frowned and focused on Haji again. Just then, Haji turned and gestured for us to follow him.

Five minutes later, Jazib was knocking on a thick wooden door while keeping the doorbell pressed with his other hand. The building watchman stood beside him with a rifle casually hanging over his left shoulder, just in line of view of the peephole. There was a succession of quick snaps and slides of various locks from inside the apartment as the main door swung open to reveal a dishevelled middle-aged man. His tight grey curls were tousled, and his glasses barely rested on his nose.

"Yes? What is this?" He stared at the watchman. "At this hour?"

"Is Ranya home?" Jazib asked impatiently.

"Moin Sahib, this mister wants to see you," the watchman said. "Says he's your relative."

"O Bhai!" Moin cried. "I've never seen him before." Then, he turned to Jazib, "Who are you? I don't know you."

"I'm Jazib."

Moin gasped, forgetting to glue back his mouth, and proving that he knew exactly who Jazib was.

"We're really sorry for dropping by unannounced," I said. "We only want to see Ranya. May we please come in? Only for a few minutes."

"But…" he paused, and looked at me from head to toe, perhaps trying to reconise me from the way I was dressed. "Wasn't it your wedding today?"

"Moin Sahib, I'll go back to my post now," the watchman said. "Looks to me you know them very well."

"Yes, I'll come with you," Haji replied and patted the other man's shoulder amicably. "Got some tea at this hour? I've had a long drive."

"Oh yes, I was about to make some when you came in," the watchman replied. Their voices faded away into the distance as the two men turned a corner and were lost to the sound of chirping crickets in the night.

"Who is it?" A woman appeared from behind Moin and gasped as she saw us. "You're Jazib, right? I've seen pictures of you," she told him, then looked at me. "And you…are you Maya? Wasn't it your mayun today? What are you doing here? Did you elope?"

"Is Ranya home?" Jazib interrupted the interrogation. "Please, I must speak with her."

"She's sleeping at this time. I suggest you come back in the morning," Moin said, partially blocking the doorway with his arm. He contorted his face in an expression that I'm sure he believed to be threatening, but it only made him look pouty, adding to his benign vibe.

"I will force my way in if you don't allow me to enter," Jazib said icily. "I don't have time and I must speak with her."

"What he means is…" I dug my fingernails in Jazib's shoulder to stab some sense and control in him, "we'd be eternally grateful if you could wake her up. This is important."

"I told you to come back in the morning."

"It cannot wait till morning." Jazib glared at him. "Didn't you hear? This is important!"

"Now, look here, *son*." Moin's puckered brow got even more pregnant. "This is Karachi. Not your ancestral land where you're the law. I'll call the police if you create a racket here."

"I did warn you." Jazib shrugged my hand off and burst past Moin, straight into the apartment's living room. "Ranya? Ranya!"

"Hey, hey! You can't just barge in here!" Moin was yelling at him while Jazib paced back and forth yelling for Ranya. I just shrunk into a corner trying to think fast of how to remedy all this. I'd totally failed in containing him. I never should've tagged along. And now there he was, wreaking havoc. Add to that the humiliation of Ranya's rejection, which I was sure she would dish out to him. Again.

Oh dear!

Maybe I could keep a knife handy to scare or threaten him or something in case he tried to abduct her or assault her relatives and such. I mean, I could cut him – a little bit, like a scratch – if he tried grabbing her. Instinctively, my eyes started searching for their kitchen.

Maybe I should ask where they kept the knives…

Suddenly, Jazib stopped shouting.

Ranya stood, pinned to a wall, quietly staring at him with eyes that glistened with tears and questions. And then she tiredly sank in a nearby chair.

"Ranya…" Jazib's voice was breaking. "I'm not here to make a scene. I just want you to know I'm sorry. So deeply. I was a jerk! And you don't have to forgive me or ever see me again but…I love you. I always have. That's all I wanted to say."

"You left your wedding just to tell me that?" she asked.

"I'm not getting married," he said. "I work on my farm now. And I got my law degree. I'm…oh, God…" he closed his eyes, then as if with a burst of fresh energy, he said, "I have to ask, Ranya, even if you say no, even if you toss me out, I'll live with all that but I have to ask! Will you marry me?"

Moin, the woman who I was now sure was his wife, and I stood in that living room as though we were sculptures created to stare with bulging eyes and gaping mouths. Jazib was down on one knee, proposing to Ranya.

"Yes! Yes, I will!" she cried, laughing through tears as Jazib locked her in a passionate embrace.

"Hai Allah, Mubarak! Congratulations! I'm so happy!" Moin's wife was now yelling in my ear.

"We must marry right away," Jazib said, putting Ranya down. Her face had lit up like a candle. "My father could come barging in here any second."

"Hold it, hold it!" Moin's loud protest silenced everyone. "I forbid this!"

"Moin, don't be a party pooper," his wife chided him.

"You don't understand, Seema!" He was so upset he was gesticulating with his hands all over the place. "Didn't you hear? His father could come barging in here any second. And do you know who his father is? Shah Farid Sultan! He'll have us all killed."

"No, he wouldn't." I rolled my eyes at him. "You're exaggerating a wee too much."

"I can't approve of this on a number of levels," Moin said, levelling the air in front of him with a horizontal swipe of his hands. "I'm not Ranya's legal guardian, I can't just give her away in matrimony. Her sister doesn't even know what hell is breaking loose under my roof right now, and when she does, she'll kill me. When Farid Sultan finds out that I assisted in marrying his son off, he'll kill me!"

"I'm twenty-two," Ranya said. "I can legally give consent to my own matrimony."

"There!" Jazib smiled. "Let's do it."

"It's one o' clock in the morning, you can't just *do it.*" Moin frowned at him. "I can't find a molvi at this hour to officiate your nikah."

"You can officiate our nikah, Moin Bhai," Ranya suggested.

"Oh yes, Moin, it's only a few verses." Seema delightfully clasped her hands. "Every able Muslim has that power vested in him to officiate a nikah. Oh, how fun it would be! A clandestine marriage ceremony in our house."

I loved how she was excited at the prospect of a wedding while her husband constantly reminded her of every possible scenario in which they both died horrible deaths at the hands of an angry feudal and a furious big sister.

"Oho, what about registration and legal stamps and reconigising the vows in law and nikahnama to sign?" Moin said. "I have none of that. Only a certified cleric carries all that."

"Then, we should leave here," Jazib said urgently. "We need to go somewhere where they can't find us."

"You want to elope?" Seema gasped. "How romantic!"

"I think I have a way," I said, dialling up my voice to get attention before Moin got another panic attack. "I know someone who can help." Everyone in the room had their eyes on me as I clutched my phone tightly, weighing my decision to make that call. I knew it wouldn't go to waste. He would come if I asked. I turned away from the interrogating stares that made me nervous and stepped outside the apartment, and waited as his phone rang…one, two…

"Hello?" His voice was heavy with sleep yet alert. "Maya? At this hour? Are you okay? What is it?"

"Arhaan," I said. "I need your help."

Moin's living room accommodated all five of us, but dense silence hung in the air. His small apartment, that probably cost millions in real estate because of its location, could be summed up in one glance from anywhere you stood in it. The living room was almost parked in the entryway and opened into a dining space that was adjacent to a hallway with a breakfast area and kitchen on the other side. The hallway led to a cove that cradled three bedrooms with presumably attached bathrooms since that was the norm.

"How much longer, Maya?" Jazib impatiently tapped the screen of his phone. "It's been two hours."

"He said to wait," I said. "I know he'll find someone. Trust me. It's so late at night. Obviously, things will take more time than they would during the day."

"I told you we should've left," he said agitatedly. "We could be in Lahore by now and I could've gone to a number of friends who—"

"And your father would've killed us for letting you go and Arju would've hanged me for getting her sister kidnapped," Moin deadpanned. "I'm sorry but I can't die for you. We don't know each other that well."

"Moin," Seema said, rolling her eyes, "you're speaking as if there's no law here."

"There isn't for his kind."

Just then the doorbell rang.

"It's him." I sprang up to my feet and was about to get the door when Moin physically put himself between me and the door.

"How do you know?" he whispered harshly. "What if it's Farid Sultan with his henchmen about to open fire?"

"My uncle is not like that." I whispered back just as irritably. "You're constantly insulting him."

"Is that why you ran away from home? Because he's so *kind?*"

I was just about losing it with him when the bell rang again, and this time, there were knocks too. "Would you at least peep through?" I sternly pointed at the hole behind him.

He reluctantly heeded my request. "I don't know who it is," he said, panicking. "I don't see any guns. Maybe he has a dagger?"

I brushed past him, peeped through myself, and unlocked the door instantly to let Arhaan in. "Oh, thank you for coming," I said to him as he entered. "I knew you would..." I stopped and stared at the other two men with him. One was a cleric by description, obviously there to officiate the nikah vows, and the other... "Abba?" My voice trailed off weakly into silence as he stared back at me.

"Abba?" Moin went pale. "Saeen Farid, forgive me for not recongising you. You look quite different in person."

"Sorry for disturbing you at this hour," Abba said to him, extending his hand for a shake that only met with a confused stare. He waited for another second before realising that Moin was too petrified to move and took his hand in his and shook it hard, as though jolting the man to life. "I'm Mir Badruddin, Arjumand's husband. I'm sorry we've never met despite being in-laws. I'm Maya's father and Jazib's uncle-in-law."

"Oh! Yes, we relocated a few months ago from Dubai," Moin explained with a relaxed smile this time. "How did you...get here…so soon? Weren't you in Gurhkot too? For your daughter's, uhm…wedding?"

"Turns out Farid has a plane." Abba smiled. "And he was too perturbed to ask questions when I told him I wanted to use it. It was good Arhaan called me. If it were Farid standing here, nothing would be quite as peaceful."

"He'd have us all killed." Moin sighed knowingly.

Jazib hadn't been able to meet Abba's eye. I understood how he felt. It wasn't exactly a proud moment for a man to meet the father of the bride he'd decided not to marry after proposing to someone else instead. As for Ranya, she'd gone crimson and probably wished she could disappear. That would've been better than to forever be known as the girl who stole her almost-father-figure's daughter's groom.

"I'm sorry my kids have been so rude as to burst in on you like this." Abba took turns glaring at us again.

"Abba, Ranya and Jazib love each other," I said. "They should be together."

"Then why the entire ruse of this wedding?" He frowned.

"Because!" I started to say but immediately pursed my lips. There was no way in hell I could spill my secret for why I accepted Jazib's proposal. Especially not when Arhaan stood right there. Besides, that was immaterial now. I was revoking my consent, and everyone needed to accept that. "Because we had a change of heart," I said, lifting my chin. "And that is all there is to it. I will not marry Jazib, so he might as well marry anyone he wants."

"I meant no disrespect," Jazib said cautiously, his voice low and tactful. Not a trait I would usually acquaint with him. "Maya and I could never make each other happy. And I love Ranya. I promise to always."

"And you, Ranya?" Abba asked her. "Do you want to marry Jazib?"

She didn't look up, but her entire body seemed to shiver.

"Abba, you're scaring her." I started to say, but he held up his hand to tell me to stay in my place and shut up.

"I need to hear it from you, Ranya," he said to her again. "Do you want to marry Jazib?"

"Sounds like a nikah to me," Seema muttered. "Might as well let the nikahkhwan do it."

I had to swallow a giggle as my gaze floated off towards the clueless cleric, a black-bearded man perhaps in his forties, who stood levelled against a wall in a corner. He slowly nodded at Seema's suggestion and looked at Arhaan as if appealing to please let him do the job he was probably dragged out of bed for at this hour.

"Badr Bhai," Ranya's meek voice cut through the awkward atmosphere. "I do love Jazib. I never meant to disappoint you. I'm so sorry."

"You haven't," Abba said, softening instantly. "I'm not upset. I respect your wishes. I'm just…why didn't you tell me?"

"And what would you do if she had?" I asked. He was surprised, registering the disappointment behind my question, because we both knew the answer to that. He was there that night in Kesar. He *knew* about them. He'd always known about me and Jazib too, yet did nothing. "Abba, please, we need your help."

"Guys, we're pressed for time," Arhaan said, looking at his wristwatch. "It'll be morning soon and Molvi Sahib would want to be home in time for Fajr prayers. If anyone wishes to get married here, they need to hurry."

"Very well," Abba said. "You have my permission. I'll give Ranya away."

His words spread like a happy wave through the room. Seema scampered off to one of the bedrooms and emerged holding a bold red gauzy dupatta dotted with golden embroidery and a wide shimmering border. She helped Ranya settle on a couch and draped the dupatta over her head in a bridal style. Jazib, Abba, and the cleric took seats too. The cleric who'd been quiet all this time was now speaking fluently. He drew out sheets of legal documents, asking about the bridal couple and witnesses, their names, ages, and other relevant information, his pen quickly filling in all blanks and checking all appropriate boxes.

"Haq mehr?" he asked, "Your obligatory gift to the bride?"

"My Karachi apartment," Jazib said instantly. "That's the only asset in my name right now. I will transfer it to Ranya first thing in the morning."

"No," Ranya said, "I don't want it." She looked at Jazib and smiled. "I want whatever Jazib's first paycheque brings as my mehr."

"Oh, how romantic!" Seema was choked with happy tears while Moin frowned and objected at the silly notion, but Ranya was adamant.

With the mehr sorted out, it was time for the vows. The cleric asked Ranya thrice if she would take Jazib to be her lawfully wedded husband, and after she consented all three times, he repeated the same with Jazib. Both the bride and groom penned their signatures on the marriage contract, we made a prayer for their blissful future, and it was done.

"Luckily we have dates!" Seema said, offering everyone the traditional celebratory nikah sweet.

"I'll register these with the court first thing in the morning," the cleric said, gathering all the documents and left after popping a date in his mouth.

Seema fawned all over Ranya, while Moin grilled Jazib some more. They were an interesting couple. They'd been married for fifteen years, were eight months apart in age, and had no children despite trying several times. Moin's family had often implied that he should take a second wife, a younger woman who'd bear him children.

"How can they be sure that wife number two would bear children?" I asked. "Would she come with a guarantee from God?"

"That's exactly what I say!" he exclaimed. "And then, if she doesn't bear me children, then what? Wife number three, then four?"

"And she better bear sons or she's no good either." Seema dished out another salty fact about the regressive mindset she'd spent a lifetime fighting. "People are just ridiculous!"

I saw Arhaan inch towards the exit, so I excused myself and hurried after him, catching him outside in the parking lot. "I just wanted to thank you," I said. "I couldn't think of anyone else to ask."

"That's alright," he said. "It was no trouble. Big surprise though."

"Bigger surprise was you bringing Abba."

"He needed to be here. Nobody could've done what he did." He looked at me intently. "He loves you, Maya. You should have called him for help yourself."

"Maybe." I sighed. "It's been so crazy. I should write a memoir on the wedding I almost had."

He agreed and we both stood smiling at each other for a few seconds as the night breeze tickled the senses. It was quiet, but not lonely. Dark, but so refreshing as the leafy scent of palms and jasmine filled the air. And the dancing lights of the lampposts did justice to Arhaan's profile. I could stand there and look at him forever. It was sad that, despite his stern rejection, I still felt this way.

"Was it your mayun?" he asked, taking note of my clothes and henna.

"Yes."

"You would've made a beautiful bride." My heart skipped a beat. I couldn't even say a thank you. "So," he said. "What will you do now?"

"I don't know. I don't even know where I'll be an hour from now. Everything is so…messed up."

"Do you want me to stay?"

Yes!

"No!" I said, a bit enthusiastically to drown out my inner voice. "No, you have things to do, I'm sure. I'll be fine. Thank you."

"Okay." He nodded slowly. "Take care, Maya."

And he walked away. He made no promises to see me again, nothing about staying in touch. He walked away just as he'd walked in that night after a single phone call from me. He'd do it again if I ever asked him to, but that was the part that irked me. He wouldn't initiate. He was there if I needed him. Did he not ever need me back?

25

THE NEXT FEW WEEKS passed like a whirlwind – rapid, tumultuous, erasing all signs of what used to be.

Jazib took Ranya to Gurhkot the same day they'd married to deal with their own maelstrom, which cast them both out and forced them to pitch camp in Lahore. There was news of Mamu-Jaan redrafting his Will and disowning Jazib. His mother was down with her own version of panic attacks. The entire haveli was in mourning over such an unexpected turn of events and disobedience.

Arjumand threw a tantrum and shut herself in her bedroom for days – mad at Abba, mad at Moin, mad at me, mad at the universe in general, and grieving for Ranya as if she wasn't married but dead.

Then, there was Ammi. She had an entire haveli to shut herself in and shut everyone else out. She refused to speak to me. She told Abba to either go kill himself or divorce her – he'd done neither. And the last thing I heard from Aya-Ji, who hadn't returned from Kesar since the day I left it, and was our sole line of communication from that world, was that Ammi had fallen ill. She had been sick since I'd run away. Had become sicker when Mamu-Jaan tossed Jazib out and now, as winter turned to spring, her body gave in to new allergies and she became even more frail.

I'd moved in with Abba again as he refused to let me be by myself in my house. I suspected he almost believed what Moin said about Mamu-Jaan sending over his henchmen to obliterate us all. Sort of boggled my mind he'd let me marry into such a family if that's what he thought of them.

"Gohar isn't taking her medicines properly," Abba said one early morning at the breakfast table.

"You should visit her," I suggested.

There was a loud clank of a fork being dropped on casual china. Arjumand sat staring at me. "Why should he?" She raised her eyebrow. "Especially since she doesn't want him there."

I decided not to butt horns with her and spoke to Abba instead, "She would listen to you."

"I called her, but she refused to take the call," he said, sipping tea.

"It's easy to ignore a call, but if you're there, she'll have to hear you out."

"Out of the question!" Arjumand said hotly. "Her nephew kidnapped my sister and you want my husband to go care for her?"

"He's her husband too."

"Only because he's too nice to leave her!"

"Arjumand," Abba said, calming her. "We talked about this. There's no need to be upset. I don't have any plans of visiting there just now. I don't think it'll do any good to anyone."

"Abba, she needs you now." I stared at him. "You can't ignore her like this. She's not well."

"He won't go there ever and that's final!"

"You don't get to decide that." I glared at her. "It's best for you to keep your nose out of our business."

"Maya." Abba frowned. "Be polite."

"I am polite. I left out the expletives."

"Maya!"

That was it for me. I pushed my chair back and stood up, grabbed my cellphone, and hollered for one of the maids to fetch my bag.

"Where do you think you're going?" Arjumand, emboldened by Abba's lack of a good spine, barked at me. When I didn't answer, Abba repeated the question.

I took a long hard look at his face. "To Kesar," I said. "To right your wrongs because you never will."

"Maya, you can't drive there alone!"

He was still shouting objections when I hopped in my car and drove out.

Life at Kesar was quieter than I'd ever experienced. Or perhaps in contrast to the way I'd left things there – festive and noisy – it felt lifeless in comparison.

At first, Ammi refused to see me. I was too tired to argue with her, so I went to bed. The next morning, the battle began, and it continued for a few more days. She was reduced to her bed for over a week, not because that's what the doctors strictly prescribed but because that was how she wanted to be. Aya-Ji would trolley in all the meals to her on time, took care of her meds, helped her with her bathroom trips and showers, and basically was at her beck and call while Zaytun ran the house as she was entrusted to. After I arrived, I insisted on taking over the responsibilities that Aya-Ji was fulfilling. Ammi didn't agree.

"I don't need anyone else," she said crossly.

"Well, you don't have a choice," I replied. "Aya-Ji has other duties now."

"I don't want to see you. I don't want to talk to you!" she was yelling at me. "Why are you here?"

"Because you're not acting rationally like an adult."

"Maya!"

"Do you realise that your yelling isn't working?" I looked at her coolly. "Besides, you're mad at me for not marrying a man who didn't want to marry me at all. Is that fair?"

"I'm mad at you for deceiving me, for running away and insulting me!" Now she was crying. "You should've told me!"

"I did, Ammi. Don't pretend that I didn't. Jazib did too when he brought Ranya here the first time. None of you listened."

"So you decided to teach us a lesson by running away? Rubbing our noses in the dirt? All I had was my brother, but you took him away from me. He hasn't set foot in this haveli ever since. He hasn't called me ever since. And his own family is destroyed. It will never be the same, Maya. Do you even understand?"

Honestly, I hadn't before with quite this clarity.

Mamu-Jaan was a big name, had a grand reputation that was greatly damaged when his only son ran away from home and returned with an unknown girl as his wife a day before the wedding to his eligible fiancée. People gossiped everywhere. The newspapers and tabloids printed the story across the front pages as if it was a national catastrophe. He used his influence to prevent further details from forming more headlines for any newspaper, but he couldn't control social media. Luckily, the universe moved way too fast for one story to stick for long and soon nobody remembered the scandal. But Mamu-Jaan refused to forget. He cut off Jazib from everything, and then he locked himself inside his haveli.

Ammi lost her only supporter. She didn't have to tell me how utterly useless Abba was for her, not even a number she could call to talk. "I thought if you married Jazib, you'd be closer to me," she said amongst sobs. "And if you lived closer, you'd come here often. And then I wouldn't be so alone."

I understood her sentiments. She'd had a lifetime of emotional abandonment and dreamt of filling up that void by pairing me with Jazib. But we destroyed that dream. Instead of widening her support group, we denied her the only crutch she had left, her brother.

Gradually, things between us eased off a bit. She finally ventured out of her bedroom and resumed her routine of lounging on her divan, and since it was spring outside, I occasionally took her for walks too.

"Ammi," I said one morning as we sat in the backyard. "You should call Mamu-Jaan."

"You think I haven't tried?" She frowned, shading her eyes from the sun. "I want to apologise to him. I'll kiss his feet and plead until he forgives me."

"His own son ran away from that wedding. Why is he mad at you?"

"It doesn't excuse what you did," she said. "And he's kicked him out. He lost his only son because you wouldn't marry him and left him all unprotected to be hunted by that gold-digging witch."

"You're not helping yourself by ranting like this."

"And I suppose you have a better idea?"

"You should call Jazib. Invite him over."

"Over my dead body!" she cried. "Bhai-Jaan will disown me too if he heard I accepted Jazib in my home."

"Not just Jazib, but Ranya too. She's his wife now."

"That's enough!" She stood up in a huff. "You're more stupid than I thought. Or you're just insensitive like your father. You should go back to him and leave me alone!" Then she marched back inside the haveli.

I lay sprawled in the lawn chair, listening to the birds sing for a while. Then, I picked up my cellphone and called Jazib. "You have to come here and make amends with her." I told him. "She'll talk to Mamu-Jaan for you. Get the family back together. This is the only way."

"Ranya will be with me," he said. "I don't think this is a great idea."

"I won't force you, but I do think this might work."

He didn't sound convinced and I could sympathise with that. I wouldn't want to force my wife to face more insults than she'd already endured.

I sighed and disconnected.

Ammi crawled back into her shell of silent treatment after our exchange. I was quickly running out of ideas and patience to bear a situation that shouldn't have dragged on for so long. What exactly was the crime here? That I refused to marry a man I didn't love, or that he fell in love with someone else and married her, or that Ranya dared to love a man who was supposed to be out of her league? Why were our elders a bunch of unhappy people who understood nothing?

I feared the negative aura of the haveli was getting to me, and instead of brightening Ammi's world, I was letting her mindset darken mine.

One afternoon, I got in my car and went for a drive around Kesar. The town was an assortment of mud and brick houses with thatched roofs scattered between ripe fields of mustard, corn, and wheat, and a marketplace that was a single row of shops on a single street selling limited choices of household staples. Kesar had a smooth network of canals that ran down from Gurhkot. I parked on a dirt patch by the banks of one and sat under a tree, taking random pictures. There was laughter from a small group of children playing in shallow waters. Two girls and three shirtless boys – their burnished brown skins and tiny figures wrapped in wet clothing, bright smiles lined with perfect teeth; they splashed water on each other and giggled with the most carefree vibe.

I asked if I could take their picture.

"For a magazine?" a girl asked, rolling her dupatta, and squeezing water out of it. She seemed to be the oldest of them.

"Would you like me to publish it?" I asked her.

She exchanged glances with the other children, and they all broke into peals of laughter, shaking their heads.

"No!" A little girl giggled. "Amma will spank us!"

"Because you're a girl," a boy said to her, then looked at me. "But she'll be okay with mine. I'm a boy!" He flexed his arms like a wrestler, only there weren't many muscles to impress with. But he had plenty of charming cuteness to make up for that.

"How old are you?" I laughed. Wrestler boy was six. The little girl was his sister and she was five. The older girl was ten and she was their cousin, and the other two boys, both eight, were their neighbours. "I'm Maya," I introduced myself. "I'm from the haveli."

"From Bano Bibi's haveli?" one of the eight-year-olds asked.

"Yes, I'm her daughter."

There was a loud gasp, and then the questions came pouring in.

Was it your wedding?

Where did you go?

We wanted to see the bride so much!

I almost felt sorry for disappointing them by not getting married. "Let me make it up to you by taking your pictures." I tried to entice them. "You can keep these if you like. I won't take it to a magazine."

They consented and I clicked frame after frame. They volunteered to give me a tour of their village and I followed them around like a puppy, completely intoxicated with their innocence. They spoke without filters, inviting me to explore their world through their eyes. I saw the frugality in which they lived. Their clothes were old and faded, sandals were worn-out, and their homes told many stories of destitution, the likes of which I'd heard from Jazib on my trip to his farmlands. Yet, the children smiled.

The older girl insisted that I meet her mother. Her house wasn't much different from Karam Din's, only smaller. A woman sat scrubbing a large steel pot under a hand pump. She stopped as she saw us come. The girl introduced me, and her mother's face twisted into a surprised smile. She left the pot, washed her hands at the pump, and drying them with the edge of her dupatta, asked me to sit on a charpoy in the shade. "What brings you here, Bibi? It's been ages since Bano Bibi stepped out of her haveli. How is she?" she asked.

"She's doing fine, thank you," I replied.

She told her daughter to bring some sherbet and sat down in a cane chair, fanning me constantly with a hand-fan. "We don't get power at this hour. Load shedding. It's springtime and temperatures are bearable, but in summers, one would die in that heat."

"You don't have generators?"

"Ours burnt out last year. Then winter came. Now we'll buy one near summertime," she explained. "We want that other system, what's it called…?"

"Battery system, Ammi," the girl supplied the answer as she handed me a tall glass of yellow sherbet. "It's mango squash, Maya Bibi."

"Thank you." I smiled and took a sip. The chilled liquid, as it cascaded down my esophagus, reminded me of just how parched I was. "It's delicious!"

"We've always lived in Kesar," the mother told me. Her name was Izzat, meaning *respect* in Urdu. She had five children, including a six-month-old baby. The family owned a few acres of farmland that her brother-in-law took care of while her husband ran a tire shop in the market street. "I would've liked my boys to get some schooling," she said. "But the one here is no good and we cannot afford to send them elsewhere. So now they help their father at the shop."

"What about your girls?" I asked, finishing off my drink. "They say education is the real jewel anyone will ever need."

"Oh, Bibi." She sighed. "The only jewels that women need are in the kitchen. Husbands don't want jewellery as much as they want a hot home-cooked meal."

I didn't like her response, but it was her truth and that of many women in my country. I asked if I could take more pictures. She allowed me to. It was only when I was back at the haveli, in my bed, browsing through the pictures, that Izzat's words resounded in my ears and a bulb lit up in my brain.

I immediately called Yasir.

"I mean, it's just an idea," I said. "We're not selling utensil-shaped jewellery for women. I just thought it would be a good message to give in line with the project that Kulsom did."

"No, no, I get it," he said encouragingly. "And we don't need actual ornaments shaped like utensils or kitchen tools. We can make such pieces with cardboard or wood and paint them or put them through filters to give the look."

"That sounds doable."

"Let me pitch this to Kulsom. The last project stirred the pot just enough for her to want more."

"That's awesome," I said. "But Yasir, this isn't to discredit all the work these women do."

"We'll have to think about what we dish out. But don't worry, we'll figure it out. When are you coming back?"

"I'm not sure." I sighed.

"That's okay. By the way, you have anyone in mind to model?"

"Kishvar," I said promptly.

"To be honest, she'd be my pick too."

"We could be a team to shape these social messages." I laughed. "Kulsom, Kishvar, you, and me."

"I'd like that," he said, and I could hear the excitement in his voice. Yasir craved to be part of anything related to social justice, the good fights, meaningful revolutionary changes, anything to shake the status quo. I shared his passion too, more now than ever.

I spent the next two days roaming around the rest of Kesar, trapping life into a series of candid frames that spoke volumes of what was perceived and what was real and where they overlapped. I had pictures of women cooking, cleaning, quilting, sewing, embroidering, at home and out in the fields picking crop; of men tilling the land to get it ready for the next harvest and selling goods in shops. They packed so many colours around them in their food, their clothes, their language, like little pockets of mirth that burst open at the oddest of times. You could be almost in tears over their impoverished circumstances and a toddler climbs up in your lap and shows you a flower he picked for you, smiling as wide as the sun with just two teeth in his mouth. Or a nervous bride of an arranged marriage, hugging her family goodbye as a stranger's palanquin awaits her, and some dear old woman or a friend whispers something happy in her ear and she blushes and shyly steals a glance of her groom to find him returning her smile.

I was thankful for every moment that I got to spend with the people of Kesar, and for every slice of their life that I got to capture.

It was one such well-spent afternoon I was returning from when I saw a familiar silver Benz parked in the haveli driveway. I found Ammi sitting on a cot bed on the patio, all huffed, red in the face, and crying. Jazib sat beside her, head bowed in apology as he clutched her knee, begging for her forgiveness. Ranya stood motionless in a corner, trying to blend in with the wall behind her. Ammi took another minute to blame him for the collective shaming of the Sultan brand, for the breach of trust, for the collapse of the universe, and then she let her voice dwindle into soft sobs as her anger ran out of steam.

"Phupo, I only came to see you," Jazib said as a final note. "I'll leave now."

"I don't think so," I said, deciding this was my cue to step in. "You're staying with us in this haveli. For as long as Mamu-Jaan continues to ban you from his."

"Of course not!" Ammi said. "He can stay for dinner, then leave."

"He will stay here for as long as it takes Mamu-Jaan to come to his senses." I said. "And you will talk to him to make him realise that he needs to come to his senses."

"I will do no such thing!"

"Yes, you will." I smiled at her and took my seat in a nearby chair, maintaining my gaze on her face. "Because if you don't, you will lose Jazib forever because he will go away to some unknown location and you will never be able to find him. Mamu-Jaan will lose his only son and you will have to live with the guilt of never trying to make things right while you had the chance. And if Jazib leaves, I'll leave too, because it'd be very unfair for Mamu-Jaan to lose his only son while you still had your daughter. So, just to make things even, I'll leave too."

There weren't even crickets chirping at the end of my speech. Ammi was stunned while Jazib stared at me in confusion. He wasn't the type to go missing. At most, he'd go to his apartment in Karachi and wait out the emotional storm. Luckily, none of that occurred to Ammi.

"Cut it out, Maya." He frowned at me, then turned to Ammi. "I'm sorry, Phupo. I'm sorry I hurt you. But I'm not sorry for marrying Ranya, because that was an honest thing to do. If you want us to leave, we'll go. Come on, Ranya."

"Wait," Ammi suddenly cried, but instead of speaking to him directly, she told me, "He can stay here. And I'm doing this for my brother!" Then she stood up and walked away, leaving behind breathable air and quiet.

"Well." I smiled at the exhausted couple. "Welcome to Kesar."

26

AMMI FORGAVE JAZIB ALL his sins after only two days. All it took for him was to show up in her room with morning tea and the bowlful of colourful pills she took with it. Twice. And he was readmitted in her good books as the best boy she'd ever known. Meanwhile she still looked at me with mild disdain.

What did he have that I didn't?

That was a question I'd long stopped pondering over. He was a male child, and that trumped everything else. He could be whimsical. I had to be sensible. He could be outspoken. I had to measure my words, my tone, my stance, my place, my gender, my family, my neighbours, my neighbours' pets, and mostly rule in favour of silence. He could take his time to grow up. I was expected to be mature at birth. He could sin, repent, and be forgiven. I was destined for hell as a precaution. And since I was none of those things I was supposed to be, I deserved none of the clemency.

The same rules applied to Ranya. Jazib could be forgiven for falling for her, because boys will be boys and boys make mistakes, but her original sin of "seducing" him would forever follow her to the grave.

"You can stop trying to climb that slippery slope to pardon," I told her while we stood in the kitchen making soup for Ammi.

"You'll never get it." Lately Ranya had taken it upon herself to spend time with Ammi, even though it earned her nothing but cold stares and silence. She insisted on cooking for her and trying to help her with her cross-stitch tablecloth. Ammi didn't allow her to read to her, so she'd given up on it for the time being. "I'm not sure how long she'll let you help with that tablecloth, Ranya," I said, ladling the soup into a bowl and placing it onto a tray. "And why on earth would you learn embroidery? I mean who in their right mind does that?"

"It's very therapeutic." She smiled. "Like seeing a garden sprout with every movement of your hand. There's rhythm to how the point of a needle breaks through fabric and comes out the other side, pulling the thread like a colourful trail as it moves across the surface, and then, there's a pattern."

"Wow, you make it sound so soothing. I tried it and felt nothing."

"Your calling is photography," she said. "I hear you're very good at it."

"Really? Who told you that?"

"Arhaan did. He said you were a natural."

"I see." I wondered if I'd ever get used to hearing his name being dropped into a conversation like that without my heart skipping a beat. "I didn't think he knew. I've only just started."

"Didn't you do some back in college? You'd shown me some of his close-ups you took. Remember?"

"Oh, yes." I allowed myself a stiff smile. "Silly times."

"You know I interned for Arhaan for a while," she said, picking up the food tray. "One of his clients talked about how she was interested in opening small-scale vocational training centres in urban areas. I was thinking we could do the same for places like Kesar and Gurhkot…especially for women. I've seen their embroidery and their cooking and other skills. They can have their own businesses."

"You've really immersed yourself in this culture, haven't you?" I said, admiring her stance. She was dressed modestly in a simply cut shalwar kamiz, with a large dupatta covering her head just like Ammi did. She looked mature and calm, with a certain poise that comes naturally to our housewives. "I love it. You should totally work on that idea."

Her face lit up. "We must talk more about this later."

"Talk about what?" Jazib asked, sauntering in and giving his wife a peck on the cheek. "Trying to impress my totally tenacious aunt?"

"I can be tenacious too." She smiled in her signature sweet way and let herself out of the kitchen towards Ammi's bedroom.

"What have you done to her?" I asked him. "She doesn't look like the fashionista we met at her sister's dinner."

"I didn't do anything," he said. "Ranya just knows what to do, and she knows how to do it right. That's why I was so sure she'd wow my parents. She's exactly the kind of girl for me and the kind of daughter-in-law for them, but…" he sighed.

"I wish I could help, Jazib." It hurt my heart to see him pay such a heavy price for choosing love.

"You've helped tons, Maya." He smiled. "I wouldn't have done any of this if you weren't there. I thought I'd lost Ranya forever."

"But what now?"

"Honestly? I have nowhere to go," he confessed.

I already suspected that much. He'd run off to Lahore, which was never his city even though he'd spent years there. But that town had Mamu-Jaan's stamp everywhere Jazib went. His father was his introduction and it was his father's name that determined how people dealt with him.

"I've been staying with friends this entire time and it's just not how I want it," he said. "For the first time in my life, I thought I had everything figured out. I was farming, doing something meaningful, and I was happy. I had plans, but now, it's all gone."

"You're a lawyer," I said. "Why not apply at a law firm?"

"I did. But the guy chickened out after he learned who I was."

"What about your friend?" I recalled the tall towers of boxes in my office at Edits & More just because Jazib wanted to help a friend.

"Nobody wants to get in the middle of a family feud like ours. It's nothing personal," he explained.

"You can move to Karachi. You have an apartment there."

"I don't have a job, Maya." He looked at me with a seriousness that was new to his face. "There are bills to pay, and groceries. And what if we have a child?" He ran a hand through his hair. "Karachi would've been great. It's my city. I don't have to live under Baba Saeen's shadow there, but I need money to make that happen."

I looked closely at his face. He'd grown up since that night at Ranya's cousin's apartment. He was thinking in concrete terms of family and responsibilities and a good future. And I realised he tried not to worry Ranya about it. I hadn't seen him turn off his sunshine around her yet. I believed even when they discussed their future, he probably displayed a brave look and told her that everything would be fine.

"You can come stay with me," I offered, but he shook his head.

"I'll be here for a while, with Phupo. She's asked me to stay and I think it's best. I can help her with her estate while I look for a real job. Ranya agrees too."

"Yeah, I guess it's best," I said. "Ammi was always nicer to you than she was to me. She'll be okay with Ranya in time. Plus, she won't be alone if you're here."

"You're going back? When?"

"Soon." I shrugged. "Maybe tomorrow. Maybe the day after. I've decided to pursue a career in photography."

"Photography?" He looked surprised. "But I thought you were with that editing company."

"That wasn't a real job, what I did there. I've been working at a studio for some time and I really like it. This photographer I was assisting really thinks I have potential. I need to enhance my résumé with some certifications too so…" I completed the sentence with a shrug.

"Okay." He looked a little bummed out that he never knew about it. "But what about settling down? I mean, I have, so now…you should too."

I laughed. "That's not how this works, Jazib. You know that."

"Is that all?" He looked at me oddly.

"What do you mean?"

"Maya…there are only a handful of people I'd sacrifice my sleep for and go running wherever they were at ungodly hours."

"Okay." I stared at him. "I know where this is going, and I don't want you to go there."

"Arhaan is a great guy." He squeezed my hand. "And he's crazy for you."

"No, he's not."

"He came running at three in the morning. For you!"

"Because he's a good friend."

"I would never do that for just a friend."

"Jazib…" I tiredly looked at him. "He isn't interested, okay. He told me so. So just let it go. And please don't tell anyone. Please?"

"Okay," he said. "But if you ever need me—"

"I know," I said, and gave him my bravest smile. "Right now, I'm happy that you're happy." And that was true. It gave me comfort to know that he had some stability in his life. And who knew, Mamu-Jaan just might forgive him and take him back. In fact, I was sure that would happen soon.

It took me two more days to pack my bags for Karachi. Truthfully, I wasn't exactly ready to insert myself in the grind of city life, but the lull of Kesar's monotonous routine scared me. It felt like a time capsule where everything came to a standstill. I didn't want to be the next Rip Van Winkle with a hundred years of reality to catch up with.

But of course, Ammi wasn't happy to see me go.

"You'll leave me at the mercy of that girl?" She was frowning.

"She's Jazib's wife and she's nice to you. I'm sure you'll be fine," I said, stuffing my last-minute items in my bag. I wanted to leave in an hour. It was a good sunny morning, and I wanted to make the best of it so I could rest at home that night.

"Jazib said you want to study photography?"

"I'm good at it, Ammi."

"What about marriage?" she asked testily. "You're twenty-four years old. Soon to be twenty-five! When I was your age, I had you. Who do you have?"

"A career? Or trying to have one."

"What about marriage?"

"What about it?" I said, feeling frustrated with her. "You of all people should know that marriage is the least reliable thing in life."

"Just because I had a bad experience doesn't mean you will too." Unexpectedly, she was calm. "Look at Jazib. He's married and he's happy. And Ranya…she isn't like her sister. I'm not saying I like her, but she isn't a complete disaster."

"You don't say."

"Tsk!" She rolled her eyes. "I always imagined you to be where she is today. It'll take me some time getting used to the change."

"It's nice to know that you're willing to try." I smiled at her. "Thank you."

"But don't change the subject," she said. "It's time you got married."

"To whom?" I chuckled at how childishly she was insisting. "I don't have anyone in mind and I'm pretty sure I won't like the ones you might have in mind."

"What about that boy?"

"What boy?"

"That boy you were in college with?"

"Ammi, there were a lot of boys in college, and none had my attention that way."

"He was a teacher."

Oh...no...but how'd she...?

"Jazib told me," she said, apparently reading my mind.

"Well," I said stiffly. "Didn't he tell you there's nothing there?"

That tattletale!

"Maya, come sit by me," she said, tapping the mattress. Then she took my hands in hers and smiled. "You are the only child I have. Life has been so crazy that I may have missed out on being a storybook-perfect, supportive mother. But I do love you. Whatever happens, and even though we don't see eye to eye most of the time, I still want you to be happy."

"Ammi, we have very different definitions of happy."

"Yes. So now, I'm thinking let's go with what happy means to you. And I think that boy means—"

"No, he doesn't! And you couldn't be more wrong." I slid my hands out of hers and stood up. "His name is Arhaan, by the way. And he isn't interested in me. He's divorced and I think the very idea of commitment makes him run for the hills." I stopped to collect myself. It was infuriating that the mere thought of him made me breathless. "Marriage is not a priority for me. I want to focus on my career. And if you really want to be there for me, then support me in this. Don't tear my confidence down with how you think I should live my life."

She looked at me quietly for a second, then bowed her head, nodding slowly. "Okay," she said softly. "I just wanted to make you feel better. Jazib went and did what he wanted, got what he wanted, and he's happy. But you, Maya...it's like you're left behind."

"I'm not left behind, Ammi." I sat back down beside her. "I never wanted to marry him. You know that. So just remove him from the picture and look at me. See *me*. I want to pursue a career in something I know I'm good at. And yes, I did love a man, but he said no, so...until he changes his mind or I'm ready for someone else, that's all there is to that topic." I looked at her face, searching for signs of acceptance. "Please, don't push me."

"Okay, I won't. But you will visit me often, yes?"

"Of course I will." I smiled, sensing the tension between us dissipate. "In fact, you should come stay with me for a while."

"I will. As soon as I have Jazib's problem solved." She smiled. "I called Bhai-Jaan last night. He's terribly angry but I'm sure he'll allow Jazib to come home soon."

"That's great! I knew you'd bring him back to the right side."

She laughed, kissing my forehead, and then wrapped me in a tight hug. It had been a while since she'd done that. I let her warmth wash over me, and I prayed she'd always be this way...

27

MY ARRIVAL IN KARACHI didn't go unnoticed. Abba visited me the very next morning. Made me breakfast even though it wasn't the weekend and sat for hours listening to every detail about my trip. I didn't fail to read between his comments that he'd been in touch with Ammi all this time, despite Arjumand's strict curfew on it.

"Are you really that afraid of Arju that you must keep your contact with your first wife a secret?" I asked him. "Isn't it enough that you rarely visit her?"

"It's complicated," he said. "Honestly, it's all my fault. I never should've married Gohar. Or I should've never stringed Arjumand along after I was married. It's all a little too late for regrets though."

I didn't grill him after that. The dynamics of his married life were better left alone to him and his wives. What was more important was that he approved of my bid for a career in photography and promised to pay for my education too.

"I think I'll make enough working for Yasir to afford it myself, Abba."

"No, I'll pay," he said adamantly. "I'm still your father and I still take care of all your major expenses."

"Well, I have zero issues with that." I smiled at him.

Aya-Ji, who'd travelled back with me, made tea for the third time in the six hours that Abba had been at my place. Among other things, he'd asked me to move back in with him. I'd declined. He filled me in on some of his new projects and mused over why I wasn't interested in construction like he was and how it pained him to see no heir to the future throne of his legacy.

"To whom will I leave this empire to?" He pouted.

"Charity?"

"Leh!" Aya-Ji frowned as she placed individual bowls of her homemade custard trifle in front of us on the coffee table. "He made all this with the sweat of his own brow and blood. This all belongs to you."

"But I won't run it," I said. "Abba needs someone who can learn the ropes so he can leave the business in those trusted hands and retire in peace."

"Exactly," Abba agreed, taking a spoonful of the dessert. "This is delectable."

"Mir Saeen," Aya-Ji said in her best thinking tone, the one that always meant she had a brilliant idea to present. "Why don't you engage Jazib?"

I gasped in excitement, almost choking on the bits of cake in the trifle. "Abba, yes! She's right. He has no place to be at this time anyway."

"But this isn't a part-time thing," he said. "I need someone who'll stay in this, and don't get me wrong, I'd love for him to join me, but I'd like that permanently."

That made sense. Jazib wasn't a builder and I was quite sure he didn't want to be one either. If only there could be a way to tie Abba's expertise with construction to Jazib's love for farming.

Or maybe if not him, then...

"Ranya said something about being interested in opening up vocational training centers in urban areas," I said. "She has this plan for helping the women of Kesar and Gurhkot with their domestic skillsets. But it doesn't have to be just that…" I remembered the young farmer from Jazib's sugarcane fields who was completely thrilled at the idea of learning how to farm better, "…if these people had access to an actual campus where they could learn various skills…" I hunched my shoulders trying to grasp and express the idea as it formed in my mind, "…if you could build a place for them to get this education, that would be something relevant to what you do, right?"

"You mean building a school?" Abba knotted his eyebrows in thought. "For vocational training?"

"It's construction."

"How does it help me find someone to handle my business?"

"I meant you could engage Ranya. She's interested in this project. You can invest in this, help build vocational centres or shops where these people can teach, learn, and sell their particular brands and products. And you can teach Ranya your business. I'm sure she'll make a great partner."

"I don't know, zindagi, this is all very vague." He shook his head, wrinkling his forehead. "Sounds to me she wants to engage in a humanitarian project dealing with skills and services. Construction is, well, different."

"I know but she wants to *build* vocational training centres," I insisted. "That's construction, isn't it? You can at least talk to her. What if she really has the acumen for it? And if she does, she can actually work with you on your projects."

Abba sank into the cushioned back of his chair, slowly nodded, and chewed his lower lip. That was his signature expression when he was letting good ideas marinate in his mind. "I like it," he finally said. "This gives me a chance to be part of something philanthropic too. I like it!" He laughed. "I'll get Arhaan to get me a report on this."

But of course, *Arhaan* had to come in too. I tried not to make a face. "Why do you need a report if you're doing it for Ranya?"

Because wasn't that the main reason? To get her interested in Abba's business through this project?

"Feasibility, zindagi. A learning campus needs students. I need to know how and where to market those products the people would be learning to make in our centres so they'll profit and ensure more students for us in the future. It's not for me or Ranya. It's for them too," he replied. "And this way, I'll have a solid reason to visit Kesar. And who knows, Maya, this may even bridge things between Arju and Gohar. Jazib and Ranya might mend this breach."

I hadn't thought of that, but it made sense. And wouldn't that be just the sweetest cherry too.

Abba travelled to Kesar quite a few times after our chat and things looked positive on that project. Mamu-Jaan forgave Jazib and arranged for a big feast to celebrate. Much to Ammi's joy, Abba agreed to attend. However there was no news of where Arjumand stood on all this. My guess was "outside".

My photography classes had begun and I had a shoot to prepare for. Yasir and Kulsom had endorsed my idea of utensil jewellery and Kishvar was on board as my model. She also knew someone who crafted unique metal jewellery in gold, silver, and stainless steel. Gulzai was a rising artist, who agreed to not even charge for his work if I just put his name in my project. Yasir, on the other hand, was also toying with the idea of using actual kitchen items to wear as ornaments, just to add depth and layers to the project.

"Like, we can string together different cooking spoons and spatulas like a necklace," he said.

"And how about onion rings as bracelets?" I said. "She can hold a knife over it like she's chopping onions, but it's almost cutting into her arm...hinting towards how the housewife puts her blood and sweat into her work."

"That's dark. Yet true."

"And heads of garlic for headbands? Because…that's mostly the perfume surrounding her?"

"You're weird," he said, after staring at me for five seconds. "I like it."

But why were we doing this?

I was still unsettled about the purpose. I recalled Izzat's words that had sparked this project.

…The only jewels that women need are in the kitchen…

I'd felt the truth of her statement. But it wasn't joy. It was pride. But why was there pride in something essential, but known to be taken for granted? Because it was *essential*…and only women knew how to do it.

"That's it!" I'd looked at my team. "Survival skills. These are essential survival skills that only the women in our culture have mastered, are expected to master, and have passed on from woman to woman, and without which the men would die. The men would die if women didn't cook for them."

"Now, hey, not all m—"

"Yasir! I'll destroy you with a belan if you complete that ch***** thought," Kishvar said, threatening him with the rolling pin in her hand. "Shut your face!"

"I know it's not all men," I said, sympathising with my mentor because he was one of the good ones. "But exceptions and minorities don't make the rules. Women in general are keepers of the kitchen and they do it with pride, regardless of how and why they were handed the keys to that kingdom."

There was also an angle of being forced into housework that I didn't want to ignore. Not all women were experts in the kitchen. Not all women wanted to be in the kitchen. But all women had to be. To depict this, I decided to dress Kishvar up as a bride, in traditional red, and instead of gold jewellery, I adorned her with stainless-steel ornaments, a necklace of wooden spatulas, onion rings for bracelets, and a tiara of garlic heads. Kishvar's expression was that of fear of the unknown in one shot, of disappointment in another, and of utter helplessness in the next. This picture, unlike all the rest, was a kick in the gut, the kind that brings in the tweets and reactions.

"This sums up everything," Yasir said the first time he saw it on my camera. "Maya, you're gonna kill it with this."

My project had progressed quicker than I expected, and I was luckily sponsored. Kulsom and Yasir's hotshot business partner were splitting the cost of renting a new photo gallery for a day where they decided to showcase my pictures. It was a large rectangular space with blank walls and lots of light, and it was next door to Yasir's studio. That street was already lined with and famous for its artsy shops. It had a woodturner's studio, a paint and pottery studio, a bakery and a café with French-looking décor serving Pakistani and English fusion foods, Yasir's photography studio, an upscale beauty salon, a unique home décor store, and now a gallery.

Yasir helped me select frame sizes and arrange the display. Our guest list included anyone and everyone the team knew, from personal friends to professional colleagues and media personalities. I couldn't be happier.

However, there was one thing.

I hadn't invited Arhaan.

He'd always pushed me to build a career of my own. I knew he'd be extremely proud…and that was exactly the problem. I'd had enough of him being *proud* and *fond* of me. He wasn't my father. He was the only man I'd fallen in love with. If we couldn't be lovers, I didn't want to have anything to do with him. For a week I writhed in physical pain, battling nausea, and tension headaches, trying to be resolute. Then I fell apart. Who was I kidding? The only scenario worse than not being his love interest would be to not exist in his life at all.

A night before the exhibition, I texted him.

My showcase fell on the same day as the celebrations at Gurhkot marking Jazib's return. Ammi kept sending pictures of the event by the minute to keep me posted and asked for a livestream and pictures from my end. I sent some, posing with friends, with my work, with food so that she'd know I ate. Jazib and Ranya video-called me and we spent the next twenty minutes looking into each other's worlds. Ranya was dressed like a bride, glowing and more beautiful than ever in gold and silver tones.

"I called Arju," she confided, her eyes reflecting her excitement. "At first she wouldn't even talk, but yesterday we cried every grievance out. She said she would never visit Kesar, but Gurhkot is different."

"Of course, she will visit." Jazib chuckled. "Arju is part of the family now."

I suspected Abba might be behind this timely change of hearts. He was quite the peacemaker. I wished my two happy newlyweds a good life and hung up. It felt so good to finally see them together. And better still to see hordes of art lovers notice my work, helping to kick start my own career.

"Maya! Girl, you rock!" Somebody hailed me. "How much is this piece for?"

"How did you come up with this theme? It's quite bold." A blogger whose pieces were candid and entertained topics close to my heart was eager to know more about me.

"Can we have a picture?" a group of youngsters asked.

"I put in all my love in this piece," Gulzai stood by one of the larger frames, explaining his stainless-steel pieces to a fan group of his own.

I looked at every energetic face around me. People were busy being together, being present, and being alive. And yet there was a knot tightening in my heart. I entertained my guests, smiling all the right smiles and saying all the right things. But the more I did that, the more I ached. What was missing?

Or rather... *Who*...

The night transitioned from dusky hues to midnight colours. I took stock of the number of red dots next to my pictures and was pleased. For a newbie, even a singular sale would've spelled success. The crowds had thinned and only a handful of people were left huddled together, just chatting. The gallery manager sat behind a tiny counter playing on his phone, waiting for everyone to leave so he could lock up.

"You should ask them to leave," I said to him. "They're just talking."

"They have a few more minutes." He smiled. "It's okay, I'll wait. And Miss, your work is amazing. You should do more of this."

"Really?" Maybe he was just being polite. But it felt nice.

"I have a sister who was married very young," he said. "She wasn't good at housework, but as soon as she became a wife, she was expected to be an expert. Your pictures reminded me of her. She's an expert now though. Can cook for a hundred people with her eyes closed."

"Wow, I can't imagine the amount of practice that would've gone into that."

"She was married into a large family so that meant a lot of hands-on training. And her husband is a good man. Always helped her."

"Oh, that's nice, and thank you."

He smiled in response, then frowned, staring at the entrance. "Who is that coming now?" he mumbled.

I followed his gaze and felt my heart doing cartwheels as my eyes forgot to blink.

It was Arhaan!

"Please, just a few minutes," I requested the manager. Surely he could tell from my face that this was perhaps the *one* person I'd planned on showing my work to. He shrugged and eased back into his chair behind the counter with his phone again. "You finally came!" I walked up to Arhaan, hoping to not sound too eager.

"I was afraid I might not catch it." He smiled back. With rolled-up sleeves, tousled hair, and smelling of car leather, he looked better than I remembered.

I tried acting *normal* around him as he eyed the pictures, regarding every frame in detail, but something in his demeanor told me he wasn't interested in what hung on the walls. He finally gave up the act and turned to me. "You know I'm very proud of this."

"Of course." I smiled, swallowing his insipid yet expected choice of words. *Proud?* He could've said something else! "You pushed me to have a career."

"But aren't you happy?"

"I am. I've worked hard for this. But thank you for the push."

"Yeah," he said softly, and stared at his shoes for a second before looking up at me again.

I waited for him to say something, but when he didn't my heart began to sink. "You don't like it," I said. "It sucks."

"No, it doesn't!" He laughed. "It's all brilliant."

"Then, where's your review? What do you *think*?"

"I think we need to talk."

That line was never good no matter who said it, and the fact that I couldn't read his expression made me more nervous than I liked. "About what?" I asked, trying my best to sound breezy above the screaming questions in my head. "Why do you look so dishevelled?"

"I've been mostly on the road since yesterday. I was in Kesar. Your father has a home industry project he wants me to evaluate. And I was in Gurhkot today for the same reason…" he paused. "And I met your mother. She asked me why I said no."

"She what?"

"She asked me why I didn't love you. And she called me a cad for breaking your heart."

I blinked, just to make sure the moment was real, that it wasn't a nightmare I was trapped inside where my own mother had seriously embarrassed me for all eternity. "Oh, God..." I closed my eyes and hoped to evaporate.

"Maya—"

"I'm so sorry she said all that. She had no right to ask you anything, to say any of it! That's it. I shall go crawl under a rock, and you will never see me again."

He smiled. "Honestly, it wasn't that bad."

"Except she completely ruined me."

"Except she didn't. Because I never said I didn't love you."

"What?"

"When you said all those things to me at Kishvar's house...I saw so much of myself in you then. A starry-eyed twenty-something, barely out there with a future of her own and throwing it all away for someone she barely knew. Someone who won't even appreciate it. It put you where I had been seven years ago. And put me where my wife had been, and that scared me!" He took a deep breath. "Your mother wanted to know everything about me. Trying to figure out why you liked me. Honestly, I've always wondered that too. What could be so special?"

Everything! But I didn't interrupt. I wanted him to keep talking.

"I told her about my marriage, my divorce, my parents. Things I've never even told you, all the ugly details. But she didn't mind any of it. You were right. None of that mattered," he said softly. "She just wanted to know why I'd said no to you when I should've said yes. Why I didn't love you. And *that* was so wrong. Because I do, Maya!"

"What are you saying?"

"I'm saying I've been a fool." His eyes were warm with hope. "Do I still have a chance?"

I heard myself gasp. All my words melted into tears and, for a moment, I couldn't decide whether I was laughing or crying. I touched his face and he drew me closer, circling his arms around my waist. A coy smile played on his lips and his eyes were the exact colour of desire that I'd always wanted them to look at me with. "It's probably two o'clock in the morning," he was speaking in melted honey tones. "I haven't slept. I haven't showered, and I've driven hundreds of miles to tell you that I love you. Always have!"

I'm not sure what came first after that, me throwing my arms around his neck or the hoots and hollers of our audience of few, scattered around the gallery, including the receptionist who stood behind his counter cheering us on, not even complaining of how late it was.

Somewhere in between all this, Arhaan kissed me.

It tasted like love.

Acknowledgements

JANIL & AMBREEN, MY most amazing friends and critics who have a hundred different subtle and not-so-subtle ways of telling me, "Humi, this sucks!"

Amz, for teaching me how the camera works.

Shami, for just being herself and being there for every random thought I ever shared with her.

And finally, this book wouldn't ever be possible without my parents who passed on their love and respect for the written word to me.